FALCON'S CAPTIVE

FALCON'S CAPTIVE

VONNA HARPER

APHRODISIA

KENSINGTON BOOKS

http://www.kensingtonbooks.com

APHRODISIA BOOKS are published by

Kensington Publishing Corp.
119 West 40th Street
New York, NY 10018

ISBN-13: 978-0-7582-2947-2
ISBN-10: 0-7582-2947-X

First Kensington Trade Paperback Printing: August 2010

10 9 8 7 6 5 4 3 2 1

Printed in the United States of America

Although writers are, by nature of their craft, solitary creatures, we still need human contact to remain sane—or at least relatively sane. If it wasn't for the incredible friendships made possible by the Internet, the men in white coats with the butterfly net would have already run me down.

Thank you, thank you to the pros at Novelists Ink for sharing life in the trenches, the Bradford Bunch for laughter and understanding, other Aphrodisia writers for honesty and openness, and random souls who pop in and out of my in-box when I need to vent.

Closer to home, Rogue Writers, you know I'm talking about you.

Prologue

The wind screamed, prompting the female Falcon Jola to pull her wings more tightly against her compact body and increase her speed. Alive as only a newly mature predator can be, she dove for the ground at over two hundred miles per hour. Tiny, bony tubercles in her nostrils slowed the rush of air into her lungs while her protective third eyelids lubricated her eyes and kept her vision keen.

Jola's prey, a dark gray rabbit, hopped from one low bush to another, oblivious to the threat above it. As the earth rushed up at her, Jola spread her wings, abruptly slowing her flight. For the briefest of moments she debated letting the rabbit live, but although the bulk of her diet came from other birds caught and killed in midair, today's energy and excitement demanded expression. Instead of crashing to the ground, she spun around so she skimmed the rocks and bushes. When the now-terrified rabbit abruptly turned direction, she sank her talons into it, easily breaking its neck. Done! Instinct rewarded.

Jola had just settled to the ground when, with a sharp cry, another Falcon swooped down, grabbed the dead rabbit, and headed skyward with it. Screeching, Jola flew after the thief, but instead of fighting to reclaim her kill, she flew in tight circles around the other Falcon, a young male.

This was Raci, her mate, her life companion. And although her body had only accepted Raci's a few times, she knew his contours. She also knew the dance that was part of their mating.

For a while Jola circled repeatedly above Raci. At length, surrendering to another ancient instinct, she hovered while he flew past her. Then, turning over so she was flying upside down, she extended her talons. Timing the act perfectly, Raci deposited the rabbit in her claws. The instant the kill's weight started to pull at her, she righted herself and drifted toward the ground.

Raci watched her for a while. Then, his smaller, paler body a blur, he swept under her, grabbing the rabbit as he passed. Screaming as one, they flew upward as if reaching for the clouds.

Again and again the pair repeated the courtship flight, with Jola relinquishing her kill only to have her mate return it to her. Finally, their tiny hearts fluttering, they headed toward the top of Raptor's Craig, where they'd begun preparations for their future nest by scraping a shallow hollow in the gravel and dead vegetation.

Raci was flying ahead of her, slowed only a little by the rabbit's weight. Studying his slate-gray back and long, pointed wings, she pondered why they'd chosen each other. Yes, her body was ripe and ready to carry the three to four eggs she'd deliver and help incubate, and Raci was healthy and mature, but beyond that she didn't know what had brought them together.

Right now, as a predator, instinct was enough, but later, when she changed into human form, she'd need more of an explanation.

Later, she silently reminded herself. At the present, following him home was enough. That and scanning the sky for an eagle. Fortunately, the greatest threat to their existence wasn't around today. She and Raci were safe.

She had no way of knowing that her mate wouldn't live beyond tomorrow, his heart stopped by an arrow.

1

Dawn crouched on the horizon as if gathering strength for the day. The birds, animals, rodents, and insects who came to life with the sun's touch had begun to stir while night creatures settled into countless hiding places.

Ignoring the waning summer's heat that would soon melt the cold from high desert rock, the small group of Ekewoko warriors walked single file along an ancient path laid down by deer or antelope. As befitting their status as those their lord trusted the most, they'd painted their chests with red and black symbols representing the hills and valleys of their birth. Although none of the five, nor those who'd remained at their encampment near the great lake, had seen their homeland since spring, their hearts remained in Ekew.

In contrast, they considered this rough and raw sweep of boulders, hearty bushes, and sharp peaks as both inferior and overwhelming. How, they pondered, could any living thing choose to call a place where the wind never ceased blowing "home"? Granted, the lake and creeks and streams that fed it provided sufficient fish and drew deer, antelope, and other game to it. In addition, the creeks and streams nourished what vegetation grew along its banks, but some of that vegetation was unknown to them, perhaps poisonous.

There was another question, one that each man kept to himself. How much longer would they have to remain here? Hopefully not until winter storms threatened to suck the life from everything, them maybe most of all. But there'd be no leaving until they'd captured what both Shaman Tau and Lord Sakima said they must if they were ever going to chase the hated Outsiders from Ekew.

Nakos walked at the front as was his right and responsibility, his eyes in constant movement. Grateful for his hide leggings and thick leather footwear, he gave little thought to his weapons, which included paralyzing darts and capture ropes. If the need arose, he'd snatch an arrow from the quiver at his back and place it in his bow; either that or rely on his spear. One thing about having embraced the ways of a warrior since boyhood: his body was ready.

Fortunately, the terrain no longer dominated his thoughts, and he'd long since stopped marveling at Shaman Tau's confidence in his own ability to interpret sacred dreams about fierce predatory birds and the primitive, subhuman Wildings who lived here. This morning, Nakos's mind stalked this way and that, as restless as the wind his companions cursed. They hated the constant low moan and swirling energy, but it made him feel alive.

Hungry for sex.

Damnation but the need to fuck had become powerful! He craved the potent sense of self and power that went with having a woman's soft body under his. Bending to his will. Obeying his every command. Living to please him. Silencing his restlessness.

Shaking his head to rid himself of memories that tightened

his cock, he drew on his eyes, ears, and nostrils to tell him what he needed to know. Unfortunately, so far the expedition into this land they'd named Screaming Wind had been unsuccessful. Granted, they'd spotted a number of the illusive Wildings at a distance and had brought down enough game to fill everyone's bellies, but they weren't here simply to kill and eat. Their goal was much more compelling, rooted in what the Ekewoko had always believed about their gods and spirits.

"Damn spiritless land," his friend Ohanko muttered, distracting Nakos from his thoughts. "We've been here much longer than I thought we would be, but I still cannot understand why anyone would choose to live in this forsaken place."

Nakos glanced behind him at the man whose physique so resembled his that they could have been brothers. The two were tall for an Ekewoko, with exceptionally broad shoulders and long, muscular arms and legs. Unlike most Ekewoko men, they didn't carry extra padding over their bellies. Their hair was so dark it was nearly black and their eyes blue black instead of the usual gray.

"It has to be the great lake," Nakos offered because his earlier praise of the wind's song had failed to change Ohanko's mind. "Without that, there'd be no—"

"I know. There's no need to remind me of the lake's blessings. Maybe it's that *thing*." Looking disgusted, Ohanko pointed at the massive, desolate-looking peak to the south.

For a moment, Nakos simply studied the distant peak. Although it was more than a day's walk from here, it challenged him in ways he didn't comprehend. Maybe it was the way it extended into the sky as if trying to reach the heavens. If his lord commanded him to go there, he would, but his heart would fight to escape his chest the entire time.

"From what Shaman Tau's dreams told him, the Wildings consider it sacred," he pointed out. "Maybe they've stationed guards there."

"Guards?" Ohanko asked. "Do you really think those *creatures* know enough to protect themselves, let alone a mass of rock?"

"I'm not sure. And maybe Tau doesn't know yet. Sometimes his revelations come slowly."

"I wonder why that is. He certainly has no doubt that the spirits are commanding us to capture a Wilding."

"But he hasn't said why." Nakos looked around to assure himself that the others weren't within earshot before continuing. "Do you think he knows what use a captive must be put to, what he needs to learn from one?"

"Ask him."

Although he knew his friend was joking, Nakos had to work at a smile. "No one questions a shaman, about anything. Only a fool doubts that the spirits speak only to those they've entrusted with their wisdom."

"And you aren't a fool, are you, Nakos? Otherwise, you wouldn't have become our finest hunter."

"Finest?" Nakos teased, grateful because at least for this moment he didn't feel as if the land was trying to steal his mind. "I thought you would never admit that."

"You're right, I shouldn't have. Now you're going to become even more insufferable than you are." Ohanko was silent for a moment as he studied their surroundings. "It isn't fair. Your ability to bring down game shouldn't be that much better than mine. I'm going to tell you something. What bothers me the most about our lord's opinion of your skill is how he always made sure you were properly rewarded. That's what isn't fair."

"You're talking about our lives before the Outsiders invaded Ekew. That no longer—"

"I know, I know! Just the same, Lord Sakima would still like nothing better than to reward you as he used to."

"You're jealous."

"Of course I am. Just once I'd love to have a captive female delivered to my bed. Is it true, by the time you were done with them, they all came crawling to you begging you to fuck them?"

"Who told you that?" Nakos demanded even though he took pride in his ability to turn a helpless woman's hatred and fear into heat. At least, he'd been able to before the Ekewoko had been turned into fugitives.

"Warriors talk." Ohanko winked. "Was it true?"

"Ask one of the females."

"I would if we hadn't turned them all free. I curse them for slowing us down and taking food and resources we need for ourselves. Ach! Everything here is the same color. How are we supposed to distinguish one thing from another? No wonder the Wildings are so illusive."

Glad for the change in subject, Nakos joined his friend in gazing at their surroundings. Within moments, he lost himself in a ritual that had served him well ever since he'd been welcomed into the warrior society. Sometimes when on a mission such as the one they were on today, he likened himself to a predator, a cougar or wolf perhaps. A predator was both simple and complex, a hunting and killing beast that did only one thing but did it well.

If he were a wolf, would this spiritless land accept him? Instead of challenging him to explore the countless valleys and stark peaks, it would stretch out before him as smooth and clean and welcoming as the lake. There'd be no need for caution, no reason to ask himself whether the simple creatures they were seeking were indeed harmless. The seemingly endless sweep of earth and rocks would reveal its hiding places and open his eyes to the nuances of color. His legs would walk sure and strong. His nostrils would understand every smell, and his ears would send clear messages to his mind. And because he comprehended his surroundings, he'd no longer ask himself why its draw was both powerful and unsettling.

Maybe most of all, his body would stop reminding him of how long it had been since he'd had sex.

"Do you know what I prayed for last night?" Ohanko said, speaking low. "For Lord Sakima to tell us that we can leave this place—and return home."

Nakos, too, had hoped that both their lord and shaman would either get over their obsession with the Wildings or explain why capturing one of the illusive creatures was so important; he just hadn't reached the point of praying.

"I've never seen either Sakima or Tau like this," he admitted. "The two of them obviously share something they don't want to tell us about. It's as if they're afraid they'll reveal too much. I can't help but wonder if something—the lake or that peak—has cast a spell over them." *As maybe it has with me.*

"Perhaps."

"What? You don't agree?"

"When it comes to this place, I'm not sure of anything. All I know is, I don't belong here. None of us do."

Instead of trying to respond, Nakos concentrated on taking in as much air as his lungs could hold. With each moment, the day was becoming brighter and the colors more distinct. Strange. At night he agreed with his companions that this area was inferior because it was so different from the rich, rain-fed land where he'd been born and grown up, but daylight always softened his opinion. Even though he'd never been where the wind was constant before, the pressure on his body made him feel alive. Granted, it wasn't the same as fucking, but at least a sharp breeze quieted his restlessness a bit.

Winter was coming. The days were becoming shorter, the nights crisper. Sometimes when the wind blew from the north he could taste snow. Surely Lord Sakima wouldn't order them to spend the winter in such an inhospitable place. Surely he'd tell them they should return to Ekew and fight for what had always been theirs. Either that or he'd say it was time to join the Ekewoko women, children, and elders near the sea where they'd fled after the Outsiders invaded.

But if he commanded them to remain here . . .

Even as he divided his attention between where his feet were going and the distance where danger might lurk, Nakos found himself not dreading but embracing snow and ice. No longer would he and the others concern themselves with trying to capture a maybe worthless Wilding to satisfy their shaman's and lord's demands. Instead, everything would be about survival. He would pit his skills against the elements. Maybe Wilding spirits and gods were determined to destroy those who, like him, didn't belong.

Who was still stalked by nightmares he refused to acknowledge.

He was pondering the wisdom of asking Ohanko if his friend ever had the same thoughts when movement overhead caught his attention. He'd seen eagles, hawks, and other birds of prey, of course, but this *creature* was different from them. Swifter.

When he first noticed it, the bird had been to his right and so high above that it seemed part of the heavens. A heartbeat later it became a brown and white blur diving toward another, larger bird. By the time Nakos's heart beat again, the smaller bird had struck the larger one in midair, causing countless feathers to fly about. An agonized shriek cut through him. He blinked. The larger bird was plummeting toward the ground. An instant later, the killer caught it and slowed its descent. The two reached the ground, then disappeared.

"Did you see that?" Nakos asked. "Nothing, not even an arrow, travels that swiftly."

Ohanko didn't respond, prompting Nakos to glance behind

him. The man he considered his brother was staring in the direction the shriek had come from. Color had drained from Ohanko's face, and his fingers were clenched.

Nakos's own nails bit into his palms. Had they just seen a Wilding spirit?

2

Her muscles, tendons, and heart working as one, Jola raced over rocks sharp enough to shred skin. Her lungs repeatedly collected and expelled air, but even when she couldn't pull in enough oxygen to fuel her system, she couldn't convince herself to slow down. Cool wind abraded her cheeks, arms, breasts, and belly, and for these moments, she wanted nothing else.

Movement. Flying—when she could. Running otherwise.

Her world was awash with colors that resonated in her soul. She loved the wind and the endless browns, greens, grays, whites, even hints of black. Most of all she loved the vast horizon with her birthplace, Raptor's Craig, in the distance. She longed to return to it and surround herself with memories, but she'd spent last night there and hadn't found the peace she longed for.

Her body and heart wanted one thing: movement. That's why she was here today, that and the need to study the newcomers as she'd done back before she'd chosen her mate and then again two days ago. While in mourning, she hadn't concerned herself with the newcomers, but when hunger had pulled her away from grief and sent her in search of prey, she'd spotted them.

Hatred had consumed her then. It still did.

As soon as she stopped running, the sweat coating her flesh would start to chill, and she'd be forced to go in search of the sleeveless hide dress she'd thrown off when too-familiar energy first lent strength to her legs. It was better to keep running, to move instead of think. To fight tears.

After pushing her long, black hair off her neck, she turned and set her sights on the great lake. Fortunately, the intruders had set up their camp on the bank opposite from Raptor's Craig. Otherwise, she would have been forced to acknowledge Raci's killers when grief had been all consuming.

A handful of the invaders was out hunting this morning. Keeping her eye on five men was easier than trying to keep track of the twenty-some who'd laid claim to the far lakeshore.

Or was it? Her Falcon senses had always worked in the past, but she was no longer sure of anything.

Angry at herself because she'd vowed to let go of what she couldn't change, she stopped and rose onto her toes. Her hands went to her breasts and she tightly cupped them as their jiggling quieted. Full breasts while in human form were as much a curse as a gift. Raci had been fascinated by them. Embracing them, her mate would whisper that they belonged to him as much as they did to her. And she'd believed him. Would still believe—if Raci hadn't been murdered.

Swamped by tears, she lowered her head and closed her eyes, sucking in oxygen. But even as she concentrated on cooling her lungs, she knew only one thing would blunt the pain: running. And when she'd returned to Raptor's Craig, which was the only place the change from human to raptor and back took place, flying.

"I miss you so much," she muttered as if Raci were beside

her. "Yes, I must come to grips with your death and walk into my future. You wouldn't want me to drown in sorrow. But you should be alive. Those newcomers—killers—had no right. If I knew whose arrow pierced your heart, I'd tear him apart!"

She should release herself, but touching her breasts felt so good. Better than loneliness. Not as exciting as Raci's hands had been and yet—

"Death stole you before the final bonding," she muttered, careful to keep her voice low. "That's what hurts so much: knowing I'm not carrying your offspring! That and knowing these *creatures* are responsible."

Barely able to stifle a cry, she pinched and then massaged her nipples into hard nubs, but no matter how much she tried, she couldn't make herself believe that Raci was holding her. Afraid that memories of finding Raci's cold Falcon body with an arrow through his heart would overwhelm her once more, she started running again. Her lungs, long accustomed to her need for extreme exertion, immediately expanded. Her heart pumped strong and steady.

Yes! This was life. Freedom. Leaving behind thoughts of revenge.

Her young, naked body made love to the air and she imagined the precious land of her birth watching her legs churn. Finding a well-worn path to run on, she fantasized that a deer was running beside her. They'd share the same heat and speed, the same confidence in their bodies. But unlike the doe or buck, she didn't have to rely on her legs to stay alive. Instead of fleeing danger, she became a predator and attacked.

That's what she wanted: images of beak and talons ripping into flesh, the newcomers screaming in pain and fear while she cried out her vengeance.

Hatred rolled through her only to be replaced by yet another emotion. No matter how long or hard she ran, she wouldn't be able to expel this sensation, and after a moment, she slipped deep into her mind and spun out what her imagination and need had spawned.

Whether they'd been in Falcon or human form, sex with Raci had been fierce and quick. They'd been so hungry for each other that they'd fairly clawed at one another. If they'd had more time together, more than a few couplings, hot starvation might have settled into something quiet that would have allowed them to savor long hours together. Instead of pushing her breasts and cunt at him and demanding he spear her, she would have taken his cock in her hands while he ran his fingers over her wet entrance. They would have gone slowly and carefully, judging each other's responses so they'd know when to slow down even more or even, briefly, leave each other alone.

They'd play games.

Taking her cue from how the simple falcons her kind shared the sky with mated, she'd tell Raci to lay claim to her body. Even though female raptors are larger than males, she'd demand he control her as a falcon brings down its prey. *I want to pretend to fight you,* she'd tell him. *To pit my strength against yours so you can teach me that you're stronger. I want you to take me, fiercely and masterfully. Teach me to respect you.*

How, he'd ask. *By forcing you?*

Yes! That's what I want. No longer feeling as if I'm in control of my world but having you take charge. Force a climax from me. Even keep it from me until I beg, or until I tell you that I hate you.

Why?

Because that way I'll always know my body is yours.

What would it be like to be a captive of the newcomers?

Startled by the question, she rubbed her suddenly cold arms. She'd seen enough of the newcomers to know they were almost identical physically to Falcon males when the Falcons were in human form. In other words, the newcomers might be as fast as she was, which meant that unless she became Falcon, she couldn't outrun them. Even more unsettling, the newcomers were well armed as witnessed by the arrow that had killed Raci.

The newcomers had no women with them, which meant that they might capture her instead of killing her. If that happened, for the first time in her life she wouldn't have control over her body or its reactions. She, who had never feared anyone or anything, couldn't flee or attack. Instead, she'd have no choice but to wait, to experience, to be handled.

To her shock, instead of being appalled, she felt her pussy became damp. Barely aware of what she was doing, she slid a hand between her legs. The instant she did, she pondered what it would be like to have a stranger's hand there. As his captive, the newcomer would have undoubtedly restrained her. Secure in his superiority, he'd set about taking control. Ignoring her curses and struggles, he'd touch her entire body. His fingers would probe and invade, tease and test. Maybe laughing, he'd strip her of all maturity and sanity. Heartbeat by heartbeat, she'd surrender to the avalanche of sensations until all battle seeped from her muscles and she became primitive, a woman wanting just one thing from this man she hated and maybe feared.

By the time her captor buried his cock in her, she'd be begging for him to have sex with her. If Raci were still alive, she might never think of him again.

Panting, her cheeks and throat hot, Jola abandoned her pussy and again sheltered her breasts. Was it possible? That those she would kill if she could were so experienced with the female body they'd turn a proud, independent woman into something else?

An icy sensation sliced through her, prompting her to release her breasts and start running again. The lake was in the middle of a long, broad valley that made sneaking up on anything around or in it nearly impossible, so she could see far ahead of where her legs were taking her. If any newcomers were on this part of the great body of water, she'd spot him long before he knew of her presence.

She'd attack, claw, and gouge.

A glance at her fingers put an end to the fantasy that she might have been gifted with talons instead of nails today. Too bad. She would loved to be able to pit her spirit-given skills against men who believed their size and weapons gave them the right to rob others of their freedom.

And turn them into sex slaves.

Sex slaves?

She should have asked her chief to explain what he meant when he'd told everyone what he'd overheard a couple of the newcomers say the other night. The two had been out hunting and, instead of returning to camp, they'd lit a small fire and sat there talking about life at Ekew where they'd come from. Not only had Chief Cheyah learned that the newcomers called themselves "Ekewoko," he'd been privy to a couple of sex-hungry men's longing for the life they'd once enjoyed at Ekew. Foremost among what they regretted losing was what they'd called their sex slaves. From what Chief Cheyah had gathered, such slaves' only value came from their use as fuck partners.

Much as the term disgusted her, it also fascinated her. Like the attraction of a fiercely burning log, lightning, or molten lava breaking through the earth's crust, she was both afraid of and intrigued by possibilities. Touching any of those things might kill her, but what if contact catapulted her into another level? She might discover that she had the power to extinguish the fire, thus saving whatever was burning from becoming ash. Being hit by lightning might grant her access to the heavens, while embracing lava could lead to a journey deep within the earth.

But what about being a slave to sex? Would she be in a state of constant arousal, chasing after men in hopes of being satisfied and using her newfound knowledge of the male animal to give him the greatest pleasures of his life? What about her own enjoyment? Would it outstrip what she and Raci had enjoyed?

Maybe, maybe not. She didn't dare forget that she'd still be a slave, which meant whatever happened to her wouldn't be of her choosing.

Slave. No matter that she tried to run from it, the word rode on her shoulders as she raced toward the lake. Many seasons ago a group of travelers had entered Falcon Land. They'd ridden on the backs of animals she'd never seen before that were larger and sturdier than deer or antelope. A few of the travelers had sat in strange wheeled structures being pulled by other animals. At first she and the other Falcon youth had been fascinated by the strange animals and had discussed at length how they might get their hands on such wondrous creatures, but they'd been forced to admit that the strangers weren't about to drop their guard when they obviously considered the animals highly valuable. Someday, she and her companions had wistfully mused, they'd find where the creatures lived and obtain some of their own. Unfortunately, no one had any idea what skills were needed to keep the creatures from running off.

Strange animals aside, the most intriguing part of watching the travelers was observing how they'd treated what she'd then believed were prisoners but now understood had been their slaves. At that point, she'd never seen one human treat another as if he was a beast of burden. Because she and her companions had gone out without their parents' permission, they hadn't said anything about their discovery. But Chief Cheyah, who'd done a great deal of traveling in his early years and knew many things, had left everyone with a clear if unpleasant image.

Slaves were considered less than human. Their needs and desires meant little to their owners, who handled their possessions as they saw fit. The slaves Jola had observed as an adolescent had been fairly well treated. At least she'd seen no beatings and the chains linking wrists and ankles together didn't look to be overly tight. Granted, a slave wouldn't be able to run, but he could walk without risking falling.

And walk they did. Of the five male and three female slaves, not one had ever been allowed to ride the strange animals.

What had bothered her the most was the slaves' unkempt appearance. They'd plodded with their heads down, and when their masters addressed them, they'd shrunk back, obviously afraid. Once, while in Falcon form, she'd flown close. Unfortunately, she'd been unable to hear what the slaves were saying to each other. A female slave had looked upward and, for an instant, life and light had transformed the dull eyes. Then, as if the female had reconciled herself to what she couldn't change, her eyes had filmed over again.

Later, a man had come up behind the female and roughly yanked her short dress up, tucking the hem under the cord that sufficed as a belt. Immediately, the female had stopped and leaned forward with her hands on her thighs and her legs spread. Without a word being said, the man had buried his cock in the female's folds. Instead of the gentle words Raci had used with her, this man had grunted loudly while slapping defenseless buttocks and reaching around to squeeze a dangling breast.

At least he'd come quickly. As for the female, Jola had had no doubt that she'd gained no pleasure from the coupling.

Jola now had been running long enough that even her superbly conditioned muscles were beginning to tire. Smelling the lake, she slowed so she could enjoy the scent. So much life grew and lived near the shore. The surface was never devoid of birds, and she could only guess how many fish lived in its depths. Most days rafts and canoes floated on it, either because a Falcon in human form was fishing or simply relaxing there. Ever since the newcomers had taken possession of the sunset side, however, the only time anyone ventured into the lake was to fill cooking pots or bathe. And no one ever went alone.

Slowing to a walk that allowed her heart rate to return to

normal, she mentally returned to the one time she and Raci had sought solitude here. They'd chosen a small inlet flanked by reeds on all sides. After making sure they had the inlet to themselves, they'd self-consciously removed their clothes and slipped, shivering a little, into the water.

"The final mating ceremony can't come soon enough for me," Raci had said as he reached for her. He might have been aiming for her arms, but when his fingers brushed her breasts, she didn't try to shrug him off. "I have to ask if you're certain you feel the same way, Falcon girl. I'll be enough for you?"

"Don't call me that," she'd chided. "My name is Jola."

"Be proud of our heritage."

"I am, just as I know you are. But when we're in human form and together, all I care about is being a woman, a woman who is with the man she loves."

As their arms floated around each other, lips had met, and she'd bent and locked her legs around him. His cock had found her opening, and she'd contented herself with the moment. At least she'd tried. Still, a part of her had stood apart to ponder the complexity of their existence until his warmth and weight and pulsing need filled her hungry hole and became everything.

Sex was belonging. Raci was hers, and she lived to be with him.

Until the day he'd bled until he had nothing left to bleed.

Trusting instinct to guide her now that tears blurred her vision, Jola reached the edge of the lake and walked into it. Cool mud slipped between her toes. After a few more steps, water began caressing her ankles and then her calves. Seeking solace, she continued until the water washed over and between her legs. When it lapped at her buttocks, she acknowledged that the water had imprisoned her. But the lake was more than a force preventing her from fleeing. It was also touch, proof that she was still alive.

Promise. Please let this life-giving water bring me peace.

3

Were there water fairies in Screaming Wind? On the tail of his question, Nakos reminded himself that if there were such things, surely someone would have seen one by now. The likely explanation was that he'd been in the right place at the right time to spot a naked Wilding female enter the lake.

From where he crouched behind a thick bush, the bright sunlight gave the creature an almost transparent appearance as if he was looking at her through a thin layer of water. Her back was to him, affording him a view of loose black hair that reached her shoulder blades. He'd never seen such thick hair, straight and glistening from the sun's touch. When he'd first spotted her standing at the shoreline with water caressing her feet and ankles, he'd been hesitant to breathe for fear of drawing attention to himself.

There'd been something unworldly about the way she carried herself, youth and strength woven together, that made it difficult for him to accept her as mortal. Her legs were impossibly long and, from what he'd been able to tell before she entered the lake, deeply muscled. Her arms, too, were long, her shoulders wider than any Ekewoko woman's. She'd yet to turn toward him so he could only guess at what her breasts looked like. Hopefully they were in keeping with her narrow waist and lushly rounded hips and buttocks.

Graceful step by graceful step, she'd made her way into the lake until it now reached her waist. Waiting to see what she'd do next, he tried to formulate a plan. She was a Wilding. As such, he should be planning how to capture her. Once he'd accomplished that, he'd turn the creature over to Tau and Sakima who, he had no doubt, could compel her to tell them everything they wanted to know, whatever those things were. But how could he concentrate on practical matters when he'd never expected to see anyone like her? Granted, he'd come out here in search of a Wilding, but it had been days since one had been seen near the lake. Why she'd exposed herself this way mystified him.

It wouldn't for long. Once he'd captured her, he'd force the truth from her, although from the looks of her, maybe that would wait until he'd used her to satisfy his sexual hunger.

Instead of the sense of power he expected at the thought of molding her to his needs, he felt unsure. It had to be, he told himself, because he was still learning about this land and the possibility of unknown danger lurking in its shadows. Just as a chill touched his spine, he reminded himself of the open land all around. He'd been here any number of times and had yet to see the slightest hint of a threat. From what everyone had determined, the Wildings were shy and peaceful, more like deer than wolves. Granted, he occasionally sensed he was being watched, but whenever he looked around, he saw nothing except a hawk or other bird of prey.

Instead of measuring the distance between him and the lakeshore, he recalled Tau's and Sukimo's reaction to what he'd told them about seeing a bird that flew so fast it was nothing but a blur—and an expert killer. They'd been both excited and nervous but had refused to explain why his description mattered so much to them.

What hadn't they shared with the others? Maybe a warning from the spirits about small predatory birds capable of killing humans?

This was insanity! He wasn't afraid of a bird. And he certainly had nothing to fear from a naked woman with long, black hair, a straight back, and womanly hips.

After mentally shaking his head, he studied the distance between them. They were too far apart for a dart to reach her, but among his arrows were two with tips he'd soaked in paralyzing brine. If she was on land, he'd have no hesitancy about using one, but if he fired it now, he'd have to hurry to make sure she didn't drown before he reached her.

Of course, he could wait until she was done with whatever task or whim had taken her into the water, but what if others of her kind arrived? He'd be compelled to fight them, which meant she'd escape. Another possibility struck him. Even if no one came upon them, she might spot him. If she was as strong a swimmer as she appeared, what was to stop her from setting off for a distant shoreline?

He was still debating that possibility when she lifted her arms over her head and leaned forward. Her lean form sliced into the water and she disappeared. Cursing, he took off at a hard run, reaching behind him for one of the treated arrows as he did.

After too long a period of time, she appeared again, arms moving smoothly and legs beating against the water's surface. He nearly made the mistake of firing and probably wasting his weapon when inspiration struck. Still running, he yelled.

As he hoped, she stopped swimming and turned toward him with just her face and arms showing. Pulling back on the bow and sighting down his arrow, he held his breath and fired. At first the arrow sped just above the surface at a slight downward angle. Then, as he'd planned, it struck the water. That caused it to change direction slightly but it would still reach its target.

Not waiting to see her reaction, he dropped his weapons and plunged into the lake. Water closed around his legs, slowing him. From this angle, he could no longer see her arms. However, her head remained above water, letting him know that the poison hadn't yet entered her system. He didn't for a moment doubt that his arrow had struck her; he didn't miss.

As soon as he was deep enough, he started swimming. His powerful arms cut through the water, and his legs propelled him forward. Still, he wondered if he'd reach her in time. And if he didn't . . .

Refusing to give freedom to thoughts of having to repeatedly dive in an attempt to retrieve her, he acknowledged how cold the water was. The unexpected chill left no doubt how deep the lake was here or how quickly the bottom dropped away.

Damnation. She might drown.

Strength surged through him. He now likened himself to a fish cutting effortlessly through the water, but he wasn't one. Instead, he was a man suddenly afraid that a valuable life might be lost. Even as he ordered his body into rhythm, he once more questioned why both his shaman and lord had been so determined to get their hands on a Wilding. Untamed the way she was now, she had almost no value.

Beyond her sleek limbs and glossy hair, he corrected. Beyond her unabashed nudity. Beyond her breasts and hips and that sweet, dark space he knew existed between her legs.

He wasn't sure he'd reached the exact spot where he'd last seen her, but he had to be close. Stopping, he treaded water as he looked around. It was impossible to determine whether the small waves and bubbles were caused by his movement or whether she was responsible for any of them. What most concerned him was that he saw no dark hair, no thrashing or even floating arms.

Needing to do something, he swam in a circle while reaching out as best he could with both arms and legs. By the time he'd completed the circuit, he was cursing himself for his rash action. Why hadn't he waited for her to come to shore before immobilizing her? It couldn't be because he half believed she'd set her sights on the shore far from where she'd gone in. No mortal could swim that far, could they?

Mortal?

He'd just begun another circle, wider this time, when something above him caught his attention. Looking up, he spotted a bird hovering some thirty feet over the lake and slightly to his right. Even as he told himself the small, gray bird's actions didn't concern him, he changed course. He stopped when he was directly beneath the bird, then curled his body into as tight a ball as possible and pushed down into darkness. His fingers reached out, fighting the water's resistance. Before long, the effort used up the air in his lungs. Still, he delayed heading for the surface.

His lungs screamed, and strength seeped from his muscles. Then, just as he acknowledged he'd gone as far as he could, his fingertips brushed something. He closed a thumb and forefinger over whatever it was.

Hair.

Pushing down yet again, he ignored his burning muscles. More strands glided over the backs of his hands, prompting him to grab them. Hair filled the palm of his right hand. Holding on with his dying strength, he executed a far from graceful turn, hauling his burden with him. His left arm clawed at the water that was killing him. Every time he kicked, his feet brushed something warm and soft. Dark pain filled his head, and fear took bites out of what remained of his sanity.

Let her go. Save yourself.

But because his actions had sent her on death's journey, he couldn't.

By the time he broke the surface, every inch of his body was on fire. Drinking in all the air his lungs could hold, he treaded water. Only when he trusted his body to obey his commands did he pull the woman's lean and limp body up next to his, careful to keep her head above water.

Turning her toward him, he shifted his hold so a hand was under her armpit. He brushed her hair out of her face and then placed the back of his hand against her nose.

She wasn't breathing, wasn't even trying to.

As a warrior-in-training he'd been taught how to place his mouth against a drowning victim's and push air into the victim's lungs, but if he tried that now, they'd both sink beneath the surface.

Time. Time was seeping away from them.

Turning her so her back was against his chest, he looped his arm over her breasts, his fingers gripping her armpit again. As soon as he was certain his hold was secure, he started for shore. She rested against his side, the back of her head on his chest and her face out of the water. Even with the passing seconds striking him like drumbeats, he forced himself to concentrate on making smooth strokes. Speed was vital but so was endurance.

Although the lake was trying to suck the warmth out of him, he felt hot. In contrast, her body was now too cool. But her skin against his was soft and smooth, and he nearly convinced himself he could feel her heart beating and her lungs filling and emptying, but maybe he was only deluding himself.

Again he looked upward. There was no bird.

Whether a bird or his imagination had led him to her became the most important thing he'd ever asked himself. At the same time, he repeatedly told himself it didn't matter. Only keeping her from dying did.

Despite his protesting muscles, he refused to slow, let alone pause and rest. When, finally, his toes touched the muddy bottom, he nearly called out in relief. Half walking, half swimming, he brought her to shore and dragged her out of the water. Lying her on her back, he sank onto his knees next to her. There was no arrow, only a barely bleeding hole in her side. Obviously she'd pulled it out.

Mud coated her legs, and her hair flowed over her shoulders to cover the top of her breasts. Other than that, he had an unobstructed view of every bit of her youthful body. Because he'd yet to be beaten in battle and so had had his efforts rewarded, he'd seen more naked females than he could remember, but there was something different about her.

Not that it mattered. Pressing his hands against her cheeks, he turned her head to the side. Next he lifted her shoulders and angled her upper body in the same direction, thinking that might help get water out of her lungs. Everything seemed unreal to him. Surely he hadn't just risked his own life trying to save a barely human creature.

Then she coughed, and relief rushed through him. After a moment, she coughed again, her slim form shaking with the effort. Water dribbled from the corner of her mouth. When her coughing became ragged, he turned her fully onto her side, holding on to her shoulder and hip to keep her in position. She spluttered and gasped, her breasts jiggling. Watching them, he tried to think of something comforting to tell her only to swallow the unspoken words. Just because he felt sorry for her and more than a little responsible, nothing had changed between his people and the Wildings. She was still his captive, potentially valuable merchandise.

When she stopped coughing, he rolled her onto her back again and released her. His arms and legs burned. His heart continued to pound against his chest wall, and his breathing hadn't returned to normal. From the way she lay with her arms sprawled and legs limp, he had no doubt that the paralyzing poison was still in her system. Maybe, he pondered, that's why she'd survived instead of drowning. Her body hadn't had much need for oxygen.

Experience told him it would be a while before she could begin to move on her own, and now that her chest rose and fell, something shifted inside him. No longer being concerned for her life allowed him to thoroughly evaluate the creature he'd taken possession of.

Her breasts were remarkable. Instead of flattening completely against her chest wall, they remained firm and rounded. Her nipples were hard, dark nubs, undoubtedly because the cold water had made them that way. Seeing no reason not to, he caught one between thumb and forefinger. Until now, her eyes had been closed. As they slowly opened, he acknowledged how much effort she had to put into what should have been a simple act.

Curiosity tightened his hold on her nipple. Her eyes widened, and she sucked in air through flared nostrils. Her lips parted, but she made no sound. Strange. He hadn't expected her to begin recovering so soon.

"I have you, Wilding," he said. "You might not yet understand what's happened, but you soon will. And when you do, you'll do everything you can to get away from me. But you're too valuable. My lord and shaman have need of you."

She still wasn't focusing on him so he pulled on her breast, drawing it away from her body. Her eyes widened even more. She went from staring at nothing to glaring at him. A chill settled against his back, nearly causing him to release her. But if she thought her dark, hate-filled gaze would frighten him, she was badly mistaken. Angry at her—and maybe a bit at himself for his reaction—he took hold of her other nipple and pinched it.

"You should have worn clothes," he taunted.

Being able to control her this way restored him. Having

control also reminded him of how long it had been since he'd fucked. He could take her now while she was helpless, spread her legs and bury his cock in her soft flesh, although maybe he'd first flip her onto her belly so he could take her from behind.

From out of the corner of his eye, he saw her fingers start to curl inward. It should be too soon for her to be able to move on her own, but maybe there was more to the Wildings than he and his companions had thought. After all, she'd survived what would have killed many women.

"Your nudity was your undoing," he informed her, although he wasn't sure she could understand him. "If you'd been dressed, I might not have decided to claim you."

Her lips thinned, and her nostrils flared even more. Seeing how much she hated him was like standing in the sun on a summer day, revitalizing, invigorating. His flesh warmed. His muscles felt restored. Most of all, his cock awoke.

"I saved your life," he said, forcing his voice to be calm. "Among my people, when one saves another, the one whose life has been spared owes a great debt to the other. As for what I want from you . . ."

Having his throat shut down surprised him. He'd been about to lay her future out before her, but he didn't know what use Tau and Sakima might put her to, what they needed her for.

She twitched, pulling his thoughts onto what he was doing to her. Because the poison numbed as well as paralyzed, holding her nipples this tightly might not cause her much discomfort, but he had no doubt she resented what he was doing.

He'd still been an untested warrior when Lord Sakima had told him that the time would come when he'd be rewarded with a sex slave. He might not spend much time with any of the slaves, but that experience would be more satisfying for him if he first reminded her that her body belonged to him, not her. Experience had taught him that the man who'd become his father in many ways was right so why did what he was doing to his captive make him feel slightly ashamed of himself?

And why was he releasing her breasts?

At first she stared at him as if she didn't comprehend what he'd just done. Then her eyes closed. He assumed that her brief *unconsciousness* was her way of regathering herself, probably in preparation for resistance. Judging by her reactions so far, he suspected it wouldn't be long before he was dealing with a wide-awake and determined prisoner. The last thing he needed was for her to injure herself trying to get free.

Placing a hand on her flat belly so he could judge her responses, he looked around for the pack he'd shrugged out of just before diving into the lake. He spotted it among some rocks a short distance away. After pressing his hand against her stomach again, he scrambled to his feet and hurried over to the pack. Snagging it, he retraced his steps and again dropped to his knees.

Good. She hadn't moved, and her eyes remained closed.

Digging into his belongings for what he needed, he studied the creature who'd come into his world. There was a warrior quality to her well-muscled arms and legs. Although her physique paled in comparison to his, he'd never seen a female in such well-honed physical shape. There was something about her long neck and broad shoulders that had him looking forward to caressing them at his leisure. Strange. Always before his interest in a female captive had begun and ended with sex.

Ah yes, sex. Her legs were modestly together, but with her left knee slightly bent, it wouldn't take much to spread her. That done, he'd take his time studying her pussy.

Her fingers twitched again, and her lids fluttered. Brought back to reality, he checked to see that he'd pulled out the leather and rope he needed to properly restrain her. When he'd first added the restraints to his pack, he'd shaken his head at what he was doing because for the first time as a warrior, his task was to capture, not vanquish. But if this was what his leaders wanted, he'd do everything he could to comply.

The rope, even darker than her tanned flesh, would contrast with it, which was why he picked up a limp arm and wrapped the strands around the wrist closest to him. Then, despite his desire to do nothing more than study her, he rolled her onto her stomach and pulled her arms behind her. Within a few seconds, he'd secured her wrists so only a finger's width remained between them.

Now what?

4

Knowing she couldn't fight him released some of his tension, but before turning her so she looked at him, he twice fed rope around her waist and then tied her wrists to the makeshift belt. Double-restraining her probably wasn't necessary, but acknowledging what he'd done might go a long way toward convincing her who was in charge. Besides, he liked the way her arms looked with her elbows bent.

After positioning her on her back once more, he scooted away a little so he could study what he'd done. Having her arms behind her had forced her to arch her back, which prominently displayed her remarkable breasts.

The last time he'd touched them, he'd been rough and masterful as befitted his stature. Now, despite the demands his cock was making on his ability to concentrate, he lightly ran his fingers over the smooth flesh. Women were remarkable creatures, soft where men were hard, filled with moist, sleek passages a man could die in.

He didn't like that that made him feel weak, damn it! She was a Wilding, a lesser being equipped with a primitive mind in sharp contrast to her magnificent body. It wasn't fair! An animal-like creature should be ponderous and slow or so fragile he could easily snap her bones.

Still gliding his fingers over her breasts, he glanced around, half believing he'd spot Wilding men sneaking up on him. Surely the men wouldn't allow her to walk about naked and alone.

Alone?

Maybe they'd deliberately sent this female out to seduce him.

Pondering the possibility, he again stared down at her. Her black eyes were open, but unlike the first time, they weren't filmed in incomprehension. Judging by the way she studied him, she understood exactly what had happened to her.

It shouldn't be like this! The poison wore off slowly. It didn't suddenly melt away.

Warned by the hatred she made no attempt to hide, he expected her to start fighting. Fortunately, he was out of reach of flailing legs—legs he should have already restrained.

Not taking his eyes off her, he picked up a short length of rope. She strained upward, lifting her back off the ground. Impressed by the way the tendons stood out at the sides of her neck, he thanked the spirits for the hand they had in his saving her life. Even with her body full of fight, he felt close to her. There were just the two of them on this deserted stretch of land in a country he might never understand or feel comfortable in. He had no doubt that this resolutely silent woman had no intention of giving up. In addition, she didn't appear to be at all ashamed of her nudity. Quite the opposite: unless he was mistaken, she was proud of her body.

"You can try fighting," he said, wondering if she understood a word he said. "But it won't do you any good."

Her cheeks and throat glistening from the strain of keeping her shoulders off the ground, she continued to glare at him. She was a wild animal, and more. Savage and sensual at the same time. What would his shaman and lord do with her?

"What are you thinking?" he asked. "Maybe you believe I intend to keep you for myself, but if you do, you're wrong. You have value beyond a man's need for a woman's body, value the Ekewoko leaders know how to make the most of."

He waited for her to react. When she didn't, he continued.

"Do you know what I'm saying, wild one? I'm speaking the common language of travelers but maybe it makes no sense to you. Maybe my words are beyond your comprehension." He reached out as if to touch her, only to withdraw his hand when she tried to scoot away. "My shaman says that Wildings are little more than animals. If that's true, you are valuable for only one thing."

Fury flashed in her eyes and, although she settled back down, he sensed no lessening in her resolve. Her reaction also told him a great deal about her comprehension.

"I saved your life. If I hadn't come after you, you would have drowned."

"You tried to kill me."

Hearing her voice for the first time caused a lightninglike current to slam into him. Her voice was low for a woman, soft and yet resolute. "So you understand what I'm saying. Maybe I underestimated you."

"You tried to kill me."

"No, I didn't." The current continued to tease his nerve endings, prompting him to caress the rope he was holding in order to have something to do. "If I'd wanted you dead, you would be."

"Your arrow—"

"Had been treated with the sap from a bush with the ability to paralyze."

A blink was all she gave him in the way of a response, but he had no doubt she was waiting him out, studying him to see what he was going to do. Without the use of her hands, she had no option but to react to his actions; but what would happen if she was free? Strange, he didn't see her trying to run away.

She was a worthy opponent, one with legs designed for running and a secret place where those legs joined. One moment stretched into another as he stared at the soft curl of dark hair standing guard over her woman's place. He'd soon have access to it and wouldn't turn her over to the others until he'd rewarded himself for having captured her.

His cock, which he'd been struggling to ignore while taking his measure of her, tightened. Wanting to gauge her response, he adjusted himself under his loincloth. Clenching her teeth, she shook her head.

"Yes," he countered. "I *will* have you. When and how I want."

"Unless I kill you first."

"You, kill me? With what, your weapons?" He punctuated his sarcasm by sweeping his gaze over her nude form. "Where have you hidden them?"

She didn't answer, and something in her expression made him wonder if she wasn't certain what she was doing here alone wearing nothing. Maybe she was even more animal-like than he assumed.

The wind had picked up. It brushed morning cool and sharp over his still-wet skin, causing him to shiver. Certain she must be even more uncomfortable, he studied her, but she gave no sign of being cold.

Damnation, he didn't understand her!

And what he didn't understand, he didn't trust.

Determined to make sure his captive realized how profoundly her life had changed and how much power he wielded, he held up the rope for her to see.

"No." She scooted back a little.

"No?" he taunted. "How are you going to stop me, *slave? How?*"

"Do not call me—"

"I'll call you what I want," he said as he stood up. Not sure how to best restrain her legs, he loomed over her. If she was afraid, she gave no indication. "Because you belong to me." *For a while.*

"No," she repeated albeit not as forcefully as the first time. "I will never—"

Just then a shadow passed over her face, and she glanced upward. Prompted by the change in her expression, he did the same. A bird, maybe the same one that had alerted him to her location in the lake, drifted overhead.

She muttered something that was either nonsense or in a language he'd never heard, and although he wanted to see what the bird might do, his attention was drawn back to her. The sharpness was gone from her features, replaced by a softness, a love even. Although he longed to know what was responsible for the change, he resented the notion that she wasn't thinking about him.

Anger driving him, he straddled her so his body was between her and the damnable bird. In the space of a single blink, the softness in her died, replaced by a warrior's courage and determination.

"No!"

He sank down on top of her until her hips were under his buttocks.

She tried to buck him off, prompting him to press down even more. She continued to struggle. The way her elbows were positioned worked to his advantage because she couldn't easily turn onto her side. Unfortunately, her flailing legs were behind him and out of reach.

He'd been right. She was strong. Even more important, she

impressed him as determined but not desperate. He would have understood terror. All the captives he'd ever seen had been frightened out of their minds, begging and crying, pleading to their gods and spirits to save them—not that begging had ever changed anything. Instead, she seemed to be drawing on her own inner resources, resources that comforted and assured her even in the face of helplessness.

Something gathered inside him, a coming together of his resolve. He was determined to win this one-sided battle, not just because losing was incomprehensible, but because victory led to fucking.

Foreshadowing nothing of his intentions, he leaned to the side and then off her. Instead of letting himself fall, he pushed off the ground, grabbed her sharply bent elbows, and yanked her up and around so she was now on her belly. When she started to turn her head to the side, he grabbed a handful of hair and pull upward, forcing her to arch her back.

Although she tried to jerk free, she put little strength behind the effort, proof that she had no intention of risking having her hair pulled out. When she stopped struggling, he drew her upper body even farther off the ground so her breasts now hung down. The lines and curves of her taut body fascinated him. He longed to cup her breasts, to kneed and tease her nipples back into hardness. At the same time, he imagined stroking her buttocks until she moaned and went limp. He'd run his fingers lightly over the lush flesh while slowly closing in on her ass crack. Not caring how long it took, he'd caress and stroke, teaching and learning at the same time. Eventually her legs would part in primitive invitation and he'd slide a finger into her.

She'd begin to belong to him, only him.

However, instead of sighing in contentment as he'd fantasized, she breathed raggedly, coughing at the end. Realizing he was compromising her breathing, he released her hair. After lowering her head a bit, she turned her head to the side, then rested her cheek on the dirt. That done, she stared up at him. As before, he sensed no surrender in her. Quite the contrary, he had no doubt that she was gathering her strength as she waited for him to make the next move.

A worthy opponent. Maybe that's why claiming her intrigued him so.

He'd dropped the rope while positioning her on her belly. Now he made no secret of what he was doing when he picked it up again. Mentally calling himself a bastard for teasing her, he trailed the rope over the backs of her thighs and then up and along the rounded buttocks he could hardly wait to get his hands on. She'd started when the end first touched her. Then, every line of her body tense, she'd lain there and taken it.

Only he couldn't believe "taken it" adequately described what she was feeling.

"This is what's ahead of you," he told her. "My touching you every way I want to, whenever I want. Reminding you what it is to be a woman and being unable to shut down that part of yourself." *Teaching you how dependent you are on me.*

If she understood what he was hinting at, her eyes didn't give it away. Thinking to distract her from what he had in mind, he patted her shoulder. "Such a healthy specimen. A little on the skinny side, but your breasts make up for a lot."

She continued to glare at him. As he was trying to decide what, if anything, to say next, a now-familiar shadow again darkened her features. Eyes wide and nostrils flared, she strained to look beyond him and into the sky.

Seizing the opportunity, he climbed back on top of her but faced her feet this time. She again bucked under him, her fierce movements stirring a cock that didn't need any more stimulation. Fashioning a loop in the rope took longer than it should have because he had to fight to keep from being unseated. But by the spirits he loved her fight!

When she bent a knee in an attempt to kick him, he tried to snake the rope around her ankle. However, she yanked free before he could tie a knot. In addition to trying to wiggle out from under him, she thrashed from side to side. Her every movement registered throughout him. This was battle, war, strength against strength with the winner claiming everything.

He refused to lose.

Sweat slickened the feminine flesh under him, and he felt the effort every time she took a breath. He half believed he heard her heart beating. He could do this forever, certainly longer than she could. He'd ride her and ride her until she exhausted herself. Then, not for a moment letting her forget how helpless she was, he'd explore every part of her body. And he'd keep his sexual heat under control, somehow.

And he'd exploit hers.

Turn her into his possession.

His forehead pulsed, nearly screamed. His entire body felt as if it belonged to a savage beast. A determined beast.

Growling, he leaned forward and forced the loop over her foot. Then he quickly tied a single knot. Convinced she couldn't shake it off now, he pulled up, forcing her to bend her knee once more. Keeping the pressure going, he took his time to secure a knot that wouldn't come loose or tighten too much. His original intention had been to tie her ankles together, but now he wasn't sure how he'd accomplish that without risking a punishing heel in his face.

She'd stopped trying to yank her leg free, which gave him an idea. The trick was to keep her knee bent. He couldn't hold onto the rope indefinitely, but if it was secured to the rope around her waist . . .

"Battle over," he informed her as he scooted back, not stopping until he could see her waist. Settling onto her back, he was careful to keep most of his weight off her.

Sliding the ankle rope under her waist near her tethered hands took a couple of tries because she kept trying to jerk her leg free, but at length he had her. She was his.

5

Helplessness spun through Jola in endless waves. Maybe she should be relieved now that he was no longer sitting on her, but reality was, it made no difference. She couldn't move. Couldn't turn over.

Freedom was no longer part of her world.

Tears thickened her throat, but she forced them back into whatever dark place they'd come from.

How had her day taken this turn? It had begun as a hard, healing run that had pushed grief from her heart. Then, thinking to cool down, she'd plunged into the lake, fully believing that nothing else bad could happen to her.

She'd been wrong.

"No more struggling," her captor said and patted her buttocks. "I don't want you injuring yourself."

Let me go! You don't know what I am. "Is this what it takes for you to feel like a warrior?" she threw at him, unable to stop the words. "Ropes and greater strength. And something to weaken my body so I nearly drowned?"

He remained silent and remote, thinking thoughts she couldn't access. He'd positioned himself near her waist, undoubtedly so he could reach every part of her. As a result, she had to crane her neck if she wanted to look at him, which she didn't.

Those of her kind who'd gotten close to the newcomers had described them as ugly creatures with small eyes and short arms and legs, but her captor wasn't ugly. She wanted him to be, but he wasn't.

Most of all, she wanted to hate him as she'd never hated, but she couldn't. Even the possibility that he'd been responsible for Raci's death wasn't enough to freeze her heart.

"I don't understand what happened in the water," he said, the words low and slow as if he was talking to himself. "You weren't breathing when I found you, and you'd been under the water a long time. The way you recovered, so fast . . ."

To her surprise, she wanted him to know she was different from anyone he'd ever met, that the mystical qualities flowing through her and other Falcons gave them inhuman strength, but the large warrior had done nothing to deserve the truth.

"What do you want of me?" she demanded. Even as she spoke, she steeled herself for his answer.

"Whatever I want, when it pleases me."

"Kill me?"

"What? If that had been my intention, you'd already be dead."

Standing, he walked out of her line of sight. The last thing she'd wanted was to fall into the grasp of those who'd invaded Falcon Land, but it had happened. If she was going to survive, she needed to learn everything she could about her captor.

Him?

Where were the others?

As awareness of the hard ground under her and the bonds around her limbs grew, she acknowledged that only this man mattered.

Waiting for him to come back into view, she reminded herself that he couldn't possibly know who and what she was. As a warrior, he'd probably captured other women or been presented with slaves. He probably believed she'd be so terrified that she'd meekly comply with whatever he required of her. As long as she pretended to be what he wanted, she was safe.

Maybe.

Surely he wouldn't keep her out here for long because even a seasoned and successful warrior surrounded himself with his companions. She'd let him take her back to the enemy camp and wait for her chance to escape. In the meantime, she'd listen and learn and if she discovered who had killed Raci . . .

Careful not to look up at the sky so she wouldn't risk giving anything away, she reassured herself with the knowledge that at least one Falcon knew what had happened to her. Whoever it was would take his knowledge to Raptor's Craig and . . .

And what? The Falcons didn't risk their lives unless they had no choice. For now, they'd study what was happening to her but wouldn't try to rescue her unless they believed they had no choice.

A warning crawled up her spine. Holding her breath, she ordered herself to assess and appraise, to learn everything she could about this man while giving nothing away. Being robbed of the use of her arms and having a leg tightly tethered was something she had never expected to experience. Much as she wanted to tell herself that this temporary helplessness changed nothing, she knew better. He was right. He could do a great deal, maybe everything he wanted to, to her.

More important, as long as she was tied she couldn't reach Raptor's Craig.

As another warning slithered along her spine, she twisted as much as she could in an attempt to see behind her. Her captor appeared as a dark, strong shadow. She'd noted his bare chest earlier. Now it seemed to dominate not just his physique but her world. If she'd ever seen greater strength in a man she couldn't remember. Trying to tell herself that it didn't matter did nothing to lessen her nervousness, although if she was being honest with herself, nervousness, didn't adequately describe what she was feeling.

She didn't want to be this close to a man. Didn't know how to handle the emotions crashing through her.

"What are you going to do?" she demanded, determined to bring herself back to reality.

"I haven't decided yet," he said and lowered himself onto his knees beside her. Although he'd been closer when he was sitting on her, this was different, more overwhelming. Maybe it was because for the first time she could study his expression. His dark eyes carried the smoldering heat Raci's eyes had had as the two of them explored each other's bodies.

It doesn't take much for a man to get sexually excited, Raci had told her. Even before their bodies joined for the first time, she'd been tempted to tell him that the same was true for women, at least for her, but something had held the words back.

Determined not to acknowledge her captor's cock, she willed herself to wait him out. The long nights since Raci's murder had threatened her sanity. Foremost had been grief and anger, but she'd also wondered if she was destined to spend her life alone, to never mate. Now whether she did or didn't have sex had been taken out of her hands. She had no doubt what her captor wanted.

"You must feel superior," she snapped.

"I do?"

"Of course. There's little I can do to stop you. Right now you're telling yourself that I belong to you. You are, aren't you?"

She couldn't be sure but thought he'd winced when she

threw the last words at him. Maybe, if she kept on talking, she could change his mind about raping her. He might even let her go.

No, he wouldn't.

Instead of responding, he positioned her on her side. Maybe he thought she'd be grateful because she no longer had to crane her neck, but with her tied leg closest to him and the other stretched out to help her balance herself, her crotch was within his reach.

Why had she taken off her dress earlier?

Because she'd needed wind-life on her skin.

"You aren't what I expected," he told her, his hands resting on his too-solid thighs. "Your courage—why aren't you afraid of me?"

Because I'm not what you believe I am.

"You're not going to answer, are you," he said a few moments later. "My lord and shaman won't know what to make of you, and getting you to tell them certain things will be more difficult than they believe."

"Your lord? What's that?"

For an instant she thought a Falcon was flying overhead. Then she realized that the shadow stealing across his features came from within him. His eyes narrowed, and his mouth seemed to soften a bit.

"Sakima. He has led the Ekewoko since I was a boy. More than that, he became a father to me after . . ."

Where was your father? she nearly asked, but if he told her, she might hear something that made hating him difficult.

"Do you have a name?" he abruptly asked.

The way he'd posed his question . . . did he think her people were too primitive for names? About to respond that he couldn't be more wrong, she held back. If he believed she was a simple creature, he might let down his guard around her.

"Answer me! What do they call you?"

"Nothing."

A harsh breath warned that she'd pushed him too far. Before she could decide what to do, he closed a hand over the breast closest to him. His fingers pressed against her flesh, hurting and awakening it at the same time. Disconcerted, she divided her attention between his face and what he was doing. His grip was firm and secure. No matter how she might struggle, if he didn't want her to be free, she wouldn't be. Drawing in a ragged breath of her own, she vowed to wait him out. She'd give away nothing of what she was feeling.

"What is it?" he taunted. His hold tightened until she was certain he'd leave finger imprints on her breast. "You want me to think this is nothing to you? You don't feel it here." Using his other hand, he fingered her nipple. "But you do, my slave. Your body is giving you away."

No! she wanted to scream. *You're wrong.* But her nipple had already hardened, as had the one on her other breast.

"There's so much you don't know about me," he informed her. "You may think I'm only a warrior, but you're wrong."

He kept fingering her nipple, causing her to curl and uncurl her toes. She longed to thrash her head about, to run or, if necessary, crawl away from him. At the same time, a warmth that had nothing to do with the day licked over her body. He wasn't hurting her; if he had been, she'd have concentrated on his cruelty and hated him.

Instead he was reminding her that she was a woman.

At least partly.

"I can do this all day and into the night if that's what it takes." That said, he bent low over her and licked her too-sensitive nipple.

"Ah," she moaned. Shaken by the sound, she tried to dive back into silence only to moan again when he ran his teeth over her nub. "Stop, stop!"

"Why would I do that?" His breath washed over her breast.

"In fact, I see no reason not to continue this—" He released her breast but only so he could suck much of it into his mouth.

Her head suddenly felt as if it was going to burst. Even more upsetting, the drawing sensation encompassed her entire body with too much heat settling between her legs. Every muscle tightened as she struggled to not let him know what he'd done to her. He'd lightly raked his teeth over her flesh while swallowing her breast, the promise of injury and pain teaching her a lesson about him she'd never forget. Within him lurked the capacity for savagery. Although he was now tonguing and sucking her, she didn't dare move.

Caught in ways that threatened to shatter her mind, she again struggled to divorce herself from her system. Fought and failed.

Please, please, please.

If he heard her, he gave no indication. Either that or her trembling body had told him how close she was to falling apart, which was why he continued to hold her as she'd never been held. His ropes were nothing compared to his teeth on her skin.

Moments ago her muscles had protested the position he'd forced them into, but now nothing registered except for damp heat over and around her breast and an even greater heat in her pussy. The wonder.

She hated him, hated! Feared. But her emotions weren't that simple. Much as she wanted him to do something to make a lie of her thoughts, she half believed he knew more about her than she did. He'd restrained her leg the way he had not simply so she couldn't get away but because he had easy access to her sex.

Desperate for something, anything to think about, she tried to bring the sky into focus, but his form was in the way. If a Falcon was watching, she couldn't see it.

Make him pay for this! Punish him!

Diving into the act accompanying her silent command, she imagined Falcon digging his talons into her captor's back.

Blood would leak around the long gashes, and he'd scream. Keep on screaming.

Instead, he suckled on her breast. Shocked and disbelieving, she twisted her wrists in a desperate attempt to get at the knots, but even as she strained to escape the inescapable, the drawing sensation grew stronger. He wasn't hurting her. If he had, her loathing of him would be simple and clean. Instead, the chasm between the two of them was blurring almost as if they were becoming one.

No, that couldn't be his intention. Could it?

"Stop it! Stop it!" She struggled to turn away only to have him plant a hand against her collarbone. Her breast was starting to throb, whether from discomfort or pleasure she couldn't say. Most upsetting, she no longer understood what she was feeling. In many ways, her body had turned against her.

"Don't!" Digging her free foot against the ground, she struggled to get out from under him. "You can't—don't!"

Using his tongue, he pushed her breast free, but before she fully comprehended what had happened, he'd rolled her about so he could cup a hand around the other breast and position it near his mouth.

"Attack! Kill him!"

At her outburst, he froze, his system hard and unmoving. Even as she struggled to comprehend what she'd said, she likened him to a predator—a cougar, maybe, or a wolf. Much as she loathed admitting it, the thought of him being ruled by instinct sent energy shooting through her. He could become an animal. More than human, like her.

Still holding her in place, he rocked back on his heels and looked all around. Because she couldn't not, she studied him. Yes, this enemy warrior had become more animal than human.

"Who were you trying to command?" His voice was cold.

Careful. "Do you think I'd tell you?"

"Maybe not now but you will, once I've taught you."

Could he? she pondered while he continued to study his surroundings. She couldn't fathom him altering her from what she'd always been, but then until today she hadn't believed a man would ever control her as he did.

Moving with a speed beyond her comprehension, he gripped her chin and forced her to look at him.

"There's no one here. Nowhere for someone to hide."

Someone? How little you know. "Isn't there?"

"No." He cocked his head to the side, smiling faintly as he did. "But you want me to think differently. You want me to believe I'm about to be attacked so I'll let you go, but that's not going to happen. Think about this, Wilding. Maybe the time will come when I have no use for you. When and if that happens, I'll discard you. But until that happens, you won't know what freedom feels like."

Left tied and immobile? Was that what he was hinting at? Fear dried her throat, and it took all her self-control not to look toward distant Raptor's Craig for reassurance.

"What's this?" He touched his fingers to the sides of her throat. "Your blood is racing. What I said frightens you, doesn't it?"

"No."

"Don't lie."

He thought she'd tell him the truth? As one moment became another, her heart rate slowed, and she no longer found it so difficult to swallow. Her momentary fright confused her because even though right now only she and her captor shared this area, she suspected that the Falcon who'd been watching earlier was on his way to Raptor's Craig to tell the others. Maybe instead of just waiting and watching, her kind would defend her, find a way to free her.

Maybe they'd kill her captor—unless his arrows found them first.

"I didn't expect you to say what you did, that's all," she admitted, her tone as unemotional as possible. "If you've never been tied up, you can't comprehend what I'm going through."

His hold on her chin let up. The way his fingers now moved, she almost believed he was trying to soothe away whatever discomfort he'd caused her. The man confused her. Maybe that's what had been behind her irrational fear.

"You're right," he said and turned his attention to her useless ankle. "No one has ever done anything like this to me. I'd hate it, and whoever did it to me." He continued to regard her. "Do you have a name?"

"Do I—of course!" she snapped, recalling that he'd already asked the question. Damn him for lightly running his fingers over her anklebone and calf! She could barely think.

"What is it?"

She wasn't going to tell him; revealing something so personal would take what existed between them in a direction she didn't want. But if he didn't call her by name, he might think of her as "slave," and that was even worse.

To her surprise, he didn't demand a response. Instead, he studied her deeply bent leg and barely concealed cunt. His eyes were like fire against her skin, somehow touching tissues that had never felt this alive or vulnerable. Much as she wanted him to know how wrong he was to call her kind "Wildings," much as she needed to see awe and disbelief and pain and even fear in his eyes, she needed other things from him even more.

"Don't look at me like that!"

"Haven't you figured it out? What you do or don't want doesn't matter. I'm in control, not you."

Not once I'm free. Although she was tempted to warn him, she didn't. Let him discover for himself what he'd begun when he'd captured her. Before she was done with him, he'd regret having ever seen, let alone touched her.

"You think you've won something by not speaking?" he demanded, his scrutiny increasing. "You haven't. And to make sure you understand—"

Before she could begin to guess what he had in mind, he grabbed her free ankle and bent her knee forward toward her belly. She fought him, of course, but all too soon, he'd forced her heel against her thigh. He only grunted when she cursed him, only held on as she struggled against his greater strength. All too soon, she was drenched in sweat and exhausted. Still, she continued to try to straighten her leg. She refused to ask herself what he had in mind, and although he was looking into her eyes now, she resolutely didn't return his stare.

When she had no choice but to rest her head on the ground and pant, he closed in on her until he'd anchored her leg under his knee. With both hands free, he turned his attention to caressing her thighs, buttocks, and belly. She had no doubt what he was doing: proving his superiority. More than that, he was giving her an unforgettable lesson in how much he understood about her body.

Once again she went from loathing everything about him to anticipation. His fingers, although rough, were also gentle. He knew exactly how much pressure was needed to keep from tickling her and used his knowledge to slowly work his way through her resistance.

He toyed with her navel, first filling it with his thumb pad and then his knuckle. When he did, she jumped and shuddered, not that it changed anything. He repeatedly focused on her navel, but when he wasn't there, his fingers slid over her belly to what he could reach of her pussy.

Maybe he was only pretending he couldn't penetrate her opening so she'd be forced to wait. To anticipate. To silently cry out.

But what did she want? To be free of him or something—intimate?

He no longer had to force her leg up by her belly; surely he realized he'd stripped resistance from her. Surely he knew, what, everything?

Despite her determination to resist and rebel, she went limp and weak under him. The closer he came to her core, the harder it was to wait for that exciting and terrifying moment. Sensations swirled through her, some she'd experienced before, others beyond her comprehension. Nothing about her body still belonged to her but not just because he'd robbed her of the use of her limbs. It wasn't that simple.

When he rested the side of a finger along her labial lips, she tried to rest with him so she'd have the strength for what came next. Tried and failed. He was under control, damn him. In contrast, she was flying into tiny fragments. At the same time, her thoughts drifted back to when she'd been in the lake. Probably because of the poison raging through her system, she remembered only bits and pieces. Most of her memories centered around sinking beneath the surface.

Until she'd summoned up the strength to close it, water had threatened to fill her mouth. Even as she'd taken comfort in her small victory, she'd acknowledged the water around her eyes and drifting through her hair. The sinking sensation.

She was drifting now, floating, surrounded and supported by something without end. A magnificent and powerful force touched every inch of her being and, even though that force frightened her, she wanted nothing else. The past faded into nothing, and the present swarmed around her. She was lost. Sinking down.

Forceful hands on her shoulders pulled her back to reality. Before she could fully center herself in the here and now, however, her captor flipped her onto her belly. The leg he'd bent against her belly was now caught under her weight, and the ground flattened her breasts. Tugging uselessly at her bonds, she lifted her head and looked behind her. Yes, there he was, still looming over her. Still controlling her world.

Then he ran his hand along her ass crack and from there to her sex, and she understood why he'd done what he had. Her earlier vulnerability paled in comparison to this.

"You're beautiful," he muttered. "I never thought I'd think that of a Wilding, but you are beautiful."

His hand hadn't moved but, with a finger resting against her entrance, it didn't matter. She couldn't think how she might straighten her leg, but maybe she didn't want to because this way he had full and free access to her.

Careful! You risk losing yourself.

"Your strength intrigues me." His deep tone silenced her inner voice. "Yes, I've taken that away from you, for now, but it's still part of you. Something I want to explore."

Speak! Tell him he has no right!

"This is what you're about."

His words began to penetrate only to shatter like a thin layer of ice. She'd just begun to wonder why that was when she realized his hand no longer lay quietly along her sex. A single finger was sliding into her, moving slowly and yet surely, touching inner flesh, gentle and masterful at the same time. Her mind blinked, stayed closed. There was nothing to her beyond his finger inside her. And her pussy weeping for him.

"Please, please, please," she moaned. Her breath stirred the dirt.

"Please what?"

6

What are you doing?

Nakos's cock felt as if a knot had been tied in it, making it all but impossible for him to think. Yes, he knew what he was doing, barely. The energy coursing through his hands was impossible to ignore, as was the pressure in his temple. He'd fingered females before, of course, but they'd either been willing participants or had reconciled themselves to a man's mastery. Today was different. Not only hadn't this Wilding ever experienced ropes, she'd yet to acknowledge that he was superior to her in any way.

She was like a meadow painted with a fresh dusting of snow: virginal.

Shifting his position brought him closer to her. Much as he wanted to see her reaction to being finger fucked, he couldn't shake off her impact to his senses. Her skin was coated with the sweat of her struggles, her mountain of hair tangled around her. There was something otherworldly about the positioning of her useless arms, and he couldn't tear his attention from the contrast between her coloring and that of the rope he'd put around her.

He loved accepting that she was his and she'd never again taste freedom unless he chose to hand it to her. Maybe it was because he'd gone too long without sex, although a part of him expected that life-weariness and old nightmares played a part. So much of his existence revolved around staying alive and being a valuable Ekewoko, but he'd recently shrugged off that weight so he could concentrate on his possession. The gift that the spirits had handed to him.

"You're soft here," he observed in a whisper as his finger sank deeper into her warmth. "Soft and ready for me. Sleek."

"No, no," she chanted.

"Don't deny the truth, Wilding. Feel yourself." Bending his finger, he stroked her secret walls. "Feel your response."

"No. No."

She was on the move, not fighting but, he believed, trying to stay on top of whatever she was experiencing. He debated pointing out that her pussy was flooding itself, but she might call him a liar, and he needed a measure of honesty between them.

"My name is Nakos," he told her. "Nakos of Ekew, although I haven't seen my home for many moons. I'm here with my fellow warriors because our lord and our shaman told us this is where we must come if we're to ever reclaim Ekew."

She might not care about what he was telling her now, but she'd remember. More important, she'd never forget what Nakos of Ekew had done to her. Fighting what raged through him, he concentrated on milking her responses. If only breathing wasn't so difficult! If only fantasies of burying his cock inside her didn't threaten to engulf him.

His finger retreated and advanced, twisted and stroked. Her scent seeped into him, almost as if she was gifting him with her essence. He took the smell of female arousal deep inside him, then opened himself up to the way that scent pushed into his veins and pulsed within his heart. Lost, he ran his other hand over her thigh and buttocks. Dirt clung to her in places, but he didn't care. Dirt was part of their world, part of this strange thing they were sharing.

"By the spirits." She jerked her body in one direction, stopped, then rocked herself back to where she'd been. "I—I . . ."

His mouth remembering how her breast had filled it, he bent low over her so he could run his tongue over her backside. The moment he did, he felt as if he was being pulled into a whirlpool. Startled by her power over him, he pulled out of her pussy and sat up.

She was whimpering like some small, lost animal, her arms and legs trembling, hips moving.

"What's your name, Wilding? Tell me and I'll give you what you need." *Maybe.*

For long seconds her silence pushed against him. Then she took a strangled breath. "Jola."

Jola. "Do you have a mate, Jola? Someone you share your life with?"

A shiver ran through her. Even as he studied her taut muscles, he sensed that this new reaction had nothing to do with her being sexually stimulated. Instead, no doubt about it, hatred rolled out of her to press against him. He wasn't surprised when she wrenched herself around so she was on her back once more and staring up at him. Her glare reminded him of a predator's single-mindedness.

"He's dead."

What? "How?"

"At your hands. Yours, or one of those you're part of."

"We call ourselves 'Ekewoko.' "

"I call you murderers."

Leaning back, he rested his hands on his thighs. Although she still fascinated him, he had no desire to break through the barrier she'd thrown up around herself. Her hard glare told him that her pussy no longer welcomed him. He could have taken her, of course, but she'd only hate him more, and for reasons he couldn't fathom, he didn't want her loathing.

If only he understood what he wanted.

Jola walked behind Nakos of Ekew. The man who called himself an Ekewoko had released her leg, thank goodness, but because her wrists were still tied, her resentment of his superiority continued. Perhaps she should be grateful because her arms were in front of her instead of still anchored to the waist rope. Instead, she cursed the soft leather around her neck and the rope he'd fastened to it so he could lead her wherever he wanted.

The day was going to be warmer than the last few, almost as if winter wasn't going to come after all. The breeze she suddenly noticed seemed to come from all directions, cooling and heating her skin at the same time. Determined not to give him the satisfaction of hauling her along like some dumb beast, she matched her pace to his. Because when she was in human form she always went barefoot unless the ground was frozen, her soles barely noted what she was walking on. She kept her head up in part so her tangled hair would stay out of her eyes but mostly because she didn't want him guessing how defeated she felt.

Not just defeated.

If only she could ignore what was taking place between her legs. She should have been able to relax as soon as he'd stopped sexually teasing her, but if anything, her sense of anticipation and need had increased. Every step sent her tissues gliding against each other. Sex juices coated her labial lips, and she occasionally caught a hint of what she smelled like there.

Every time she let down her guard and stopped reminding herself of how much she wanted to see him dead, vivid memories stole over her. He knew too much about her body, too much about what excited a woman.

He called himself a warrior, so did that mean he spent much of his time in battle or preparing for war? If so, she didn't know how he'd found the time to become an expert about the opposite sex. She wouldn't ask him about his experiences with women, of course. She certainly didn't care! But until she'd gotten free or her people came to rescue her, she and Nakos would be together. Only a fool wouldn't realize how vital it was to probe him for his strengths.

Weaknesses? Did he have any?

Studying the way his legs worked forced her to contemplate that he might not have any physical weaknesses. He certainly hadn't demonstrated any. In fact, the longer she regarded him, the more she acknowledged that her captor was built for his role in life as a warrior. Yes, he was well armed, but without muscles, sinew, and bone capable of responding to every need, his weapons might not be enough to keep him alive.

Ah! The heat, the fire in her pussy! Even being thirsty did nothing to tamp things down.

His ass was hard and neat and muscled beneath the short leather garment that hung from his waist. She'd been so focused on herself during their struggles that she hadn't taken note of how the garment was constructed. Most men took care to protect their cocks so maybe there was more to what he was wearing than a skirt that barely reached his knees. The logical conclusion was that his cock rested inside a pouch of some kind, but maybe not.

His hair brushed the tops of his shoulders. It was slightly curled and nearly as dark as hers. If anything, his eyebrows and lashes were even darker than what was on his head, which, although she didn't want the thought, led to musing about the hairs at his groin.

Damn him! He'd seen her sex. Touched it. Invaded it.

Awakened need. In contrast, she was forced to stare at a sun-kissed back made for battle and legs designed for an active life. He wore leather shoes.

She'd slowed while deciding how to get around an ant mound when something tugged at her mind. Grateful for any distraction, she immediately looked skyward. Yes, there it was, a Falcon. It was so high that someone who didn't know what he was looking at might not know what it was, but she had no doubt that this predator was one of her kind and not just a bird, because her heart and nerves never lied about the difference.

As hunters, Falcons were solitary creatures so she hadn't been surprised to see only one earlier. Just the same, she'd tried to believe that her rescue would come about when a large number of Falcons attacked Nakos.

Obviously, her kind didn't believe that time had come, if it ever would.

The strap around her neck pressed against her, reminding her that she'd slowed down. But although she picked up her pace a bit, she didn't take her attention off the bird. Watching it filled her with a sense of belonging. This was *her* land. Nakos was a stranger and as such unwanted. He and the other Eke-woko should return to Ekew!

But he'd said they couldn't.

Why?

And why had his leaders commanded him and the other warriors to come to Falcon Land?

"What?" he asked, startling her.

Responding to the second tug on her leash, she glared at her captor. Back when she'd dived into the lake, she'd been so intent on regaining her love of life that she hadn't cared whether she was naked or dressed. Now, because of *him,* her nudity seemed to stalk her. She felt defined by her lack of clothing.

"I asked you a question." He stopped and pulled, making it

clear that he expected her to join him. "What were you looking at?"

"Nothing."

"You're lying."

By way of response, she turned as far away from him as she could. He could force her to swing back around, of course, but she hoped she'd made her point.

"What is it? You think your *people* are coming to rescue you?"

"*People?* Why do you say it that way, as if we're less than human? You call us Wildings when you know nothing about us."

"Tell me, then, starting with what you call yourselves."

That she'd never willingly do. "It doesn't matter. What does is that when they surround you, you'll regret what you've done to me—for as long as you live."

If he was alarmed, he gave no indication as he studied their world. On the verge of laughing at his attempts to see behind boulders and bushes, she tried not to react when he suddenly looked upward. Certainly his eyesight wasn't as keen as hers but—

"That speck. What is it?"

"I see nothing."

"Yes, you do!" His hand snaked out and around her throat. Although she resisted, she couldn't stop him from pulling her against him. They touched from shoulder to hip. "It's a bird, maybe the same as before."

"Maybe."

If she planted her hands against his chest, she might have been able to push away, but somehow it was easier to sink within the contact.

"Something's happening here." He sounded a little in awe. "The speed with which you recovered from the poison and that bird—it's as if it's following you; us."

Of course she wouldn't, but she was tempted to tell him what it meant to be a Falcon. Instead, she let his strength enter her. What she felt went beyond sexual awareness. It was deeper somehow, a tentative joining of two people with nothing in common.

"I didn't want to come here," he told her. "I did because I would never refuse to follow my lord's lead, but I don't understand why this place we call Screaming Wind means so much to him and Tau. I still don't."

"Tau?"

"Our shaman."

From the little he'd said, she'd concluded that they'd been forced to leave Ekew. Born and raised in Falcon Land—or Screaming Wind, as he called it—she couldn't imagine ever living anywhere else.

But if he forced her to leave . . .

Alarmed, she straightened. He didn't pull her back against him, but neither did his grip on the leash relax. Looking at the man who was so close that his features blurred, she again wondered if she simply hated him. She'd expected him to be a monster, a beast. But there were so many layers to him.

"Your lord," she tried. "Are you taking me to him?"

"Yes."

"And Tau?"

"Yes."

Soon she'd be turned over to other men, and they might indeed be monsters or beasts. If she'd been truly human, the thought would have terrified her. As it was, she had to tamp down fear, yet she told herself that she was grateful for what he'd just told her. Knowing what he planned for her future made it easier to shrug off her conflicted emotions. She and Nakos were enemies, nothing more.

"Aren't you going to ask me what Sakima wants of you?" he questioned.

"Sakima?"

"My lord, and the man who took me from boy to adult."

There, another layer to this complex man. "I don't have to," she evaded. "I know."

Shaking his head, he wrapped his fingers around the rope holding her hands together and lifted. "You can't possibly know what his or Tau's intentions are, because they haven't confided in us yet. Tell me something, Jola. Why are you naked?"

"I'm a Wilding. Do you expect anything different?"

"I'm not sure."

"Maybe I—wanted to get close to myself," she blurted, "To feel the sun everywhere."

"And that would, what, make you feel more alive?"

Surprised by his perception, she said nothing. Falcon Land was a place of great contrasts, but most travelers didn't note those contrasts. The mostly flat terrain struck most of those who traveled through it as monotonous, even barren, but she'd spent her life appreciating the nuances of color and the impact of each season. She couldn't help wondering if Nakos would ever see it the way she did.

Probably not, especially if he soon left, taking her with him.

She didn't want to be his prisoner! She wanted back freedom of movement and privacy and the ability to go to Raptor's Craig whenever she needed to. She wanted to not think about him.

"It's still here," he said.

Certain what he was talking about, she nevertheless glanced up. The speck that she had no doubt was a Falcon was still circling above them. Again and again it traced the same pattern while drifting a little lower with each circuit. Falcons flew like that when they were searching for prey or learning what they needed to about something in their world. In Falcon form, they were ruled by instinct and not intelligence. Just the same, she told herself that the creature above her cared about her well-being. The creature was assuring him or herself that she wasn't in danger.

And perhaps deciding to leave her alone so she could learn everything possible about the newcomers who called themselves Ekewoko.

"The way you're looking at it," Nakos went on, "it's as if you love it."

"You think I shouldn't?"

"It's only a bird."

Only a bird. Under other circumstances, she would have laughed at his ignorance. Instead, she let her gaze drift back to him. Because he was still looking skyward, she felt free to study his features. Nature had set his eyes deep in their sockets. His cheekbones were high and his chin firm and square, which lent him an air of confidence and added to his strength. Even his mouth struck her as strong. If he hadn't taken her breast into it, she would have never guessed at the soft sensuality beneath the firm line.

Yes, her breast had been in his mouth, sheltered and teased.

Just then he shook his head as if dismissing the circling predator and met her gaze. They stood staring at each other, enemies probing beneath the surfaces for weaknesses. At the same time, she sensed something else behind the relentless stare: a questioning, perhaps, or maybe simple acknowledgment that she was female and he male.

Unwanted warmth pressed against her throat. The sensation swept over her breasts to harden her nipples. Caught in the grip of an emotion beyond her control, she shifted her stance, but her attempt to plant her legs more securely under her only sent fresh warmth to her core. Her mouth sagged, and her lids became so heavy she could barely keep her eyes open.

Sensuality danced around and through her, stroked her arms and caressed her legs. Her knees were on the brink of collapsing. Believing she was going to drown had been nothing compared to what swamped her right now. She ached to rub her body against her captor's and with the act let him know how desperately she needed to fuck.

Yes, that! The hunger she'd lived with since Raci's death.

When Nakos released her wrists, she tried to quiet the inner rage by telling herself that Raci's death was responsible. Raci had shown her what it was to be a woman; he'd awakened her to a woman's needs. With him gone, she wanted only one thing: a cock. Any man's cock.

Even her captor's?

"Don't look at me like that," he snapped.

"Like—what?"

Wrapping his arm around her waist, he again sealed their bodies together. "If you think you can buy your freedom with—"

"I don't know what you're talking about." How could he think she was trying to seduce him when it was he who had the power to melt her.

"The hell you don't! That damnable body of yours—" He thrust his pelvis at her. "Is that what you're after, is it!"

His cock ground against her, a spear, promise, and threat all at once. Maybe his urgency prompted her to lean into him; maybe her own need drove her. Whatever the reason, she widened her stance and locked her knees. Instead of looking up at him and risking a reminder of the difference in their height, she fixed her attention on his chest. He'd questioned her nudity, but wasn't he all but naked himself, the lack of clothing screaming at her?

"Damn you," he growled. Gripping her upper arms, he turned her so they faced each other square on. Then he forced her against him, his cock pressing against her belly. If she stood on her toes, maybe it would slide between her legs, but no, he was too tall for that and she too short, feeling frail and female for one of the few times in her life.

Her eyes closed. Darkness slipped in around her edges to quiet her senses and free her to concentrate on the only thing that mattered. She no longer saw herself as this man's captive. Rather, they'd become equals with their hearts racing and the fire she sensed in his belly licking out and blending with hers. Her mind spun and her legs trembled, prompting her to lift her arms and work them over his head. Rope pressed against the back of his neck.

She had no intention of kissing him, wanted nothing to do with that kind of intimacy. At the same time, she couldn't stop herself from wondering what touching her lips to his would be like, what he'd taste like.

"You're a devil," he muttered. "A dark spirit."

"Not me. You."

When he didn't respond, she pressed her cheek against his chest. The sun had baked his flesh there, and the warmth seeped into her. Heat met with heat. Spun together.

Dizzy, she struggled to clear her head. Instead, it filled with the image of the slowly circling predator. She delighted in the joy and freedom that came with flight. What she didn't comprehend, and barely acknowledged, was how an enemy warrior could fill her with the same excitement.

"I hate what you're doing to me." Despite her words, she pressed her heavy breasts against his chest. "Let me go, damn it! Leave me."

"Let you go?" His laugh was harsh, nearly cruel. "You don't want that, I know you don't."

He gripped her buttocks and his fingers became her world. They pressed into her soft flesh, somewhere between painful and a sensation she refused to name. Even though she knew it was insane to do so, she focused fully on his strength and mastery. Then his grip strengthened, and he pulled her ass cheeks apart. Exposed her.

"No!"

"No? What are you afraid of?"

Fear wasn't supposed to be part of her world. Even when she'd wondered if she was drowning earlier today, she'd accepted the inevitable, but this was different. Out of control. "Just because you've done this to me"—she pressed the ropes against the back of his neck for emphasis—"doesn't give you the right to—"

"I disagree, Jola." He continued to manipulate her ass cheeks. "Everything in life goes to the victor. I've decided you will go to me."

To her shock, her pulse quickened. Possessed, by him? What would that be like? Even though she might have been able to lift her arms off his neck, she didn't try. Instead, she rocked from side to side, her breasts gliding over him as she did. Because he still held her buttocks, the drawing sensation on them increased. Her effort was hardly strong enough to jeopardize his hold on her, but that wasn't what she wanted.

Then what was?

7

With every turn, the pressure on her buttocks intensified, only to drop away as she straightened. Anchored, he took in a long and slow breath, grunting a little at the end. When she stopped her restless movements, he waited her out and then worked his fingers into her crack. Something exploded inside her mind.

"You're so warm in there, wild one. Your moist heat catches my fingers on fire."

Sucking in a breath, she sought a way to put distance between herself and his knowing hands, but all she accomplished was to seal her belly to him.

"What is this, wild one? Whatever it is, it doesn't feel like fighting."

Fighting? She'd struggled at first and should still be but wasn't. Couldn't think how or why to begin. Fascinated by the human blanket against her from breasts to pelvis, she rose onto her toes. Her mouth was so close to the side of his neck that she could have bitten him, if she'd wanted to. But biting was the last thing she could imagine herself doing. Instead, she clung to him.

He gripped her in turn, his muscles taut and breath now hard and quick. Was he on the brink of coming? He didn't need to be inside her in order to climax?

"Capturing you was the best thing I've done in a long time," he informed her. "You're like a just-opening flower."

"A—I don't know what you mean."

"It doesn't matter because I have every intention of showing you."

Even as she gave herself up to sensation, fear nibbled at her. She would have given a great deal to be granted a measure of freedom.

Then a finger found the entrance to her anus and her mind again exploded. "No!" She hated the whimpering note, hated her inability to do more than tremble.

"You don't like this?" He slid his finger over her puckered opening. "Feel nothing?"

Her toes and calves ached and her breasts continued to harden. Aching away from him and holding on at the same time, she gave up trying to keep the world in focus. If this was the way the Ekewoko treated all their female captives, she didn't want to know about it. Still, she didn't see how any woman could resist.

She'd taken a chance on settling onto her heels when he began a swirling movement against and around her rear opening. Her ass muscles clenched, but the longer he handled her, the less her resistance. Nerve endings seemed to spring to life everywhere he touched. Her cunt leaked.

Help me! Spirits, please help me!

He was now applying pressure to just one buttock, keeping it from settling into place. The constant movement, the burning sensation caused by his flesh grinding against her filled her head.

"By the spirits, I—I can't—"

"What, Wilding? What can't you do?"

How had he become so big and powerful? What had happened to her strength and will? And why didn't she try to shake him off the moment he left off her anus and ran his fingers over her labia?

Why was she standing there whimpering, drooling even?

She still didn't have the answer when he returned to her rear opening, coating it with her own fluids this time. She tried to see behind her, then reared back and gave him a beseeching look. "Don't, please, don't."

"You don't know what I have in mind."

Something broke down inside her. She was no longer aware of Falcon Land's existence, and if a small part of her remembered that one of her kind was watching, it didn't matter.

How could it, when this man who'd stormed into her world pushed a fingertip into her, bringing her sex juices with him? His finger stretched her, the sensation nearly painful and wondrous at the same time. Undone by her response, she again rose onto her toes and risked a wrenched spine trying to see what he was doing. Even though she couldn't see beyond her body's curves, she knew what was happening.

His finger was fucking her ass, going where no man's had ever gone, where she'd never imagined one would rest, pulling her apart and filling her all at the same time. She was certain he could reach clear to her belly this way, sure she'd die if he did.

"I can't—I can't—"

"This isn't your decision." Cupping her buttocks with the hand not engaged in fucking her, he pressed. "I'm your captor. As such I can and will do whatever I want to you."

Her captor. Owner and master.

Any other time she would have fought with every bit of strength in her, but even though she couldn't comprehend how it had happened, he'd stolen her will. All he'd done was place a single finger against her and her wings had been clipped. No longer could she fly. Or fight.

However, much as she wanted to beg him to return her body to her, she didn't. Instead, she nearly bit her tongue as the invasion deepened. No matter how many times he worked his finger back and forth, her muscles clamped down on what she couldn't expel. Sensing his determination, she struggled to relax and let *it* happen, but instinct refused to give way. The probing wasn't painful but so much more than her system could deal with.

No, it wasn't that at all.

Instead, she wanted his fingers elsewhere, in another hole.

Maybe he understood why she vacillated between trying to escape and offering herself to him every time he drove into her. Off balance and lost in sensation, she could no longer distinguish between her separate body parts. Indeed, everything seemed connected to her ass, which he controlled.

Up until now she'd believed she could withstand whatever he tried to do to her, that she'd never surrender. But she'd made that vow without knowledge of how weak and hungry her body would become or how little will remained.

Something about his larger size and the restraints he'd put on her worked in tandem with his take-charge approach. She barely understood what was happening to her. Only his touch, his power and control, mattered. He could hurt her; she'd be a fool not to acknowledge the potential. But instead of breaking her down, he was turning her body against her.

Lighting it on fire.

Suddenly ashamed of herself, she pressed her hands against the back of her captor's neck. Cursing, he lowered his head. As he did, she drew her arms over and off him and forced them down between their straining bodies.

"What the hell—" he started.

"No! Do you hear me, no!"

She'd barely gotten the words out when he withdrew his finger from her rear entrance, leaving her ass lost and lonely.

Free, if that's what she truly wanted. "Think you've won, do you?" he taunted. "Listen to me, Wilding. I've just begun with you."

If he'd thrown the words at her, she might have been terrified. Instead, she detected a teasing note behind his challenge. Remembering childhood wrestling matches with her siblings, she pondered whether he intended to turn things into a game between them, but she'd be a fool if she let that happen. Her future was at stake, her life even, surely her freedom and self-respect.

"You have no right," she retorted after a short hesitation.

"I don't need a right. Not with might on my side." His mouth twitched. "And coupled with proof of how much of a woman you are."

A fresh sensation seared her. She was still trying to make sense of it when he turned her to the side. At the same time, his leg struck the back of her knee, buckling it. He pushed down on her shoulders, and she wound up on her knees on the ground. Joining her, he captured her wrists and flattened her useless hands against her belly. He kept up the pressure until she toppled backward with her legs trapped under her. A quick, strong yank on her bonds and her arms were over her head.

Helpless.

"That was easy." His breath heated the side of her head. "In case you didn't understand, that's what I mean by might. Say it: I'm stronger than you."

Admit his physical superiority? After what he'd just done, what was the point?

His mouth twitched, and his eyes took on a cast she'd never seen. Maybe he'd been distracted by the sight of her breasts stretched over her chest wall and her ribs silhouetted under her skin. Although the position he'd forced on her was far from comfortable, she was strangely content to remain where she was. His hands on her bound wrists served as an inescapable reminder of their unequal relationship while a certain heat between her legs comforted her. He could have hurt her, but he hadn't. Every time he touched her, she responded. Felt alive.

Alive.

"All right," he said in the same challenging tone. "So you don't want to say anything. I could force it from you, but I don't believe that'll be necessary. Do you want me to demonstrate what I'm talking about?"

Before she could respond, if she was going to, he cupped his free hand around the breast closest to him. Lifting it, he closed his fingers over its fullness. "This is an example, little wild one. Feel my strength." Giving weight to his words, he pulled on her hands until she felt the strain in her armpits. "Acknowledge how easy it is to turn you into what I want."

She couldn't move, couldn't focus on anything except his bulk over her and his knowing hands, her utter helplessness.

And willingness.

"Your body is your undoing," he continued. "No, don't shake your head. It's the truth. Damnation, I want what your body offers. And I'm going to take it."

"By raping me?" She waited for the words to drive her into loathing, for it to be that simple.

"No."

"Then—"

"Because it won't be necessary."

"Not—let me up!"

"Not until I have no doubt of how you're going to respond when I do."

There was something ominous to his tone. At the same time, she sensed a promise behind what he'd just said; either that or she wanted a promise. Although she couldn't see herself, she had a clear mental image of what she looked like. Among the Falcons were several craftsmen. One created exquisite wood carvings of everything from wolves to flowers while another painted wonderful pictures on hide canvases. She'd long envied not only their skill but also their ability to find beauty in so many things.

Today her body had become something beautiful, sleek health stretched and curved so his eyes could feast on it.

"I've never seen anything like you," he muttered as if reading her mind. "Perfect."

His praise sent a wave of heat-energy through her. He released her wrists but kept ahold of her breast, lifting and compressing it at the same time. A delicious tingling swam through her. Feeling as if she were sinking into a bottomless pool, she struggled to turn away until she'd discovered how to reach the surface again but was forced to stop when he shifted his grip so her nipple pressed against his palm.

"Hmm," she whimpered, nerves and muscles jumping.

"Like that, do you?"

"Hmm."

"That sound. You don't have any idea what it does to me, do you?"

Too much pressure and muscles short-circuiting, a climax building. Bucking under him, she tried to kick.

Shaking his head at her futile attempts, he flicked a finger over her nipple.

"No!"

"Why should I want to stop? You are perfect; absolutely perfect."

Whether she perceived his words as a compliment didn't matter because the pressure against her breast now radiated throughout her. Once more he was laying claim to her and taking her deep into herself. She heard herself sigh.

"That's right, wild one. Let it out."

"Let—what?"

"Everything you're feeling."

She couldn't, couldn't! That much honesty would leave her unbelievably vulnerable and lost. Desperate to take back pieces of herself, she struggled to sit up. Instead of pushing her down again, he switched hands so his right now cradled her breast. Resistance died.

"I'm not done with you, don't you understand that? Everything I want to do to you is going to happen."

Unable to determine whether he was threatening or promising, she collapsed but kept her hands on her chest instead of over her head as they'd been earlier. Her thumb brushed his.

"What's this?" he asked, rotating his hand a little and abrading her breast. "Maybe you think you can pull me off you."

"I won't let you hurt—"

"Have I said anything about pain?"

"You said I can't stop you from—"

"From doing not just what I want, but what we both do. No, don't deny it." His mouth twitching again, he ran his left hand over her ribs. His touch was too light, too sensual, full not of threat but promise. Because he still claimed ownership of her breast, she had no choice but to acknowledge and accept everything he was doing. Inch by inch, rib bone by rib bone, he traced a path she sensed would only end one place: at her pussy.

"No, ah, no!" She again tried to heave herself into a position only to fail once more. If only she could straighten her legs! That way she wouldn't be so off-balance.

"I love the way you struggle. The way your breasts move when you're gasping for breath, the look in your eyes."

"What look?" Was the Falcon still around?

"A little fear. Nervousness. Uncertainty. And something else: anticipation."

He was wrong, damn him, wrong! She wasn't looking forward to being manhandled, and she certainly didn't want to have sex with him.

Did she?

Sex, fucking hot and hard, ecstasy raging through her and flying. Alive. So alive.

Although his hand had stopped moving while they were talking, it had occasionally twitched, which added to her inability to concentrate. And when his fingers headed toward the valley where her belly lay, she broke out in a sweat and clawed ineffectively at the hand covering her breast.

"Is that all you're capable of?" he asked.

Determined to rise to the challenge, she slapped him. If she'd caused him pain, he gave no indication.

"Whatever you are," he told her, "it isn't a warrior. You'll never get free this way."

Did she want her freedom back? Right now the only thing she was certain of was that he was lightly drawing his nails over her belly and pelvic bones as if painting them. Shuddering, she sucked in a breath even deeper than the last one. She'd lost command of her body to a man who had no right to it, who knew nothing about her. But although she should be battling him with every bit of strength she possessed, resistance would have to wait until her awareness no longer centered around him.

"You're no innocent." Even with her head turned from him, she knew he was staring at her. "This is no virgin's body. Because it knows what it's capable of."

Much as she wanted to retort that he couldn't possibly understand what she was experiencing, she couldn't force the denial past her lips. Her cunt was coated with proof of her arousal. More than that, he'd earlier gathered some of her seemingly unending fluid and had spread it over her asshole. Some of her juices remained on his fingers and were now drying, adding a roughness that lightly scraped her flesh—flesh he showed no sign of leaving alone.

"You think I'm wrong?" Catching her nipple between

thumb and forefinger, he kneaded it while she squirmed and tried not to moan. "You're getting ready to tell me I have no idea what I'm talking about?"

"Let me go!"

"Why do you keep saying that when you know it's not going to happen?"

Ever?

She was still gathering the courage to ask when he suddenly and firmly gripped her mons. Not giving her time to comprehend, he shook it.

Sparks from an inner bonfire shot down her legs and into her pelvis. Sobbing, she again tried to sit up, only to collapse when he pressed down on her breast. His hold on her mons tightened. Her breath hissed. Her mouth opened and then closed.

He had her.

"I don't have to tie your legs, do I? As long as they're bent under you, they're useless. More to the point, your pussy is exposed. Open to me like a gift."

She'd never gift him with her sex, damn it! If he thought she wanted anything to do with—

"Ah my wild one, what an exquisite creature you are. Full of the need for sex." A finger, maybe his middle one, led the way to her slit.

Gasping again, she acknowledged her flaming cheeks and throat. She, who'd never thought of herself as a sexual object, suddenly had no other identity. Most disconcerting, she didn't want anything except this—and him.

"Is there anything softer," he said with a bit of awe in his voice as he slid his finger into her. "Anything that affects a man more?"

With the invasion, she trusted him; not just trusted, but knew deep inside that he wouldn't hurt her. Whatever his intent, he wanted no part of injury or cruelty. She'd always been told that the enemy had no humanity to them, but here she was within the enemy's grip and more alive than she'd ever been.

Granted, the strong masculine finger working its way into her flooding channel had a great deal to do with what she was experiencing, but even in her befuddled state, she acknowledged it was more than that. Not just a man, but *him*, this stranger who called himself Nakos of Ekew.

"Soft, like the feathers of a small bird, like the first grass of spring."

His voice was music, flutes and other wind instruments. At the same time, she heard something that reminded her of heartbeats, a quiet drum perhaps. She vaguely comprehended that his palm still covered her breast and was stroking and massaging it, but next to the clawing hunger in her pussy, the *abuse* didn't matter. She couldn't keep track of everything he was doing, just that he'd brought his entire hand into play. His gentleness seemed right. She should want no part of it, but too many nights and tears lay between her and the last time a man had touched her as a woman.

She wanted one thing. Wanted it not from Raci, who was no longer part of her world, but from her captor.

"I can't—by the spirits, I can't . . ."

"What can't you do, little one?" he whispered. Something, maybe a knuckle, rolled over her clit.

"Ah!" she fairly screamed. Her fingers fastened onto his arm, and she used him to lift her back off the ground. Still off-balance, she clung to him, depended on him.

Something firm again walked over her clit. At the same time, his finger remained in her, covering her in proof of his existence. Throwing back her head, she dove into sensation. "I can't—"

"Take any more of this?" He flattened his hand over her cunt. Owned it.

"No, no! Falcon, please, help me!"

"Falcon?"

8

It was too late for Jola to take back her words, too late for anything except this moment. As she blinked Nakos into focus, she comprehended that he'd released her breast and wrapped his arm behind her back so he could help her sit up. She felt cradled by him.

Vulnerable and invaded.

"I don't know what I was saying," she blurted. "Let me stand, please."

"No."

The single word settled against her heart and mind. She, who'd always embraced the land's colors, saw only black and white with a deep red vein running through it. Her pussy muscles contracted repeatedly as if determined to keep him inside her. Wondering if she'd ever fully comprehend what was happening, she tried to look beyond her belly to her sex, but all she saw was his arm.

Diving deeper into her, he bent his knuckle, his fingertip sliding along the front of her pussy. She screamed. Wild, she tried to buck free only to collapse against him. The side of her head resting on his chest and his arm holding her in place, she made sounds like a newborn cougar.

"Your body wants me," he muttered. "Don't try to deny it."

"I—can't."

He chuckled although there was something melancholy about it. Before she could decide whether to ask him why, he began to pull out of her. Although she repeatedly, almost desperately, tightened her inner muscles around his finger, he escaped.

"What?" she gasped, eyes burning and mouth numb.

"You don't know?" That said, he laid her back down and straightened her legs.

The sudden end to the strain in her spine briefly held her attention. Then an undeniable throbbing drew her focus to her pussy. She lifted her pelvis toward him only to have him shake his head.

"I don't dare touch you anymore."

"What?"

His frown pulled her thoughts off her insistent and hungry body, reminded her of who had done this to her.

"You really don't know much about a man's body, do you? And yet you aren't a virgin."

"No."

Judging by the look in his eyes, she knew she hadn't satisfied his curiosity, but as long as the darkness engulfed her, she couldn't say more than she had.

Did he have a wife or mate? Not long ago it wouldn't have mattered. Now, although she needed to believe that his personal life had nothing to do with what existed between them, she wished she knew more about him.

But if she asked, he'd expect the same from her, and before they were done, she'd demand to know whether he'd killed Raci.

Raci, I'm sorry!

Desperate to escape her questions and the shadows stalking her, she swallowed. "Tell me about this man's body of yours."

"You really want to—"

"Yes."

"It isn't patient. It wants what it wants, now."

Cursing herself for not having caught on earlier, she stole a glance at his crotch. Beneath his single piece of clothing, his cock strained. Huge and trapped, it demanded to be set free.

"You do understand," he muttered as he cupped himself. "At least a bit."

Riding instinct, she lifted her bound arms and stroked his tip through soft leather. Although he tensed, he didn't put distance between them. "What's that about?" he demanded.

"I'm doing to you what you've been doing to me."

His expression a mix of skepticism and anticipation, he closed her fingers around his mound. "If you try to hurt—"

"You're afraid of me?" Only a few seconds ago she'd been so lost within herself that she'd barely been aware of him. Now she felt stronger—not in control, of course, but more of an equal. "How can that be when you consider me a wild animal, inferior?"

"I never—"

"Yes, you did! Otherwise, you wouldn't be calling me a Wilding."

He glowered down at her. "We shouldn't be here. I should already have you halfway back to my camp."

"Then why don't you?"

Although it would have been a simple matter for him to drag her hands off him, he didn't, and the longer the contact continued, the darker his expression became. She understood. After all, his handling of her had taken her into a deep and personal place.

Her heart beat on, seconds stretching out until maybe a minute had passed and still he hadn't responded to her ques-

tion. Having him looming over her like this continued to intimidate her, and more.

"You belong to me," he muttered. "What a strange feeling,
knowing another human being—"

"You're admitting I'm human?" *Belong?* Was he right?

"Maybe."

Her hands were so on fire that when he pulled her off his
cock, the burning reached all the way up her arms. She tried to
jerk free only to have him settle her hands over her belly and
hold them in place. They'd gone back to approaching each
other as the enemy, danger and potential at the same time.

"I've changed my mind," he told her. "I don't want you
touching me after all."

About to again accuse him of being afraid, she decided to
wait him out. There was something deeply arousing about
being manhandled this way. She didn't want her life to be in his
hands, never that, but what if she turned her body over to his?
Surely he'd take her, and in the taking she'd find release and relief.

The lake's aroma still clung to her, making it easy to remember why she'd wanted to be in it. He'd been right to call her
human. What he hopefully didn't comprehend was that there
was another layer to her, a primitive and raw one. He'd brought
out that side with his hands and ropes.

"I've been a warrior long enough that I know what it's like
to both win and lose a battle." His voice had taken on a hyp-
notic tone; either that or her hungry body had affected her ability to process. "Fortunately, I've never been badly wounded or
taken prisoner."

A life that revolved around opposing others was alien to her,
yet when he changed his position so he was closer to her hips,
instead of trying to shrink away, she slid toward him a little.
His gaze intensifying, he studied her from the top of her head

to her legs. She was being touched everywhere, turned on with nothing but a look—that and the hand over her wrists and fingers lightly brushing her belly.

"I've taken prisoners and hostages. All tried to hide their fear from me, but their eyes and bodies lied."

Why was he telling her this?

"What they most hated was being helpless. Without his weapons and strength, a man is nothing. He loses his self-esteem."

Nakos's singsong tone hadn't changed, which maybe was why she barely reacted when he ran his hand down her inner thigh.

"Their fear comes from the same place, that helplessness. Maybe, for a hostage, there is no difference between terror and loathing. Hopefully someday I'll know, without having to experience it myself."

She still didn't understand why he was confiding in her. However, she had no doubt about the reason behind the rough and strong fingers stroking her soft and too-sensitive flesh.

"It's different for the females we capture."

A blip of awareness somewhere deep in her befuddled brain hinted that he was finally getting to the point, but he was touching her, sometimes stroking one thigh and then the other while her breath hissed and her legs inched apart.

She wouldn't lift her pelvis toward him and beg, she wouldn't!

"They know they have little value as hostages. As females, they're seen as strong backs and the bearer of babies by their people, but they don't help insure the safety of their tribe. They don't hunt."

"You're wrong," she blurted, undone by a thousand lightning strikes going off inside her.

"You don't agree?" he asked as a finger separated her sex lips.

Him, everywhere. Everything. Yet, pushed on by the sky above and everything it represented to her, she fought for sanity.

"Why am I wrong?"

"I never said—" she started but couldn't think how to weave a lie together. "I know what you're going to say, that you and the other Ekewoko warriors keep the women for yourselves. Turn them into . . ."

When he didn't finish what she'd started, she accepted that there was no need because they both understood. Vanquished women became sex slaves. Much as she needed to concentrate on his hand, to anticipate, she couldn't shake the chilling image of a terrified woman kneeling before him and begging him not to hurt her.

Barely aware of what she was doing, she closed her legs and dug her heels into the ground. He didn't stop her from scooting away a little, but neither did he remove his hand, compelling her to cradle it between her hot thighs.

"What are you thinking?" His tone, although commanding, was low.

"About all the things I hate about you," she threw at him. "Treating a woman like an animal—"

"I've never done that."

Recalling everything he'd put her through so far, she nearly laughed. She didn't, because heat refused to leave her thighs and her pussy pulsed with the need for his touch. He'd somehow suspended her between sanity and madness with maybe only one way of returning to the existence she'd always taken for granted: by having him fuck her.

"However, I've seen the change take place," he told her. "I know the techniques sex slave trainers use."

"And you reap the rewards once those *trainers* are done."

His silence told her more than she wanted to know. At the same time, knowing she'd been taken by a man skilled in such things pulled her farther into the dark vortex swirling around her.

"Maybe this"—a nail glided over her clit, tearing a sob from her throat—"is something I understand simply because I'm a man. Maybe I didn't need to watch a trainer."

"No." Who was that weak woman and would she ever find herself again?

"No? Why do you say that, Wilding?"

Words flowed from her mind to be absorbed by the ground and air. Even when she forced herself to stare at him, she couldn't find her voice. How could she, as long as he kept touching her clit? Mewling like the newborn cougar she'd likened herself to earlier, she arched her neck so she stared upward and not at him. Her fingers dug into her belly, leaving indentations, and his hand defined her world.

Where had gentleness gone? What had happened to the slow glide along her heated tissues? Those she could stay on top of, almost. Those she understood, nearly. But the finger suddenly jammed deep inside her had turned harsh. It prodded and commanded, moving more quickly than she'd thought possible. His breathing become hard and quick. His finger rode her, creating a deep burning sensation that plowed through her.

Every time he buried himself in her up to the base of his finger, fear swept over her, but her sex was swollen and drenched and accommodated him. Through a haze, she realized he was no longer holding her hands in place. Relishing the relative freedom, she scratched her belly and pinched the taut skin over her pelvic bone. Pain dove into her only to collide with the pleasure radiating out from his hand. The sensations swirled, taking her with them.

Caught in the middle, she hissed and sobbed and whipped her head from side to side.

Suddenly she stopped thrashing, her body frozen by something she didn't comprehend. She fought the untold sensations rampaging through her, determined to hold them back. She was still fighting herself when the pressure against her opening increased. Mesmerized, she closed her fingers around her breast and waited, learned.

Yes, two of his fingers were now inside her. They lay there unmoving and yet full of promise and challenge. This new fullness demanded something from her; she just couldn't comprehend what it might be. Maybe it was the feeling of being invaded, of not knowing how to expel him, or if she wanted to.

Then, as she'd known he would, he again began moving inside her. Both fingers worked as one, slipping deep and deeper still, pausing, retreating a little only to push on.

"Ahh, ahh," she heard herself cry. She clamped down on her breast, pinching it. Her head started thrashing again. Even though her temple pulsed, she picked up the pace.

Think about what he's doing. Prepare. Be ready.

But did she want to anticipate? Maybe it was better and certainly easier to float in the middle of the storm he'd created. Once again he gave no hint of the gentleness he'd demonstrated earlier, and her pussy wept with each thrust. Her tissues gave way, then surrendered even more, flowing around the masterful fingers.

She sensed that he was leaning low over her, his back bent and the hand that was not between her legs braced against the ground. Damp heat slammed into her chest. His face was a blur, his body a dark mass over hers. And he was coming closer, his breath drenching her much as her flooded cunt soaked him.

"What, what?" she managed.

His response came in the form of something warm and wet settling over the breast she didn't have hold of. She hadn't yet acknowledged what he was doing when he sucked her mound into his mouth and closed his lips around it. His tongue pressed against her already hard nipple.

"Ahh!"

The fingers skewering her pushed home and held, pressure coming at her and staying, promising and taunting.

Swimming, much as she relished the experience, had never made her feel as weightless as she did now. Flying had been a part of her for as long as she remembered, a wonderful experience, but that, too, had nothing in common with the soaring, burning sensations swamping her.

Twisting under him, she scraped her nails along his forearm. Although he grunted, he didn't try to shake her off. Still scratching him, she opened her mouth, but instead of saying anything, she licked her lips. Sometimes the wind at Falcon Land blew in tight, violent circles, sucking up dirt and leaves and throwing them into the sky. She was in a cyclone of her own making, hers and this man's.

Determined to pull him into it with her, she spread her legs wide and bent her knees. A potent scent assaulted her.

Pushing her breast out of his mouth, he sucked in a breath, then grunted. "You smell of sex, of wanting."

"You—made me."

"I couldn't force something you didn't want on you."

Although she wasn't sure about that, at the moment it didn't matter. Her legs continued to gape. Watching him pull in another breath reminded her to do the same. She was beyond modesty, beyond fear, ready to plunge.

"I need your cock in me!"

"You're sure?"

"No, no!"

His slow blink endeared him to her because for the first time she saw something hesitant in his expression. Maybe he wasn't the consummate warrior he'd wanted her to believe after all.

"I don't have to ask permission," he said after a moment. "Whatever I want, I can take."

"I know that."

A hot wave washed over her. She was still trying to come to

grips with it when another threatened to drown her. Desperate for a death she was positive would lead to a new birth, she rocked up and clamped her hands over the wrist between her legs. Instead of pulling him off her, she pushed, pressing his fingers even more firmly into her. Her back burned, leaving her with no choice but to fall back again. Her hands slid up him to his forearm.

"Please," she begged. "I only want this one thing from you, please."

"One?" His chuckle lacked warmth. "And after we've fucked, we'll each return to our people, is that what you're saying?"

She couldn't think beyond killing the great hunger in her, that and acknowledging his mastery over her. Both hating and worshiping him, she tried to soothe away the scratches she'd inflicted on him. Having his fingers still in her bonded them together. Either that or the invasion increased his control of her.

"Nakos, please!"

"A warrior loves to hear a woman beg," he muttered and leaned over her again.

His tongue slid over her damp nipple. Then his teeth scraped the sides of her swollen nub. She started to buck only to lose all strength as he once more pulled her breast into his mouth. He owned it just as he did the rest of her.

She'd become his slave, his sex object.

9

The fingers filling her had been quiet while his attention was on her breast. Now they were on the move again, plowing and withdrawing in a motion that should have become familiar but wasn't. She felt as if she were sinking into her own cunt, becoming it, being defined by it.

The cyclone returned to pull her into its center. She spun in helpless circles. Heat and then more heat seared her. Her mind filled with images only to reject them. She saw a Falcon, then countless small birds. A curtain of snow was followed by light rain followed by the relentless sun. Next the moon, cool and full, filled her vision. She stared at her people seated around a cooking fire, but when she tried to join them, they became Ekew warriors. The enemy reached for her, grabbed her, threw her to the ground, and wound ropes around her until she couldn't move. Then a man stepped into her vision, big and naked with knowing eyes and possessive hands.

In a dim and unimportant way, she acknowledged that Nakos was no longer sucking on her breast; not that it mattered because he still owned her pussy, filled it, and gave it a reason for being. Then he pushed her soft, swollen flesh out of his mouth and moved down between her legs. Dizzy, she blinked him into focus. His naked chest made it all too easy to imagine him without any clothes, stripped of everything except the power inherent in his muscles.

I want to trust you.

"Say it again, Jola. Beg me."

Any other time, she would have thrown the words back at the damnable man who'd spoken them, insisting she wanted nothing to do with him, but he'd taken her far beyond the independent woman she'd always been. Forced her. Either that or she'd allowed herself to be brought into this space. Not caring which it was, she squeezed her legs against his thighs. Her breathing put her in mind of a desperate deer trying to outrun a cougar.

"Beg me for sex."

Yes, yes! "Damn you!"

"You may say that, but it doesn't mean you don't need me."

"Need? This morning I didn't know you existed."

"You do now." His voice was low, thick, and heavy. Not only had he kept the two fingers inside her, he now stroked her mons, the touch light but inescapable.

Mewling, she ground her knuckles into her belly. She *wouldn't* surrender; she wouldn't!

To her shock, he pulled out of her only to run his hands under her buttocks and lift her onto his thighs. Her mind shattered.

"Such an exquisite creature, all sensation and hunger. Your hunger is your undoing, Jola. If you're ever going to win this battle between us, you have to learn how to control yourself."

"I hate you. Hate you!" Even though she wanted to claw him, she lifted her arms over her head. The moment she did, she acknowledged that she had indeed surrendered everything to him.

As if agreeing with her, he pulled her even tighter against him. Staring at the sky, she bent her knees yet more and planted her feet under her. His cock ground against her burning tissues, forcing another primitive sound from her.

"Hate me if you must. It doesn't change your needs, or mine."

Need. More powerful than anything I've ever experienced.

Her senses splintering like thin ice, she grabbed her hair and yanked. Pain poured through her only to slide away.

"Stay with me, Wilding."

Stop calling me that! she wanted to scream, but he was right. She'd never felt more wild. The pressure against her pussy increased. Then her sex lips parted and he slipped in. Only his tip invaded, yet the promise of more arched her back and opened her mouth. A low moan escaped. She again tugged at her hair, then pushed her fingertips into her scalp.

"My lord told us that the Wildings might not have been created like humans," he said in a strangled tone. "That their sex might be part animal, or bird."

A chill instantly cooled her fevered body. "Bird?" she got out.

"Those were my lord's words, his and Tau's. No one questioned them, but they were wrong."

"You say that because . . ."

"Because my cock knows what a woman's sex feels like." His breath brushed over her breasts. "And this"—he pushed in a little more—"is a woman's cunt."

Relief slowly washing over her, she ran her fingers along his throat. If he was concerned she might scratch him again, he gave no indication, but then a rutting man was a single-minded beast.

His hands slid from her buttocks to her hips, and he drew her yet closer. Her pussy, stretched wide from his bulk, caught fire.

More images filled her mind, but she couldn't make sense of them. They, maybe, were part of the world she'd always known, although there was something foreign about them. But could she expect anything different? With everything in her world new, frightening, and exciting, no wonder nothing was familiar.

The thick, heavy mass inside her—she'd never experienced this, never!

A small voice insisted that Raci had taken her virginity, yet she felt like a virgin again, not scared as much as untested and unsure.

And eager, so eager.

She couldn't stand, couldn't even sit up. Her hands were all but useless. This big, tall man might easily outrun her; he'd certainly overpower her.

Overpowered. Forced down onto her back with her legs splayed, waiting for him to penetrate.

No, already penetrated. Skewered on his cock, thrust after thrust now pummeling her body. If not for his continued hold on her hips, she'd be sliding against the ground. Rocks might tear at her flesh and make her bleed if not for him.

Her arms were becoming heavy, compelling her to stop reaching for him and let her hands rest on her middle. Then he plowed forward, and her breasts danced, and she gripped the one that had been in his mouth. Holding it tightly, she quieted its fierce jiggling. The other still shook and shivered, but with her hands roped together, she couldn't hold onto both at once.

Didn't matter. Only her body dancing with his did. He shook her, rocked her entire length, demonstrating his greater strength, his single-minded purpose.

"Ha!" he grunted. "Ha."

Who's animal now, Nakos?

Another grunt seemed wrenched from him. She waited for

his next sound, yet more proof of how deeply he'd sunk into his cock's demands. Instead, silence greeted her.

By grinding her shoulders into the dirt, she managed to hold her ground so every time he thrust into her, his cock sank in all the way to his balls. His scrotum became a hot kiss along her inner thighs.

His features were twisted in the way of a man lost. If she didn't feel the same way, she might have believed she'd won something. But they were both on the same journey, almost.

Fighting the rope around her wrists only caused it to bite deeper into her. Besides, she wasn't sure she wanted to be free, didn't know anything except the pummeling her body was taking and the fury/fire in her belly. The tornado was back again, flinging her in all directions at the same time. She flew, fell, flew again, burned.

"Ah!" she screamed. "Ah, ha."

He said something, not words but raw honesty torn from deep inside him. His low, harsh cries hammered her.

She knew she was going to climax before the eruption struck, but although every fiber of her being ached for release, she fought to keep it inside her. Her captor's release began flooding her, proof that, maybe, her self-control was greater. Maybe that's why she fought her insistent body. She was afraid nothing would remain of her afterward.

Head thrashing, hands again squeezing her breast, she tried to push free of the hard meat invading her. Far from granting her what she needed, he loomed low over her. Her lower legs were caught against his armpits, and as he closed in on her, he bent her legs so deeply that her thighs nearly touched her breasts.

"No, no, no!" Releasing her breast, she struck his cheek with both hands.

"Yes!"

Ah, more pressure on her legs, his too-big body folded over her and his breath washing her face and throat. She tried to slap him again.

His pelvis jerked and drove forward an impossible inch more. More of his wet heat drenched her inner tissues and fed the flames she tried to tell herself she didn't want.

"Yes!" he bellowed. "Yes."

And she came. Flew apart. Shattered.

10

The smell was the first thing Jola noted when Nakos and she entered the Ekewoko encampment. Meat was being roasted, but behind the pungent aroma was something that knotted her stomach. It took her several moments to realize she was reacting to the stench of the men watching her and her captor. The Falcons saw cleanliness as a way of celebrating the gift of life, but apparently that was an unknown concept to the enemy. Either that or they were afraid of the lake. She was the only woman.

Trudging wearily behind Nakos, she dimly wondered why his aroma hadn't sickened her, then concluded that diving into the lake after her must have cleaned him. She just wished she felt as physically strong as he appeared. Of course, if his freedom had been stripped from him as hers had been, he might not be holding his head high.

Thinking about how he'd look wrapped in enemy ropes was preferable to dealing with her own reality. She tried to imagine him stripped of his weapons and surrounded by her people, but too many piercing gazes made that impossible. Although she was grateful to him for taking the time to locate the dress she'd cast off so long ago, she couldn't help but berate herself for not taking advantage of the few moments when her hands had been free. Even with him standing within easy reach of her, she should have done something.

What something? she asked as she resolutely stared at his back instead of the men seated around the cooking fire. He'd been prepared for her to attempt to escape. In fact, she'd had no doubt he would have relished the opportunity to run her down, which is why she'd refused to give in to impulses.

And because she hadn't, she was now surrounded by compact hide tents, weapons, and other possessions of those who'd invaded her country.

"You must be tired of having to keep an eye on her," one of the seated men said, nodding at Nakos. "Because I'm concerned for your well-being, I'd be only too happy to take over the responsibility."

"Controlling a Wilding is hardly a job for one man," someone else added. "Perhaps we need to take turns. I'm volunteering for the first shift, tonight."

They weren't just studying her; some were leering. If Nakos hadn't fastened a lead rope to her wrists to keep her close to him, she would have been tempted to cling to his side. He might have robbed her of her freedom, but at least he'd proven himself to be gentle, so far.

"So there really are female Wildings. I had my doubts."

"Me, too, but now that I no longer do, I know what I'm going to be doing tomorrow: looking for another."

"Not by yourself you aren't. Bodies like that—did you fuck her, Nakos? Of course you did. Any living man would."

The crude conversation made her shudder. Still trembling, she stiffened her spine and lifted her head. She expected Nakos to say something to his companions, but although he'd stopped, he only studied them.

He hadn't looked at or spoken to her since they'd left the lake. At first she'd been grateful for the silence but as time wore on, she'd silently cursed him for forcing her to live with her thoughts. She didn't understand this man who'd captured her; she might never.

At the same time, she had no doubt why he wanted her and maybe that was worse than the rope that forced her hands in front of her. He saw her as a possession, a pet maybe, a slave even. He'd keep her with him as long as she satisfied his man needs.

Years, forced to be with him?

Unable to rejoin her people.

Not being able to reach Raptor's Craig where she'd change form and fly.

Heat moved through her in a wave, reminding her all too acutely of what leaving her human body and becoming a Falcon felt like. She loved every moment of the transformation, but none brought her more joy than being able to spread her wings and soar into the wind.

But even if changing was possible anywhere except at Raptor's Craig, it didn't matter because she couldn't lift her arms.

Afraid she might not survive if she didn't face reality, she forced herself to stare at her arms. He'd crossed her wrists one over the other. Although he'd wrapped the rope around them several times, he hadn't cut off her circulation, but maybe numbness or pain would have been better than this.

"She isn't paying attention to us," an older-sounding man said. "What'd you do, drug her?"

"With a treated arrow, yes," Nakos said. "It worked quickly but wore off far sooner than it should have."

"Hmm. Maybe the Wildings are immune, at least to some extent."

Nakos nodded. "There's something about her . . . Where are Tau and Sakima?"

The older warrior pointed at a faded tent. "I'm surprised they're still in there, but sometimes when they get to talking or praying, they aren't aware of anything else."

Pulling her to his side, Nakos closed a large hand around her arm. She tried to guess what he was thinking but how could she when she knew so little about him?

Spirit, please look after me.

Sweat ran down Lord Sakima's naked chest and pooled over his well-fed belly. His gray, thinning hair was plastered to his neck, his hands folded near his flaccid cock. The shaman Tau sat across from him, steam from the heated rocks in a shallow stone bowl that contained water drifting like fog around both men. Like Nakos's lord, Tau was naked, but although he was considerably younger than Sakima, Tau wasn't as muscular.

Both men had looked up as Nakos lifted the tent flap and brought his captive in with him. They were still staring at her, two sets of eyes wider than usual.

"You did it," Lord Sakima said, smiling. "I was beginning to wonder—"

"Our chants have been answered," Tau interrupted. "My prayers—"

"Yes, of course. No one ever doubts the power of your prayers. I'd simply asked if your chants would have to be modified because we're dealing with creatures who aren't quite human."

Although he'd always revered the two men, a sudden anger struck Nakos. *She is human,* he came close to insisting.

"How," his lord asked, "did you capture her?"

He kept the explanation short and wasn't sure why he hadn't said anything about her unexpected swift recovery from the numbing drug. Out of the corner of his eye, he noticed that she was staring at him.

"You had sex with her," Tau said matter-of-factly. "How were her responses?"

"What do you mean?"

"Were they the same as other *women* you've fucked? No blunted responses?"

"None." Hopefully the shaman wouldn't ask for more in the way of details.

"Hmm. Interesting. What about her ability to comprehend?"

"If you mean does she understand what we're saying, the answer is yes, every word."

Tau's features had been impassive. Now, head bobbing, his eyes narrowed. Part of what made the shaman so mysterious was his ability to keep his thoughts to himself. Even when he was revealing one of his magic dreams, he did so without emotion. As a boy, Nakos had wondered whether Tau simply didn't care about others' reactions to his proclamations, but as he grew up, he changed his mind. Quite simply, Tau embraced the gift that set him apart from the rest of the tribe. Others might gasp at his revelations or shiver when he warned of danger, but to the shaman, he was simply sharing his truth with those that truth impacted. That was what isolated Tau from everyone else.

Tau stood, his long, slim body unfolding gracefully. He didn't put on the heavily decorated cape that had been passed down through generations of shamen before standing before Jola.

"She's slighter than I thought she would be," the unabashedly naked man mused. "Hardly any bigger than a child."

"But strong. She fights."

"Of course she does. What wild creature wouldn't?"

She isn't wild, not the way you think.

"Perfectly formed with hips meant for childbearing."

Struck by the surprise in Tau's voice, Nakos glanced down

at Lord Sakima. The older man continued to sit cross-legged and rest his palms on his knees, his neck stretched but still wrinkled as he looked up.

Jola's quick intake of breath brought Nakos's attention back to the interaction between his captive and his shaman. Tau had placed his hand on her throat, the fingers curled around the slender column. Even though he didn't believe Tau would hurt her, Nakos tensed.

"A strong pulse." Tau ran his fingers over her chin. "Strength here, too."

She didn't move. Not a muscle jumped. But her eyes had darkened, and her nostrils were flared. Wondering what it would take for her to forget she was a captive, Nakos tugged on the rope. Her jaw clenched.

"What's that?" Tau said, tightening his hold on her chin. "Don't you like being touched?"

"No."

"Ah," Lord Sakima said from his place on the floor, "she does speak. Tell me, Nakos, did she fight when you raped her?"

"It wasn't rape."

"Oh? One look at your magnificent muscles and she wrapped her body around yours? That's why it was so easy for you to capture her?"

Lord Sakima had never held back when talking about sex. As he'd pointed out back when he was preparing Nakos for his first time with a sex slave, the more open a man was about his needs and intentions, the more likely she was to submit. A man who felt the slightest hesitancy about his sexual prowess or rights had to fight her instinct to retain control over her body, but that changed once she realized the man intended on demanding his due.

Nakos might have blindly believed his lord if he hadn't been privy to Sakima's relationship with his wife. That relationship boiled down to one thing: Sakima was deeply grateful to his wife for everything she did for him. Not only had she borne his children, she was a good cook and a tireless worker. She also put up with her husband's snoring and his uneasy stomach. Of course, there was a great deal of difference between a slave and a wife.

"Initially she fought me," Nakos admitted. "And I have no doubt she will again, given the opportunity, but by the time I was done preparing her body—"

"Ha!" Sakima exclaimed and pushed his creaking body to his feet. "See, Tau. I taught my *son* well."

"So you have said, many times."

Tau still had his hand around Jola's throat, and from what Nakos could tell, she hadn't begun to relax. Although he wanted to order the shaman to release his captive, he knew better. Then Tau moved his exploration to just above her breasts. Something hard seized Nakos's chest, forcing him to breathe deeply.

"Her heartbeat," Tau said, "is no different from mine. Strong and steady."

"You didn't expect that?" Nakos asked around the pressure in his chest.

"I told you, I had my doubts. Did she—was there ever a moment when you thought she might become something else?"

Suddenly Jola sucked in air. Her fingers curled into tight balls.

"What's this?" Tau demanded. Grabbing her tied wrists, he lifted her arms so he could study her hands. "Your heart is pounding like a drum, and if you could, you'd kill me, wouldn't you?"

Although she curled back her lips revealing straight, white teeth, she said nothing. Frowning, Tau released her and stepped away. For just a moment Nakos thought he saw apprehension in Tau's small, pale eyes.

"Be careful with her," Tau warned. "Don't give her use of her arms or she'll try to end you."

Was that possible? With the memory of her soft, warm pussy around his pulsing cock, he couldn't quite believe the warning.

"We battled," he said. "I won." *Maybe.*

Coming to stand beside Tau, Sakima studied Jola with an intensity Nakos had seldom seen from his lord. "Is this what you saw in your dreams?" he asked the shaman.

"I cannot be sure. A fog covered everything."

"But you must have seen—"

"Of course," Tau snapped. Releasing Jola, he folded his arms over his chest. "A shaman's dreams are often like a new leaf unfolding, slowly revealed."

Sakima shot Tau an irritated look. "We've been talking—"

"I know what you and I have been talking about, things that are meant for your and my ears alone."

Sometimes the relationship between lord and shaman reminded Nakos of squabbling children. Both tended to be boastful, neither of them willing to admit that they might be wrong about something. He'd come to the conclusion that each was determined to reign over the Ekewoko, not share the responsibility. At the same time, shaman and lord had certain strengths and weakness and, whether they wanted to admit it or not, they often relied on the other to balance out those strengths and weakness. In short, they needed each other.

"Tell me this, Wilding," Tau said. "Are you afraid?"

Straightening her spine, Jola glared up at the shaman. "Her name is Jola," Nakos said.

"A name? I didn't expect that. So—" He drew out the word. "So tell me, Jola, were you armed when this warrior grabbed you?"

"Does it matter?"

No one opposed the shaman, at least Nakos had never seen an Ekewoko argue with the tribe's spiritual leader. Jola's sharp question and continued glare reminded him anew of the differences between them.

"I asked you a question, Wilding." Eyes dark with anger, Tau snatched the rope out of Nakos's hand and hauled her against him. "Were you armed?"

Although her tension increased, Nakos didn't believe Jola was afraid, at least no more than she'd been when she first stepped into camp. His admiration for her grew.

"Not with what you consider weapons," she said after a strained silence.

"Then what—"

"I will not tell you that. No matter what you do, I won't say more."

Nakos expected Tau to slap down her resistance. Instead, he fingered the rope, his facial muscles working. The way he and Jola stared at each other reminded him of a confrontation between predators. He understood Tau's displeasure over Jola's refusal to back down, but why was she opposing the shaman when she had no weapons or the means to fight?

This wasn't the first time her fearlessness had made an impression on him.

"Refusing to speak, are you?" Tau fairly spluttered. "Believe me, wild one, I know how to get what I want from you."

"Be careful?" Sakima warned. "If you try to break her—"

"There will be no breaking of my captive," Nakos blurted. A lifetime of reverence for his elders kept his arms at his sides, but if his shaman struck Jola, it wouldn't happen again. "That's not why I brought her here."

"Tell me, why did you?"

For a moment he couldn't fathom Tau's question, then decided the shaman was testing him. From the way Tau was watching him, he wondered if he was afraid of him, but that couldn't be. Shamen feared nothing or no one.

"Your command," he finally answered. "You, and my lord, wanted a Wilding."

"And you're the only one who has been able to fulfill our need. Your skill impresses me, not that I ever expected anything else from you."

Praise from his lord had always touched Nakos; today was no different. Just the same, he didn't relax. "What happens now?" he asked.

"Now?" Tau echoed. "You have completed your assignment, and received your reward I dare say. Even if you had to force her to—"

"I told you, there was no need for force."

"No . . ."

Taking care not to stare openly at Tau, Nakos was nevertheless struck by the shaman's look of disbelief. Maybe Tau didn't know as much about Wildings as he'd led everyone to believe. Maybe his dreams only revealed so much.

"Not rape," Tau said at length. "Then what?"

"Sex. Both of us wanting the same thing."

Jola, whose attention had been fixed on Tau, glanced at Nakos. Her sleeveless dress covered flesh he'd freely explored earlier, yet he had no trouble calling up her naked form, or what her breasts and pussy had done to him, the way they'd felt. He wondered if she understood why he hadn't looked at her while they were walking to camp. If he had, he'd have laid her out and buried himself in her again.

Or maybe let her free.

"Is that true?" Tau demanded of Jola. "You willingly fucked him?"

Although she'd held herself straight and tall from the moment they stepped inside the tent, she drew herself up even more.

"I asked you a question! You wanted him?"

"I owe you nothing."

Coming from another captive, her words would have compelled Nakos to warn her not to anger those who had control of her. Instead he silently acknowledged her courage.

"You owe me everything, most of all your life," Tau insisted. "I claim you."

"Claim?" Nakos repeated although he'd known that from the beginning.

"What is it?" A faint smile changed but didn't soften Tau's expression. "Now that you've fucked her, you want to keep her for your own?"

"I didn't say—"

"What are we going to do?" Sakima interrupted. "With her, I mean. Tau, the things we've been talking about—"

Tau nodded. Using the rope, he again lifted Jola's arms and went back to studying her hands. Nakos thought she might resist, but she only observed Tau, her expression still unreadable.

"Those things will take time," Tau said. "Force—"

"No force," Nakos insisted.

"What is this?" Sakima demanded. "You're a warrior. You know what it takes to get the enemy to reveal—"

"Maybe we're wrong to think of her as the enemy," Tau interrupted, shooting a look at his lord. "She's a female, not an armed warrior. Females are soft and as such easily broken. But broken she might be of no use to us."

Nakos had no doubt that something he didn't fully comprehend was going on between his lord and shaman, secrets maybe. He'd accomplished his mission by bringing Jola to them. His services were no longer needed, neither was his presence. But if he left, she'd be forced to remain with them.

What did it matter?

A glance at her gave him his answer. *She* mattered. She shouldn't but she did.

"It's been a long day for her," he said. "Exhausting. She nearly drowned. The walk here was a long one. She's had nothing to eat and only a little to drink."

"And she has to be tired from being fucked by a Ekewoko warrior," Tau added. "What are you saying?"

"That perhaps whatever you want from her can wait until tomorrow."

"Until she has had time to fully resign herself to her new lot?" Sakima asked. "Tau, there might be wisdom in what my *son* is saying. A simple creature like her needs time to accept certain things. Once she has, she'll put up less resistance."

Still studying Jola's hands, Tau nodded.

11

Even though she longed for the fresh air at Raptor's Craig, Jola drank deeply of the breeze drifting through the Ekewoko camp. The tent had stank of sweat, and the steam that filled it had threatened to steal all strength from her muscles.

Standing next to Nakos, she acknowledged that he'd been right when he said she was tired. The long walk had taken a lot out of her. That coupled with her dread of what was ahead of her had her wishing she could lie down and fall asleep. Weariness had fled while the men had touched on their plans for her, but now it was returning.

Where would she sleep tonight?

"That's my tent." Nakos pointed at a compact enclosure near the rear of the encampment. "But before we go there, we need to eat."

Her mouth filling at the thought, she struggled to remember everything the three men had said, but the only thing that remained clear was when the shaman had asked Nakos whether there'd been a moment when he thought she might become something other than what she was.

Did he know?

A tug on her wrists brought her back to reality and, feeling like the captured animal the shaman had called her, she trudged behind Nakos. The lounging Ekewoko, as before, studied her every move, and she found it easier to stare at Nakos's back. Everything about him touched a part of her, unsettled her, and yet he was known while the others were strangers.

Fear she hadn't experienced since she'd first become aware of Nakos's hands on her in the lake slammed into her. She stumbled, then caught herself. If he was aware, he gave no notice.

She hated being here! Hated having so little control.

Those staring men were her people's enemy. If they could, they'd swarm over Raptor's Craig trying to kill every living thing they encountered. The arrogant Ekewoko thought they had a right to Falcon Land. Maybe they believed it had been created to feed their greed.

And she was their prisoner.

A warm gust of wind slid over her like a caress. Although she knew better than to give anything away by looking up, she said a silent prayer to whoever had touched her.

Thank you for reminding me of who and what I am. I allowed myself to become weak and afraid, but no more! I am Falcon. Brave and strong.

"There," Nakos said in that quiet tone of his. "Food."

He was pointing at a circle of stones with a small fire burning in the middle. A pot hung over the fire, steam escaping from the top. A sweet, rich aroma reached her, flooding her mouth again and making her stomach rumble.

As they approached, Nakos explained that the cooking pot they'd seen when they first reached camp was manned by warriors who threw whatever they found or killed into it while a slave was responsible for this smaller one. The slave, who belonged to Lord Sakima, had proven to be an excellent cook.

"Many years ago, Lord Sakima became my father," Nakos explained. "As his *son*, I have every right to eat here."

"He won't mind if I—"

"This is my decision."

Jola expected the slave to be a woman. Instead, an elderly man with a long fringe of white hair sat cross-legged near the fire. He was so slumped over that his chin nearly reached his knees, and he was snoring.

"His name is Lamuka," Nakos told her. "I can't remember when he didn't belong to my lord. He used to help with many things, but these days all he does is cook, and sleep. He's the only slave we brought with us when we left our people for Screaming Wind."

"Why doesn't he run away?"

"Where would he go to? I don't know if he remembers where he came from or how to return to it. He's loyal to my lord, and Sakima makes sure his needs are met."

That wasn't a slave. Instead, Lamuka was as much a part of the Ekewoko as if he'd been born to the tribe. Although she couldn't imagine ever feeling that way, knowing the elderly man was being taken care of released some of her tension. As long as she didn't have to be near the shaman, she might survive her time here.

She just wasn't sure about tonight.

Nakos's tent was sparsely furnished. The woven reed mat that served as his bed was covered with a thick blanket made of bear hide. Over that was a less bulky blanket. Once her eyes had adjusted to the dark, she'd made out two more loin coverings and another pair of leather shoes. There were other mounds, which she assumed were more clothes, but her attention settled on the arrows, knives, and spears near the entrance flap.

Thanks to the bowl of venison and root vegetables Lamuka had handed her, her belly was full. That coupled with her weary legs and overloaded mind had her wondering what Nakos's bed felt like. When she'd been outside, the heavens had called to her, but now there was only this small enclosure and the man who'd brought her into it.

"Sit down."

She did so, albeit awkwardly because of her tethered hands. He'd released them while she was eating but had remained close by, his presence a silent reminder that trying to escape would end in failure. She hadn't tried because she hadn't been up to fighting him again today. Tomorrow, somehow. Once she felt restored.

"Tau is going to want you," he said once he'd joined her on the bed.

"I know."

"And I won't stand in his way. You need to understand that."

"I do."

"But not tonight."

Tonight. Locked in a small space with the man who'd robbed her of her freedom and made her scream. She shivered, then tried to flex her wrists. As before, they were crossed over each other, all but useless. Granted, her legs were free, but he was bigger than her, stronger.

"Why the questions about rape?" she asked, stalling.

"You're the conquered, and because you are, they assumed that was the only way we'd have sex."

"But they knew there would be sex. Why? Because that's the way of all Ekewoko warriors?"

It was nearly dark inside the tent, the only illumination coming from several small slits along the sides that let in the setting sun. Nevertheless, she had no doubt that his eyes had narrowed. His breathing turned sharp.

"I haven't fucked for a long time. Neither has any other warrior here."

"And that makes it all right for you to—"

"Enough, Jola!"

His anger frightened her but only a little. What, she wondered, would he think if she told him that his need for sex couldn't be any stronger than her need to become a predator right now? Just thinking about soaring into the sky and watching the moon and stars emerge made her heart burn. Determined not to let him into her thoughts, she turned from him.

His breath hissing, he grabbed her shoulders and jerked her back around. "Listen to me. When I hand you over to Tau and Sakima, they'll do whatever they believe they need to in order to get certain information from you. Now that they know we all speak the same language, they're going to demand everything."

"What do you mean, everything?"

Still holding her, he slowly shook his head. She tried to tap into his thoughts, but his fingers on her distracted her. Maybe if he hadn't already buried his seed in her, he wouldn't have this impact on her; maybe.

"I wish our paths had never crossed," she told him. "If only I hadn't gone running and then decided to cool off in the lake—"

"Why did you?"

A thousand reasons, restlessness and grief crashing together, wild energy and feeling as if her skin was too small.

That wild energy was returning, slipping into her veins and heating her heart. With predator blood flowing through her, she should want to tear her enemy to shreds. Instead, if she was in Falcon form, she'd tuck her talons against her body and fly in tight circles around him.

Compel him to mate with her.

But that would never be! He was human, the enemy, not one of her kind.

Pressure on her shoulders splintered her thoughts, and he'd pushed her back and onto his bed before she could pull reality around her. He existed as a male shape looming over her, potent muscles giving out insistent messages and his swollen cock rubbing her thigh.

"This might be our last time together," he whispered. "I want to remember it."

"What if that isn't what I want?"

"But you do."

How could a whisper have so much impact, she wondered. Then, as the tip of his cock touched here and there, she acknowledged that his voice was only part of it. Weariness still clung to her, quieting her maybe and stealing some of the fight that had always been part of her. She felt as if she was floating as she had in the lake before he'd turned her world over. At the same time, her arms and legs were becoming heavier and heavier. Instead of trying to push him away, she let the bed—his bed—support her. Her breasts were gaining weight and becoming more sensitive. Her nipples knotted.

Releasing her shoulders, he slid his hands along her hips, making her shiver. Then he took hold of her garment and tugged it up her body until it settled around her waist. She could have fought him, should have!

No, she shouldn't.

"A test," he said, "of your body."

What do you mean, she needed to ask, but letheragy had reached her throat. With no purpose in mind, she fisted the soft blanket.

There, his hand, on her hips again but this time without anything between their flesh. Pressing her nails into the fabric, she ground her teeth together.

Ah, his hand, sliding up over her pelvic bone and down to the valley where her belly lay. His fingers, gliding over flesh that danced under his touch and sent shiver after shiver into her core. Sweat broke out on her throat and between her breasts, forcing her to clench her fingers until they cramped.

"You're soft here." He stroked her belly. "Incredibly soft."

"Ah."

"You agree, do you?" His voice sounded labored, and sweat bloomed where his thigh pressed against hers. "Yours is a woman's body, all woman. No matter what Tau may have thought, this is all you are."

He was wrong, of course, but at this moment with this man over and against and on her, it didn't matter. Even as parts of her expanded, she was becoming smaller, weaker, a creature spinning helplessly in a whirlpool.

"Here," he whispered, still laboring, "what do you feel when I touch you here?"

A finger, she couldn't tell which one, slid into her navel. It filled her, pressure sinking deep and finding her core.

But she wouldn't moan, she wouldn't!

Ignoring her cramping fingers, she lifted her head off the bed only to fall back because his finger remained in her navel, taking ownership. Stripping her down so she didn't know who she was.

"I should stake you out, spread your arms and legs and tie them to posts I've driven into the ground. I'd have already stripped you naked, maybe blindfolded and gagged you so you're aware of nothing except me."

"Why?" *By the spirits!*

"Because I can. And because it's what we both want."

"How dare you say—"

"Don't," he warned and yanked her arms over her head.

Before she could think to react, he'd pulled up on her garment until it was against her armpits and her breasts were exposed. He'd released his hold on her arms, but although she might have been able to tug her garment back around her waist, she didn't try. Either that or she couldn't pull herself together enough to think how the task was completed.

Somehow he switched from a kneeling position to stretching out next to her without giving up ownership of her navel. Now, not only did his cock press against her outer thigh, his breath dampened her breasts.

"I love knowing you're on my bed. And touching you like this."

This wasn't the first time he'd taken her breast into his mouth; she could survive it, she could!

But maybe she didn't want to.

Not sure which it was, she tugged at her hair and tried to remember how to breathe. Her hips kept lifting off the bed. She kept squeezing her thighs together.

Ignoring her pitiful attempts at movement, he sucked on her breast, prompting her to arch her spine. Pain from pulling on her hair did nothing to distract her from the awful waiting, the hungry wanting.

When he removed his finger from her navel, he granted her a full heartbeat in which to try to convince herself she was going to survive. Then that same finger slid between her legs and over her pussy. A tremor dove from the top of her head down to her toes.

"There it is," he fairly growled. "Your body revealing itself to me."

She was already practically naked so what could he be talking about? He answered by swiping his hand over her cunt while she struggled to blink away the red film that had stolen her vision.

"Taste yourself, *slave*."

This time the word slave was a caress, a deep voice speaking to her heart and pussy. When he touched her mouth, she gasped, then parted her lips. His fingers tasted of sex, her wet and wanting sex.

If he'd insisted, she would have sucked him as deeply into her mouth as he'd taken her breast and maybe more. Instead, she ran her tongue over his fingers, wondering why he'd abandoned her core so soon.

No, he hadn't. Answering her silent plea, his hand returned to her traitorous pussy and drank from what might be an endless store of heat.

And then, not soon enough, he was giving her another taste of herself and she was licking, swallowing, licking some more.

He freed her breast, but she barely gave it thought. How could it matter when he was on the move again?

Handling her as if he'd been doing this one task his entire life, he spread her legs and climbed into the space he'd created for himself. She'd thought he'd waste no time positioning her for sex, asked herself if she was ready. Instead, he rocked back so his buttocks rested on his heels and rested a palm against her pubic hair.

So close, not close enough.

Much as she wanted to meet his seeming indifference with the same, she couldn't make herself relax. They were going to fuck; she knew it. So why was he making them wait?

"Some men, sex slave trainers, can condition a female so this is the only thing she wants." He rubbed her mons, stopped. "I'm not certain how that's accomplished, probably through a series of lessons. I've heard it said that females trained to heed only their bodies' needs make the best slaves."

"I'm *not* a slave."

"But that's what you'll become, if it's what my shaman wants."

Why was he telling her this? To make her fear Tau?

"Maybe you'd like that existence," he went on, sounding

cold now. The pressure on her mons increased, and it took all she had not to howl like some hungry whore. "There'd be a lot of pleasure in it."

"But not freedom!"

"Freedom?" To her surprise, he patted her thigh as if trying to ease her mind. "You're right, there's that. But it's not as if you have any choice in the matter."

"Because of you!" Hating him was easier than admitting how much she craved what he dangled before her. "You could let me go."

Before she could add that he'd had no right taking her in the first place, he slid another hand under her hips, lifting her. With his upper hand now pushing down on her core, she felt trapped by him, caught in a grip she'd never imagined. Sweat coated her entire body, and she couldn't have moved her arms if her existence depended on it.

"You don't want that," he said. It took her a moment to remember they'd been talking about her freedom. "You'd much rather stay in here while you discover and experience what you can be."

He was offering her an existence she'd never fathomed, one framed by him. Because he'd already demonstrated how much he knew about a woman's body, she, too, easily imagined night after night of fucking, sex, rutting. He'd take her in ways she didn't know were possible, each of those ways pulling her deeper into his influence.

He was right. The trade-off was knowing she'd never fly again.

Was it worth it?

The question pounded at her, tore into her, spun her around, and threatened to make her bellow. Red-hot explosions in exchange for ropes.

"I don't want—"

"Don't say that until I'm done."

"Done?"

"Taking you. Gifting you."

By the spirits, she couldn't think! And because his hands still trapped and cradled her, she couldn't move.

"That's better," he said, making her wonder what she'd agreed to. Then he drew his hands off her and let her down, and she went back to waiting. Needing.

"Lift your hips."

"What? I already—"

"On your own, if this is what you want."

He wasn't just offering sex. No, he was pushing her to the edge, taking her places she'd never been. She started to tell herself she didn't have to do this, that he'd have to force her.

But because she couldn't lie to herself, she bent her knees and arched her back so her shoulders bore most of her weight. The strain of holding this position burned through her, but she strained upward, her pussy clenching.

"Thank you," he whispered.

Then, as she'd known and prayed he'd do, he rocked forward. His cock slipped past her wet barrier and into the hot, tight tunnel that had been made for him. Having him inside her filled her with strength and energy, and she stared boldly up at his shadowed form as he stretched out over her with his arms planted on either side of her shoulders.

He became part of her, his thick, hot rod completing her. The pressure along her pussy walls took her deep inside herself, blinded her to everything except him. They were equals, two halves meshing together and becoming one. Even though he'd yet to thrust, she drank from the gift he'd given her and prayed she was giving him the same.

Her future would have to wait, as would his. There was only this tent, these moments together, these bodies.

Soft, quick heat flooded her passage, maybe hotter in front and deeper behind. How strange that one swollen, sleek organ could turn her around and empty her mind.

Mindless, yes, living in and through and around her pussy, growling encouragement when he pushed deeper, struggling to hold him in place when he pulled back, hissing each time he came at her.

The quick heat rolled deep and true, set fire to her legs and licked at her spine, shook her breasts.

She began shaking, her body screaming and threatening to break apart. Sobbing, she sank onto his bed. Moments later the shaking quieted, making it possible for her to again concentrate on being fucked.

Fucked? Attacked, more like. Her enemy hammering at her and her howling her approval.

So fast, no slow and exciting buildup. Instead, thunder roared and lightning struck. Half believing she smelled herself burning, she stared at the looming, straining shadow that was Nakos. Her pussy spasmed. Spasmed again.

12

Too fast, too hard. Everything out of control.

Although she'd pulled her garment down over her hips and rolled onto her side so her back was to her captor, Jola couldn't shake off the memory of their frantic coupling. His breathing had labored long after his climax, but now it was stretching out, and she sensed his muscles relaxing.

Sliding her hands between her legs, she lightly fingered herself. Her flesh there was so tender and yet if he'd come after her again, she would have opened herself to him. Why she'd willingly submit to sex was something she needed to examine and, if possible, walk away from, but how could she begin when her mind insisted on drifting? Night had closed over the Ekewoko camp. A few faint voices reached her, none of the words making sense. Most likely they were talking about her.

Tau, that's whom she didn't dare trust. Shamen had skill and power. They saw things others couldn't, knew things that should remain secret. From what little he'd said, she half believed he knew who and, most important, what she was. He might turn her into his hostage as his way of getting close to her people or . . .

With a start, she pulled herself back. Much as her body craved oblivion, she had to first face what tomorrow might bring. No matter how much she objected and fought, could Tau force her to go to Raptor's Craig with him and the Ekewoko warriors? True, Tau might not know that Raptor's Craig was sacred to the Falcons, but she didn't dare take that chance. Somehow she had to keep not just him but all Ekewokos away from there until . . .

Again, she shook off her growing exhaustion. How could she warn her people if she couldn't get to them? Freedom, that's what she needed. Freedom.

Her sex was warm and soft and still moist. That, coupled with Nakos behind her, made it all but impossible for her to fasten her mind around what she'd have to do if she was ever going to be free again. She wasn't even sure that's what she wanted.

Something cold touched her throat. Eyes open but unseeing, she tried to keep the chill from expanding, but it spread over her. Shivering, she struggled to understand why she suddenly felt afraid.

Although she didn't want to admit it—not tonight, not with him so close—she reluctantly acknowledged that what she was most frightened of was not wanting freedom.

Being able to fly and hunt and mate had always defined her existence. Without those things, who and what was she?

Nakos's captive. His slave.

More cold pressed against her throat and spread outward. She tried to step back from it by sliding a forefinger into her pussy, but because of the way her captor had secured her hands, she could only manage an inch. Giving into the strain in her arms and shoulders, she rested her hands against her belly.

What had she been thinking about, something to do with the

Ekewoko shaman and the threat he represented. In the morning, she'd listen and learn, plan and plot. And when her time came . . .

Fire. Flames. Screaming, endless screaming.

Darkness surrounded him, wrapped him in isolation and fear. He longed to curl into a tight, shivering ball, wanted to be a child again, needed innocence back.

More flames, growing hotter with every second. They crackled and crashed loud enough to awaken the just-dead, but the sound couldn't destroy the screaming.

One voice was high and shrill, yet weak. The other rode a deeper river with fear woven into it, the fear of the doomed.

Forcing his trembling legs under him, he ran toward the screaming. Jumping, leaping, muscles straining, feet shredding on rocks. On and on he went, pounding past night curtain after night curtain. His lungs burned; he couldn't pull enough air into them and what little entered was hot and tasted of death.

"Save us! Save us!"

"Where are you? By the spirits, where are you?"

"Nakos! Wake up."

The voice slipping into his dream was vaguely familiar, and probably more so if he'd been able to concentrate, but he was still too close to the edge. Fighting a familiar foe, he pushed back from the darkness. As he knew it would, the nightmare followed him, sucking at his sanity and insisting he return to the past.

"No!" he yelled, punching the mist. Instead of fog, however, he connected with something soft and alive.

"Stop it! Nakos, wake up!"

Even though he opened his eyes, nothing waited for him. True, it was night, but with horror pressing around him, he needed something, anything to focus on. Determined not to yell again, he struck out.

"Ah!"

What was that, a female voice, sharp with pain. But that couldn't be because his nightmares were never about women. He reached out again, not to ward off the devils this time but to make sense of the unexpected sound. His fingers touched soft flesh, prompting him to grab and hold on.

"Nakos?"

The voice penetrated deeper, splintered the dying dream. As reality rushed in, he sat up and hauled the woman against him. Her slight body was warm and alive, which were the two things he needed most in life. Something warned him not to surrender his strength to her, but how could that matter when he owed his sanity to her?

Her breasts pressed against his chest, and her arms were between them, giving rise to the question of why she wasn't trying to either push him away or embrace him. As the seconds passed, more memories emerged, and although he didn't yet understand everything, he knew he was responsible for her immobile arms.

"Don't hit me again," she said. "I did nothing to deserve it."

"I—didn't mean . . ."

"You were asleep, snoring a little. Then you started moaning and calling out. It was a nightmare, wasn't it?"

Oh yes, that was the explanation he was after and all he wanted to face about why he'd been acting the way he had. Even though he was lying to himself, he ran his hands over her back. With the simple touch, his cock awakened.

"What was it?" she asked. "Were you being attacked by something in your dream?"

An attack, yes, but undoubtedly not what she was thinking. "It doesn't matter. Where did I strike you?"

"My arm, up near my shoulder."

Relaxing his grip, he went in search of her shoulder but found her breasts instead. Fully steeped in reality now, he acknowledged he had every right to touch her there and other places because she belonged to him. She must have accepted the same thing because she made no attempt to stop his exploration Neither, however, did she respond when he rubbed her nipple.

"It's getting hard," he said. "You can't tell me you don't like being touched like this."

"My body's response isn't what this moment is about, Nakos. Your dream is what matters."

Damn her for pushing when surely she knew better! He should punish her, give her a lesson she'd never forget. But not only wouldn't he want to face himself if he did, something told him this wasn't a woman who could be broken by pain.

"Why are you hiding behind silence?" she demanded. "Do you think that's going to make a difference?"

"What?" He ran his forefinger over the hard nub.

"This isn't the first time you've had that nightmare," she continued. "Earlier tonight—"

"I don't remember."

"Don't you?" She sounded as if she didn't believe him. "I'll tell you what I believe. Deep down you know you can't rid yourself of it. It's become part of you. You've tried to make your peace with whatever stalks you, but it hasn't happened yet. Maybe it never will."

"How can you say—"

"Personal experience."

"What are you talking about?"

She sighed and shrugged. "I understand what it's like to try to get free of something, to try to convince myself that something didn't happen. It hasn't worked for me, and it isn't going to for you."

You don't know anything about me, he wanted to insist, but if he did, their conversation might take him someplace he didn't dare go.

"You call yourself a warrior, and yet a few moments ago you sounded like a small frightened child."

Anger tore at him, but before he was tempted to unleash it on her, he acknowledged that she was trying to goad him. "I doubt that," he said although she might be right. "No matter what sounds I made, they were nothing compared to you when you're climaxing."

She drew in a slow breath that seemed endless. "You aren't going to tell me, are you? That's why you're trying to change the subject."

Damn her! He'd never encountered someone with such spirit and fight. Or who put his secrets at such risk. Disappointed in himself for doing so, he nevertheless pushed her away, grabbing and straightening her legs as he did so she wound up sprawled on her back. Confronting someone he couldn't see was a strange sensation. He couldn't decide whether to shove her out of his reach or tease her until her excited cries floated through the camp and she'd forgotten what had awakened them.

"Don't," she warned as he positioned himself above her.

"Don't what?" He reached out, grazing an arm with his nails. Remembering that he'd kept her wrists bound, he drew her arms over her head. That done, he leaned close. Holding her in place with one hand, he went in search of her breasts, belly, hips, something.

"That's right, treat me like a captive," she snapped, writhing a little under his touch. "You think there's nothing to me except a hole for your cock! That I have no other purpose."

"You want that cock."

"Ha! If you think that's the only thing I need then you are a fool."

She had no right throwing that word at him, none at all! He ground his palm against her navel.

"Such a fool!"

He would hurt her! Break her down. But if he did, could he face himself? Maybe even more important, could he ever look this woman in the eye again?

"Go back to sleep, *captive*. But before you do, ask yourself what the rest of your life is going to be like. There'll be me, only me."

"What about your lord and shaman?"

"I captured you. Maybe I'll keep you for myself."

Nakos's threat settled against Jola's chest, making her heart ache. From his slow breathing, she guessed he was trying to return to wherever he'd been before the nightmare had begun. She'd been angry at him for the way he'd treated her, but only briefly. What she didn't understand was why she couldn't hate this man. If things were that simple, all her energy could go toward two things: surviving his presence and planning her escape.

Unfortunately, struggling with him had aroused her in ways she prayed he didn't know. Hopefully he'd only heard her angry words, noted nothing except her pathetic struggle to get free.

Determined to keep her hands off herself, she stared at the tent top she couldn't see and breathed when he did. She didn't care if he had a nightmare. How could she have possibly believed it mattered to her? Let him thrash and scream, sweat and shake. He deserved to be haunted by—

By what?

Sighing, she admitted that his midnight fears had impacted her. She, who had covered Raci's lifeless body with her wings, knew all too well what helplessness felt like. And rage. And grief. She didn't want Nakos to have to weather the same emotions.

Why?

Close to sighing again, she swallowed the sound and hopefully with it the damnable insistent question. Tomorrow was for clear thinking and, once she'd broken free, flinging her body into the sky.

Sleep nibbled at her edges, and she welcomed it in. She became selfish. Nakos's attempt to rest was his concern. He'd put her through enough today, and she didn't care.

The sound again. A man's harsh voice. Something between a cry and a shout. Limbs thrashing. A heel, maybe, striking her thigh.

Hopefully scooting out of reach of his leg, Jola turned onto her side and propped an elbow under her. Even though she couldn't separate his form from the unrelenting night, she had no trouble determining where he was. Unlike earlier, however, she wouldn't try to save him from whatever had seized him. Instead, she'd let it play itself out while learning everything she could.

"No! Run. Please, run. The smell, ah, the smell! Fight, don't—no! Don't ask that of—no! I can't. By the spirits, I can't!"

His voice shrilled, then dropped to a whisper. An moment later, he made a sound that reminded her of a child crying. The harsh sob tore her apart. Not caring about the consequences, she stretched herself over his writhing form. Pressing her hands to the base of his throat, she spoke into his ear, or rather she crooned and hummed, even sang a little. Mostly she hoped he wouldn't ask why she was trying to help.

"Not again. No, not again!" His almost frenzied shaking frightened her.

"Nakos, listen to me. Whatever it is, it isn't happening. It's behind you, part of the past. Nothing for you to worry about, nothing—"

"Go away!"

"I can't!" she insisted, pushing down to keep him from thrashing. "You need me, Nakos."

Maybe her words reached him; maybe he'd simply exhausted himself. Whichever it was, he stopped struggling although he continued to shudder. Her first thought was to bring him fully awake; then she decided to let him leave his nightmare in his own way and at his own pace.

Bit by bit, his body quieted, and his breathing settled down. She told herself that she didn't understand why his relaxing meant so much to her. Mostly she remained stretched out on top of him with her breasts flattened against his chest while lightly stroking his side and arm.

"That's good," she ventured. "Much better. There's nothing to be afraid of." *Afraid?* She couldn't imagine this man fearing anything and yet . . . "You're safe. We both are."

"Both?"

His unemotional tone caught her unaware, and she straightened, trying to look into his eyes. Would morning never arrive?

"You heard me?" she asked.

"What?"

"Never mind. We'll talk about it later." The moment the words were out of her mouth, she regretted them. "Nakos, you said something about a smell. What was it?"

Jola's voice came from a distance Nakos couldn't measure. He was acutely aware of her body on top of his but couldn't remember how or why or when that had happened. She was his captive, his prisoner, so why was she willingly lying on top of him?

"Nakos?" she repeated. "What did you mean about a smell?"

He could have refused to answer, but what defense could he throw up against that gentle, caring voice? Still, he ordered himself to wait until the familiar nightmare had lost its hold on him. When, finally, it did, he willed himself to relax. After pushing herself off him, she stretched out beside him. Before he could guess what she had in mind, she took his hand and rested it on her belly.

"Does anyone know what's behind your dreams?"

"No." His fingers twitched.

"Why not? Maybe your shaman could help."

Tau hadn't been the shaman back when the too-familiar nightmare had been reality. He couldn't possibly understand. No one could.

"Why don't you trust him?" she asked.

"I never said—"

"You didn't have to."

He'd never noticed how dark the tent was at night; at least, it hadn't made such an impact before. He supposed he should be grateful for it because he didn't have to look at her, but it wasn't that simple.

"You know nothing about us," he countered after a moment. "The Ekewoko are strangers to your—what do you call yourselves?"

"Falcons."

"What? Why?"

A fine tremor ran through her. "Falcons—are skilled hunters. No bird is swifter. We, ah, admire them."

"So much so that you've named yourselves after them?"

"The name came to be long before I was born. I never questioned the reason behind it."

Her voice had taken on a tone he hadn't heard before, something between strain and reluctance. Given everything that had taken place between them, he couldn't blame her for not wanting to say more about her background than absolutely necessary.

"Will you answer me one thing," she said, sounding more like herself. "What are you smelling when you're having one of your dreams?"

Her body was soft and warm and alive when he desperately needed those things. And with night close around them, he couldn't think beyond that need. Granted, he'd already fucked her twice since capturing her, but his body had recharged itself. It would take almost nothing for him to spread her legs and house his cock in her heated walls.

Maybe she knew what he was thinking because she tugged her arms free and closed her fingers around his wrist and guided his hand to that sweet place. Feeling as if he was coming home, he began stroking her nether lips. Her breathing, although ragged, stretched out.

"The—smell. Nakos, please tell me about it."

"Smoke."

"What kind of a fire is it? What's burning?"

He wasn't going to answer. Years of keeping everything locked away should have made holding onto his secrets simple. But his existence and hers had somehow intertwined. He couldn't, wouldn't tell her everything but maybe enough to satisfy her.

And himself.

"Years ago," he told her with his fingers on her and the sound of her breathing filling his ears. "We—the Ekewoko— were attacked by a fierce and powerful tribe."

"You were a warrior?"

"A child, a boy." He turned his head in the direction her voice was coming from. "I was with relatives at a camp a short distance from where the attack took place."

"Some tents were set fire and you smelled—"

"Not just any tents. My grandparents were living in one of them."

"Nakos, no."

Yes, he corrected her, yes, his father's parents' home had burned to the ground. His grandparents hadn't had time to arm themselves before fleeing the flames.

Even though he couldn't strip emotion from his voice, he didn't stop talking until he'd told her everything he was capable of. As he relayed it, he'd reached the smoldering tents while his uncle was still gathering other warriors around him in preparation for attack. His aunt had tried to hold him back, but he'd twisted out of her grasp.

His grandparents had been everything to him, second parents and the source for everything he knew about the Ekewoko past. His grandfather had taught him how to hunt, and he'd sat at his grandmother's side while she cooked and sewed. His mother had died giving birth to him. His father had turned Nakos over to his grandparents to raise and lived another six years—until he'd been killed in a battle with the same savage tribe that later set the fire.

"They were dead by the time I reached them," he said in response to Jola's quiet question. "Stabbed to death by the enemy when they tried to flee their burning home."

Silence surrounded his words. No matter how desperately he needed to get beyond them, he couldn't think of anything to say, and Jola, too, remained silent. Although he was grateful because she kept her sex open to him, even guiding his hand over her core, he couldn't take his mind beyond the too-simple sentence.

The lie.

Finally she shifted position a little. "You found them?"

"Yes."

"Touched them? Knew they were beyond help?"

"Yes."

"And your nightmare—you kept seeing that one thing in your mind."

He again told her yes. Then, determined to end the topic, he lied again, saying he seldom had that dream anymore and didn't know why it had returned tonight. Whispering, she suggested that her presence might have played a role, and he agreed.

Not long after, when she was on her back with her legs draped over his shoulders and he'd hidden his cock inside her, he told himself they'd never need to have this conversation again.

Only he knew the truth, the horrible things he'd done.

13

Jola welcomed the morning. Not only wasn't she still inside Nakos's too-small tent, the air outside was fresher and the breeze sharp. Most important, her captor's body heat no longer touched her.

They'd had sex an unbelievable three times since he'd hauled her nearly lifeless body out of the great lake. She hadn't tried to fight him off. In fact, each of those times she'd desperately needed his cock in the place only Raci should have known throughout all the days and nights of her life. Fucking had left her satisfied and satiated, for a while.

Once they'd gone outside shortly after dawn, he'd given her a bowl of stew. There hadn't been much flavor to or meat in the stew, but her stomach had welcomed it. She would have tried to identify the ingredients if she hadn't been so aware of the interest directed her way. Nakos had left her in the care of one of his fellow warriors, a husky man he'd called Farajj after informing her that he had things to attend to which didn't concern her. That might be true, but she couldn't help wondering if he wanted distance between them as much as she did.

At the moment, Farajj was sitting on the ground while smoothing the sides of a spear, but he kept stopping his task to study her. Finally he set down his weapon and faced her. "Nakos says you have a human's mind. I say you've turned him around until he doesn't know what to think or believe."

"Why would I do that?"

"Ha! The question is, why wouldn't you try? You don't want to be here. You'll do everything you can to get free, even pretend to be something you aren't."

How little you know. "Perhaps."

Farajj's expression became quizzical. "You don't deny it, do you?"

"Deny what?"

"That my friend would be a fool to trust anything you say or do. Maybe—maybe you want to see him dead. And not just him but all of us."

"By myself?" Going by Farajj's smooth features, she guessed he'd recently left childhood. In a few more years, he'd have gained the wisdom a man needs to survive and succeed, but right now he reminded her of boys who would rather play and wrestle than assume responsibility. In some ways she envied him. "How would I do that?"

"Maybe because you're more than human."

Even before she turned her head and looked up, she knew who was speaking. The shaman stood behind her, his lips thin and eyes narrowed.

"Come with me," Tau ordered, jerking his head at her.

"Nakos ordered me to—" Farajj started.

"Are you saying I have no right?" Tau interrupted.

Farajj shook his head so violently that his long, fine hair flew about. Not waiting for the young man to speak, Tau grabbed her arm and hauled her to her feet. After letting her tend to her morning needs, Nakos had retied her arms in front in such a way that there was less pressure on her wrists than before. To her relief, he hadn't placed anything around her throat. Judging by Tau's take-charge attitude, the shaman would have relished treating her like an animal. Hoping Farajj would tell Nakos where she was, she didn't resist as the shaman led her over to his tent. She reluctantly went inside.

The smell was a mix of herbs and spices along with the shaman's body odor. Unfortunately, the time she'd been forced to spend in his presence yesterday didn't make weathering his stench now any easier. She wondered why he had no use for cleanliness, then guessed it must have something to do with protecting his shaman powers.

"You and I, we need to have time alone," he said sternly. Not giving her time to sit on her own, he jerked her down. She fell onto her side but quickly positioned herself on her knees. He wasn't particularly large, yet he carried himself with a self-confidence that she had no doubt came from years of wielding power.

Settling himself onto a stool made from leather and wood, he leaned forward with his hands gripping his knees. It took all her self-control not to shrink from his commanding and suspicious glare.

"I know who you are," he said. "And what exists between your people and the birds you call falcons."

No, you can't! Please, you can't. "What do you believe exists?"

"I ask the questions, not you, understand!"

Determined not to recoil, she nodded. Her every nerve was on alert.

"I have visions," he continued. "Visions sent to me by gods and spirits. Those forces gifted me. I have seen what falcons are capable of."

"Did you?" She hoped he wouldn't notice that she'd asked a question.

"You think I wouldn't?" He filled his lungs and continued

to stare down at her as if she was something lesser than him. "Foolish creature, why do you think I wanted you captured?"

Last night's conversation had been much like this except the shaman and she hadn't been alone then. Sensing that Tau felt freer than he had when he'd had an audience, she forced herself to incline her head a bit. Hopefully, he'd believe she was cowed. She then prayed she wouldn't give away anything she shouldn't.

"Ekew is a wondrous place. The gods gifted it to the Ekewoko when the earth was made, but over time our ancestors became lazy. They stopped thanking the gods for that great gift. The gods grew angry. They sent another tribe, a fierce one, to Ekew. Their warriors, whose weapons are greater than ours, forced us to leave Ekew."

"There was fighting?"

"Of course! Do you think we are nothing but whipped animals who slink away with our tails between our legs?"

Taking his outburst as a warning to watch everything she said, she shook her head.

"Some Ekewoko died during those battles. For a long time everyone insisted we would stay and fight for what was ours, but there are so many Outsiders. We lack the warriors and weapons necessary to vanquish them."

"So the Ekewoko decided they had to leave if they were going to stay alive?"

"Yes." Tau whispered the word. "But no matter where we go, our hearts belong to Ekew. It's our destiny to return."

"What is Ekew like?"

"You think I would tell you? Ha, hardly. Someone like you would never appreciate its richness or see its beauty."

"Perhaps not."

"Look at this place," he continued, sneering. "There is little dirt, mostly rocks incapable of sustaining growth. Winters are so cold that the earth remains frozen and in summer, heat bakes everything. When our scouts described this land, the decision was made to leave our women, children, and elderly near the sea where we'd spent last winter and spring."

If he had such a low opinion of Falcon Land, or Screaming Wind as the Ekewoko called it, why had he ordered his warriors to come here?

"It seldom rains and the wind never stops."

We're used to it. We hear music in the wind.

"No gods bless this place."

How wrong he was! About to tell him so, she clamped her teeth together because she guessed he was deliberately pushing her.

"Evil spirits walk here, nothing else."

"Then why—"

"Dark spirits with a single gift."

They were getting to the heart of why he'd wanted a captive. Her heartbeat kicking up, she studied him without moving.

"Falcons."

Her heartbeat continuing to increase, she forced herself not to blink or speak.

"Magical predators with the speed of the gods."

Fighting a sudden chill, she could only pray her expression wasn't giving anything away.

"You say nothing, slave. Is it because you can't comprehend how much I know?"

But he didn't know everything, did he? "What do you want me to say?"

"Nothing, yet. First you will hear me out. And then"—he smiled a smile that didn't reach his eyes—"you will give me everything I demand."

Nakos couldn't possibly suspect what was taking place, could he? He wouldn't leave her to Tau's mercies, would he?

She was still searching for the answer when Tau began. As a favored son of the heavenly Ekewoko spirits, he'd been gifted

with a series of dreams, each more revealing than the one before. At first he'd seen only a small bird with a slate-gray back
and long, pointed wings. The underparts were white with thin,
dark brown bands. The long, narrow tail was rounded at the
end and mostly white except for a black tip and a white band at
the end. The top of the head and along the cheeks were black,
contrasting with the pale neck and throat. Most compelling
were the powerful, yellow talons and piercing black eyes ringed
in yellow. Black claws and beak completed the fierce image.

"At first I believed he was a hawk but smaller than any I
have ever seen," Tau continued. "Why, I wondered, were the
spirits handing me this vision. Then during one dream, the
hawk took flight and I began to understand."

Tau's voice lost some of its volume. Just the same, Jola had
no difficulty hearing every word, not that she needed to because she already knew what he was going to say. At least she
believed she did.

In the dream after the flying one, Tau had watched two
hawks soar and sweep around each other. The smaller bird had
repeatedly passed food off to the larger one, the larger flying
upside down and effortlessly taking a fresh kill from the small
one's talons.

"I have never seen anything like what happened," Tau continued. "They rose high into the sky as one, circling each other
as if they were dancing with the wind. Then, together, they
turned and dove for the ground. Their speed—unbelievable!
My eyes couldn't keep up."

"That dream ended, leaving me in awe. The next night there
was another vision. When it was over, I understood that I'd
been watching a mating pair. The male, smaller than the female,
killed prey after prey and took it to his mate so she could eat it
while flying. After feeding, they mated, also in the sky, their
bodies blurred. Following that, the female scraped a hollow in
dirt and vegetation on a high ledge, and they nested there. She

lay four snow-white eggs with red markings and spent every night keeping the eggs warm. In the day, the pair took turns caring for their offspring. When the chicks were born, their down was creamy white, their feet huge."

Although she'd tried to relax, her heart continued its fast tempo. Her knees ached, but she didn't want to draw attention to herself by changing position. If only she could get him to stop speaking!

"Are you ready to hear about the next dream?"

No! Knowing she had no choice, she nodded. Her hands and feet were cold, her torso hot.

"No longer did I feel as if I were standing on the ground watching. Instead, it was as if I had been given wings and was flying only a few feet away while the hawk hunted. I don't know what kind of bird the hawk caught, just that the prey was larger. He did so in midair. One instant I saw a blur of movement speeding toward earth, going faster than the fastest arrow. The next, the prey was spinning out of control, whirling in circles and dropping with its feathers swirling like a snowfall around it. It fell only a few feet before the hawk clamped its talons around the body and took it to the ground where it ate it. I have never seen anything move with such speed, not by half. I'd think if the hawk had struck its prey in the middle of its body, the blow might have killed both birds. Instead, the hawk struck a wing, which is why the prey spun the way it did."

Tau obviously expected her to be disbelieving, but although she should give him what he was waiting for, she couldn't. In fact, she was tempted to tell him the rest, that what he was calling a hawk but was a falcon had reached that great speed by folding back its tail and wings and tucking its talons against its body. In essence, the falcon became an arrow.

"There was one more dream," Tau said after a short silence. "In it, I learned two things."

Be patient. Wait him out. Say nothing.

"First, that those hawks are called 'falcons.' And second, that what we first believed was worthless land is where they live."

She'd grown up believing her kind were different from all others. Even though Falcons assumed human proportions some of the time, they weren't true humans. Instead, they were rare and special, gifts from the gods. But why would a god or spirit let Tau see as much as he had?

Even more important, what use did he intend to make of those dreams and how did his plans involve her?

"You know where falcons live when they aren't hunting," she heard Tau say despite the fog descending around her. "Don't tell me you haven't seen their nests."

Almost before he finished speaking, the fog started to lift, allowing her to comprehend it for what it was. She'd been afraid Tau knew everything about her and the rest of the Falcons. But he didn't understand that predator and human shared the same heart.

"Answer me! Where do the falcons live?"

"You've been here for several moons," she countered. "Surely you don't need me to tell you what your scouts should have discovered long ago."

Tau didn't rise to his feet with Nakos's easy grace, but he still made her aware of the difference in their size as he stood. When she was in predator form, size didn't matter. Unfortunately, she couldn't change here.

"That's what I hoped and believed when we began this quest, but I was wrong. This place"—he all but spat the words—"keeps its secrets well."

He was standing over her now, looming really. He'd spread his legs and folded his arms across his chest to intimidate her; she couldn't shake free of his impact on her senses. Her useless arms had something to do with it, of course, but her fear came from a deeper place. He could hurt her. He was capable of inflicting pain and would do whatever it took to try to strip everything she knew from her.

As suddenly as her fear had swamped her, it died under powerful anger. He might be able to control her human body, but in her heart she was a Falcon. She'd die before she betrayed her kind.

"Why do you care?" she demanded. "A falcon is a bird. Nothing for a shaman to concern himself with."

"How can you, a simple creature, begin to know of a shaman's plans?"

Spittle had formed at the corners of his mouth. But if she didn't push him, she might never learn what she needed to.

"Falcons have long been part of our world," she said, dancing around the truth. "We admire their speed and skill, but they live their lives the same as every other creature. I don't understand—"

"Of course you don't. You're incapable of seeing their potential."

The chill she'd managed to ignore swept over her again. "Potential?"

"To benefit the Ekewoko."

"How can that be? They're wild birds. No one can possibly capture them."

The way he shook his head put her in mind of a parent whose patience has been tested by a misbehaving child. About to say something to alter his low opinion of her, she changed her mind. Maybe, if she played into his ego, he might reveal more than he would otherwise.

"We have never tried—I mean, it has never occurred to my people to try—to make some use of them." She frowned. "But you are right. No other creature can match their hunting prowess. That's what you're thinking of, aren't you?"

He nearly smiled. "Think. A falcon can bring down birds

much larger than themselves as well as rabbits, squirrels, young raccoons, snakes, and rodents."

"Yes."

"And once my warriors and I have trained them to kill on command, they will turn their skills on our enemy. They know nothing of fear. The Outsiders' weapons will mean nothing to them. Ekew will again belong to us."

"Train them? How is that possible?"

"Even if I was inclined to tell you, which I'm not, only someone, like me, with spirit-given patience and understanding can mold a newborn falcon into a killer. The blood of the Outsiders will flow—"

"Newborn?"

"Enough! I've told you everything I'm going to. Now"—his joyless smile grew—"do you understand what use I have for you? The Ekewoko will reclaim Ekew, they will!"

He wanted her to take him to a falcon nest! Expected her to stand by while he stole chicks, maybe first killing their parents!

"No!"

"Yes!" His foot flew out, catching her shoulder and knocking her back so she sprawled on the ground. "Do you think your refusal will get you anywhere? My poor creature, breaking you will be far easier than training a falcon."

Although her shoulder throbbed, she sat back up. Much as she wanted to jump to her feet and pummel him, she forced herself to remain still. A single shout from him and the Ekewoko warriors would charge into the tent and overwhelm her. Maybe Nakos would join them.

"If your dreams showed falcons preparing their nests, then you must know how inaccessible those places are." She deliberately kept her tone level. "None of my people have ever tried to climb up there."

"Climb where? Where do they nest?"

"I don't know."

"You said—"

"Because my people have never come across a falcon nest, we assume they're high in the mountains far from here. We see them only when they're hunting."

"I don't believe you."

"Why would I lie to you?"

His smile had flattened even before she'd finished asking her question. In some ways she relished pitting her mind against his. Even more, she longed to stand face to face with him and see which could battle the other into submission.

"You, my simple creature, will do whatever you believe you need to to stay alive—even fuck your captor."

"That's why you think I—"

"You're not denying that you and Nakos had sex?"

Why was the conversation taking this turn? Cautious, she shrugged. The gesture sent sharp pain into where he'd kicked her.

"Don't you understand?" Although he reached behind him and touched his stool, he remained standing. "If you wanted sex as much as he did, which is what I believe, that's all the proof I need."

Proof of what? Hating this man who believed he could do whatever he wanted to her, she refused to respond.

"Interesting," Tau muttered. "You're thinking. I didn't expect that. However—yes, yes, this is better. The more complex you are, the more I have to work with."

Eyes open, she imagined herself soaring over Tau. In her mind, he was standing at the base of Raptor's Craig looking for a way to the top. She wouldn't care if he spotted her. In fact, she wanted him to see the deceptively small raptor floating in endless circles above him. She'd pace herself so it looked as if she had nothing in mind except playing with the wind and letting it play with her. She'd keep her talons close to her body and her beak closed, occasionally drifting low so Tau could make out her yellow rimmed eyes.

Eventually he'd lose interest in her. That's when she'd dive, extend her claws, and tear open his cheek. Half a heartbeat later, she'd reach his throat and rip it apart. He'd try to stem the blood flow by clamping his hands over his neck, but within moments he'd sink to the ground, weak and dying.

Just as he wanted her and other Falcons to do to the Outsiders.

"Stop it!" Erasing the distance between them in two steps, Tau slapped her. Her head snapped back; her cheek stung.

"What?" she asked, determined not to give away her fury.

"Your eyes—what was that? They started changing color, becoming—"

What? "You're an old man. Your eyesight isn't what it used to be."

She thought he'd strike her again, but he only pushed her back. Although the tent opening was behind her, she didn't try to escape. Instead, she wrapped what he'd just told her about her eye color around her. Was it possible? Could a Falcon change form anywhere except at Raptor's Craig? That had never happened, but if the Falcon was desperate enough—

"You are a wild animal," he told her, his hands fisted and his nostrils flared. "Too primitive to know when you're facing death."

"If you kill me, your dreams won't be realized."

Something flicked in his eyes only to fade before she could be sure it was fear. But much as she needed to examine the depth and length of his fear, if that's what it was, she also needed to understand what he was capable of.

"It was nothing for Nakos to capture you," he said. "If something happens to you, he'll get another of your kind."

"Maybe. And maybe my kind, as you call us, saw my capture. Maybe they're preparing to attack."

Tau's gaze flickered from her to the tent flap, then back to her. He opened his mouth only to close it. Watching his reaction was almost laughable. His dreams might have given him a sense of direction, but they'd told him nothing about Falcons. Otherwise, he'd know who and what she was.

"Do you think I haven't thought of that," he finally said. "Where do you think Nakos went this morning? He, along with several others, are looking for your kind near where he found you. If, when they spot them, they are met with hostility, there will only be one outcome: victory for the Ekewoko."

Nakos wasn't in camp; he had no way of knowing what was going on between her and Tau. At least she hoped he didn't. "Your warriors won't find anything," she said belatedly.

"How can you—"

"My people know this land, its hiding places, secret caves and narrow valleys."

Once again Tau looked at the opening. She shouldn't, but she almost felt sorry for the older man. What was it like to be ruled by one's dreams, to be controlled by powerful and mysterious forces?

She wanted to believe that the so-called Ekewoko spirits and gods couldn't possibly speak to the shaman and his dreams. Surely they were nothing more than his overactive imagination. But some powerful essence had created her kind. Anything was possible.

"Hiding places are important but not just to your people," Tau mused. "That's why we've been unable to find where the falcons nest. If Nakos and the others discover no indication that your kind will try to rescue you, then he will concentrate on you. He'll force you to take him to where the falcons lay their eggs."

"Never!"

"Never?" Tau shot back. "How wrong you are."

"I would die before I betray either my people or anything else that lives here."

Before she could escape, Tau grabbed her neck. His fingers pressed down, threatening to cut off her ability to breathe. "Your death won't be necessary, *slave*. However, once we are done with you, you might prefer that to your fate."

"Let—me go!"

"Never!"

14

Although Nakos and the three warriors who'd accompanied him had each brought along two water-filled bladders, it hadn't been enough. Judging by the way his companions sucked on theirs, he wasn't the only one to feel the sun's impact. At least they'd accomplished what Lord Sakima had ordered them to and were on their way back to camp.

"Did you think we'd find anything?" Ohanko asked.

Nakos looked over at his equally sweaty and dirty friend. "No. The Wildings are like ghosts."

"Maybe they *are* ghosts. What better explanation for why we so seldom glimpse them?"

"Do you really think that?"

"I don't know what to believe." Ohanko wiped sweat off his temple. "You're the only one I'd tell this, but I will never understand why we came here. Of all the places—"

"I agree." Even though he'd convinced himself that they were alone, Nakos again took in his surroundings. "The land is worthless. And the Wildings—"

"Are welcome to this godless place." Sighing, Ohanko

shook his head. "Something I've wondered about. Do you think the other Wildings look like the female you captured? From a distance it's hard to tell."

"Her name is Jola," he told the man he'd long thought of as a brother.

"Jola? I'm surprised she told you that."

"So am I."

"Hmm. It sounds as if the creature has caught your interest, not that I blame you. She is beautiful, in a wild way. The moment I first saw her, I wanted to fuck her." Ohanko laughed. "But then I haven't seen a woman for so long that, given the chance, I'd probably bury myself in anything with a pussy. She does have one, doesn't she?"

Although he wasn't sure he wanted to continue this conversation, Nakos nodded.

"What do you think's going to happen to her?"

"Tau insists he has use for her." He had to work the words past the tightness in his throat.

"Of course he does. He won't rest until he's done everything he can to turn his spirit-dreams into reality. But that's not what I'm asking."

Stopping, Nakos faced the other warrior. His legs ached, and he couldn't stop wondering what Lamuka was preparing for dinner. "Say it."

"She's yours by rights of capture. Not only that, you saved her life."

"Maybe."

"What do you mean?"

"Nothing, maybe. I'm just not sure—Ohanko, she might have lived even if I hadn't pulled her out of the lake."

"How? With the poison in her—"

"I know." Although the sun was heading for the horizon, it wouldn't reach it for a while, and there was no shade where they stood. Between the heat, his thirst, and hunger, he could hardly think. "From the moment I first saw her, I knew I'd have to turn her over to Tau and my lord. I told myself it didn't matter, that I had no use for a simple captive, but she fascinates me."

"Is it her," Ohanko softly asked, "or the thought of having something that's yours and only yours?"

"Don't!" His outburst swirling around him, Nakos looked to see if the others had heard him, but they were a fair distance away. "I'm not the little boy I once was."

"I know." Reaching out, Ohanko patted his shoulder. "I'm sorry. I shouldn't have brought that up. Tell me, would she make a good sex slave?"

Ohanko's question didn't surprise him. Just the same, he couldn't think how to respond. Maybe, if he could clean his mind of thoughts of what he and Jola had shared, it would be different.

"You know what I'm talking about," his friend continued. "Does she enjoy sex? Does she welcome your cock?"

"She welcomes it."

"Ah." Sighing, Ohanko cradled his flaccid cock. "With heat?"

"With heat."

"Did she come?"

If anyone else had asked, he wouldn't have answered. "Yes."

"Then I truly envy you."

Nakos started walking again, not because he wanted to see how much more he could push his legs but because his body whispered to him of a soft female form. But even as his thoughts drifted to the sight of Jola waiting for him, he faced reality.

He'd captured her not for himself, but for his shaman and lord.

No, Farajj had told Nakos a few moments ago, he hadn't seen Jola since the shaman had come looking for her in the morning. As far as he knew, the captive was still in Tau's tent, and unless he'd left when Farajj wasn't looking, Lord Sakima was in there with them.

He'd suspected this would happen, had known it would. Just the same, Nakos's first impulse was to charge into the tent and demand his captive's return. But as he made his weary way to it, he'd had to fight the impulse to turn and walk away—because no matter what he saw, he had no choice but to accept it.

Sakima was part of whatever would become of Jola. His lord, the man who'd taken him in and raised him after he'd lost everything, was a complex mix of compassion and commitment. He embraced everything that was Ekewoko without question and would die protecting his people if that's what it took to insure their survival. At the same time, his lord saw everyone who wasn't Ekewoko as inferior, the enemy.

Reaching the dusty tent, Nakos started to push the door flap aside only to let his hand drop and step back. Tau's tent was sacred. No one entered it without first receiving permission.

"My shaman," he called out. "It is I, Nakos. If my lord is in there, I need to speak to him."

"Come in," Tau and Sakima said in unison.

The invitation should have propelled him forward. Instead, he stood where he was. Then, because he had no choice, he ducked his head and entered the dark enclosure.

Tau and Sakima stood facing each other in the middle of the tent, their attention already leaving him and returning to the ground between them. Even though he suspected what he'd find there, the sight of Jola lying on her back with her body arched so her breasts were prominently displayed chilled him anew. Her arms had been tied behind her, forcing her unnatural position. A rope around her waist left no doubt that her wrists had been secured to it as he'd initially done, further hindering her ability to move. Although they trembled, her legs were pressed tightly together. She was gagged.

"She's ready for you," Tau said.

This wasn't the first time he'd seen a female captive so displayed. Once, shortly after the Ekewoko had entered a long, low valley fed by a lazy river, the warriors had encountered the valley's residents, a small, fierce clan that had no intention of sharing their land with those they considered invaders. Two skirmishes had resulted in injuries on both sides but no deaths. Instead of risking a battle against a foe they barely understood, some of the Ekewoko warriors had slipped out under cover of night trying to learn where the clan was hidden. Instead, they'd captured a couple of women they'd found picking fruit.

Because he'd been a warrior in training at the time, he hadn't participated in the women's *interrogation,* but he'd listened and learned. Although the women had been kept tied the entire time, they hadn't been physically abused. Instead, their sexual natures had been explored in depth and once that nature had revealed itself, the women had been forced to endure arousal after arousal but never allowed to climax. After a day and a night, they'd been desperate to exchange everything they knew about where their clan was in exchange for sexual release and relief.

After that first introduction, Nakos had participated in the kind of treatment of other female captives that sometimes led to vital information. He'd never carried out an interrogation on his own, until now.

"What have you done to her?" he asked.

"Prepared her for you."

Now that his eyes had adjusted to the gloom, he noted that she was taking deep and unsteady breaths, her ribs and pelvis bones standing out every time she inhaled. Moisture glistened on her pubic hairs.

"Why didn't you wait until I returned?" He directed his question at Tau.

If the shaman resented what might be interpreted as criticism, he gave no indication. "I've had to be patient a long time, perhaps because the spirits have chosen to test me. Now that the means to my goal is in my control, I grow impatient."

As long as Nakos didn't meet Jola's gaze he could concentrate. "Has she told you what you want to know?"

"Not want, need. No, she hasn't, but then, I've enjoyed the journey." Tau held out a juice-soaked hand. "Of course, bringing her along has exacted a certain toil on me." He grabbed his crotch for emphasis. "She will pay for it."

Nakos wanted to turn and walk out. Even more, he wanted to sling Jola over his shoulder and take her with him. The moment they were alone, he'd demand she tell him what the shaman had done to her; not that he needed to because her rapid breathing spoke loudly of one thing: a shaman's knowing fingers.

"Nakos," his lord warned. He jerked his head at Nakos's hands, which had curled into fists.

"I didn't expect this," Nakos said, forcing himself to relax. "You say you needed certain information from her. Why, then, is she gagged?"

Tau grunted, then smiled. "To discourage her from lying. When she finally speaks, I want there to be no doubt she's telling the truth."

More likely, Tau was feeding his need for power. Still not studying the prone captive, Nakos concentrated on Sakima. "You approve?"

"I know what you're thinking. She lives because you saved her, and you don't want to see that life jeopardized. Rest assured, she has never felt more alive, have you, slave?" Lifting his leg, Sakima ran his foot over her thigh. Her legs parted a fraction. "See? Her responses are becoming predictable. They're exactly what we expected."

"But if she's given too much time to rest," Tau added, "we'll have to begin all over again."

Trying to ignore Jola wasn't working. How could it, when

his every nerve and vein seemed connected to her? Maybe, if he didn't have the memory of how urgently she embraced her sexuality, he wouldn't now be remembering how her body had jerked wildly and one gasp after another had escaped her. That she wasn't trying to sit up or pressing her thighs back together said a great deal about how far the two men had brought her.

"She would already be singing," his lord told him, "if my thoughts hadn't been on a simple fact. This pleasure should be yours. You earned it."

From the moment he'd grasped what was happening, he'd known Sakima would say that. A slave might belong to every Ekewoko but usually one warrior had a greater right than the others. In Jola's case, there was no doubt who claimed ownership: him.

"Do it," Tau commanded. "Teach her that she has no existence beyond you."

The shaman's words echoing, he took a single step toward her, then stopped. She was still a stranger to him, and yet he'd told her things he'd never believed he'd tell a captive. One of those things had been a lie or, if not that, only a partial truth, and although he'd regretted the omission then, he was now glad for the distance between them. Another step and distance no longer factored in, at least not in the physical sense.

But because he'd stopped himself in time, he retained the vital emotional separation he'd need to accomplish his mission.

"You're certain she holds the information you've been seeking?" he asked Tau while his mind spun with possibilities. There were so many things he could do to her. So many pleasures awaiting.

"No doubt."

Two words and he knew what he had to do. His thirst, hunger, and weariness forgotten, he sank to his knees beside his possession. She rolled her head to the side so she could watch him.

He liked the way the strips of leather held her mouth open and robbed her of voice. He'd prefer it if she was blindfolded so she couldn't see what he was about to do, or find something in his expression that he wanted to keep from her, but right now maybe it was better if she could watch and anticipate.

"You used only your hands?" he asked, not looking up at Tau. "On her sex, I mean?"

"It wasn't easy. I wanted to take her."

"But you didn't?"

"You have so much to learn about a shaman's strength," Tau said. "The body must never override the mind and soul. Believe me, my hands were all I needed to break down her defenses. Besides, I wanted to explore her sex."

Jola's breath hissed. If she'd had use of her hands, Nakos had no doubt she'd dig her nails into the shaman. He also suspected that the consequences of doing so didn't concern her. In fact, imagining her attacking him like some mountain cougar made his own heart race.

"You're sure she didn't climax?"

"I'm certain."

Because Tau, like all Ekewoko, knew how to read and gauge a female's sexual responses. Ekewoko. Yes, that's who and what he was and would always be. "So you refused to give my shaman the information he needs," he said, extending his hand until it nearly touched a hard, dark-tipped breast. "How can you, a captive, believe you have the right to do such a thing?"

Her eyes flashed. More telling, her legs parted a little more. He wondered at the self-control that had compelled her to try to protect her sex from the men who'd imprisoned her arms and robbed her of speech. Soon he'd explore the depths and limits of that self-control, but first—

"You are beautiful, desirable." He grazed her nipple, then withdrew. "There's nothing more exciting to an Ekewoko than a beautiful and helpless female."

She glared at him.

"What is this?" Cocking his head, he gave her a quizzical look. "You don't think you're attractive? You are. Believe me, you are." He again touched his finger to her nipple, then pulled back. "You're like a spring flower unfolding. At this moment, you're little more than a bud, swelling life. But the sun warms you, and before long, everyone will see the truth about you."

Even though she didn't know what to expect from him, she didn't want to be draped in lethargy's blanket. Instead, dangerous as it was, she needed to feel alive.

"How does it feel to be silenced?" he asked as his fingers settled over her nipple. He held her lightly yet firmly. "To not be able to stand or fight me?"

If he wanted her to answer, he'd have to remove her gag. Until he did, she'd cling to the present. And listen to his deep tones.

"Maybe you don't have fight in you after all," he continued. "A strange concept, I'm certain, to discover that you like this." Leaning low, he fed her breast into his mouth and closed down.

Arching her back, she gnawed on the leather in her mouth. Her cheeks flamed.

A drawing sensation on her imprisoned breast forced out a low moan. Hating her weakness, she shook her head.

No! He was feeding on her, nibbling here, there, and everywhere. No matter how she tried, she couldn't keep up with him, couldn't begin to guess where his teeth and tongue would touch next. That he'd done this to her before didn't matter. As he sucked more of her into him, she tried to turn to the side, only to stop and flop onto her back again as his grip tightened.

Still firmly gripping her with his lips, he straightened a little. She stared as her blurred breast elongated. The drawing sensation increased, then built even more until another moan broke free. Instead of heeding her cry, he pulled again. Tears sprang to her eyes. At the same time, white-hot heat scored her belly and ran toward her crotch. This time she groaned.

After giving her breast a quick jerk, he released her. Her entire breast felt as if it had been brought too close to the sun.

"What did that do to you?" he asked and slid a hand between her legs. Shuddering, she struggled to remember how to close them, but even when she managed to bring her knees together, his hand prevented her thighs from doing the same. Hating herself for the thought, she drew comparisons between her sex lips embracing his cock and soft thigh flesh cradling his fingers and palm.

And when he glided a thumb over those lips as she'd known he'd do, she whipped her head to the side and tightly closed her eyes. She had no such control over her bucking hips.

"You want to be ridden, do you?" he demanded. "Yes, you must, because here's the proof."

Something deep inside her quivered. She barely acknowledged the thumb that was invading what maybe already belonged to him. This body of hers had never felt like this, had never been touched in such ways.

"Proof," he repeated, lower this time. "Sweet, wet truth flowing from you."

He was gone, leaving her empty and her mind shaking. Then he began bathing the breast he'd handled earlier with warm, sticky fluid from her pussy, forcing her to open her eyes and gape at him. She had no thoughts, no words wanting to be spoken. There were only his indistinct features and the heat sliding off him and onto her. Only that sweet, wet truth he spoke about drying on her breast and him going back for more.

One of the two other men might have chuckled as he painted her other breast with her own liquid, but perhaps she only imagined the sound.

Back he came for more, sliding past her inflamed flesh, caressing and stroking, his sleek, firm nail contrasting with his calloused fingertip and everything confusing her. Making her whimper and moan and still not care that she was being noisy. Her leg muscles burned and threatened to cramp. Why was she trying to hold onto modesty or self when both had been shattered? Melted.

"See what I mean," Tau said from someplace far away. "She's ready."

Nakos's thumb stilled. She could be wrong, but he seemed more tense than he'd been a moment ago and his breathing was louder. "Just because her legs have parted?" he asked. "Believe this, shaman, there is more to her than sex and need."

Was there? With Nakos handling her and what the other men had done to her earlier ruling everything, she didn't know.

"What about it, Jola?" Nakos asked with his mouth so close to her ear that his breath tickled. "If I remove your gag, will you tell us where the falcons breed and give birth?"

"No!" she screamed into the gag.

"I told you," Nakos said, speaking to the men, "she isn't as simple as you want her to be. Yes, she's a sexual creature." As if making his point, he slid his thumb deep into her. Her legs all but melted into the ground. "But she's loyal to her people."

"People?" Tau questioned. "They're animals."

"No, they aren't."

Before she could comprehend what he had in mind, Nakos grabbed her ankles and began pushing on them, forcing her to bend her knees. He was relentless and strong, not stopping until her heels touched where her thighs and buttocks joined. Then he drew her legs apart and settled himself on his knees in the space he'd created. Only then did he release her ankles, but with his body in place, she remained spread. Vulnerable.

"Pleasure and helplessness, Jola," he said and rested the heel of a hand on her mons. She saw nothing but his face, his dark and knowing eyes. "That's what I'm going to give you. When

I'm finished, you can either thank me by telling us what we want to know or . . ."

Or what? her mind screamed. Then he placed her calves on his shoulders, lifting her buttocks off the ground. Her weight settled onto her trapped hands and shoulders, forcing her head back so she now stared at the top of the tent. Not being able to see him even as her body recorded everything he did frightened her.

Not content with what he'd just accomplished, he gripped her ass cheeks and pulled her yet closer, yet higher. Her shoulder blades ached from the increased pressure, and her cunt muscles clenched in anticipation.

"I saw that," Nakos told her. The breath that had inflamed her ear a few moments ago now bathed her pussy. "The simple beauty of a woman's sex muscles doing what the spirits created them for."

Something wet and warm slid over her slit. Gasping, she tried to buck out of her captor's grasp. He waited her out, and when she relaxed a little, he touched her there again. Although she shuddered and gasped, she didn't try to break free this time. He'd caressed her with his tongue—his tongue!

"No more fighting, Jola?" her captor questioned almost gently. "Is it because you want this more than you fear it?"

Fear, maybe a little. Acknowledging that, if only to herself, made it easier to shake her head. However, she guessed he didn't believe her because he lapped at her once more, taking twice as long this time and dipping deep into her core. Again she fought, not for freedom, but because his touch brought her so close to the edge.

She started to thrash her head only to stop because her neck burned. Although she wasn't upside down, she might as well have been for all the control she had over her body. Not only that, she was becoming light headed.

Most of all, every time her struggling quieted, he came after her. Dragged her to the edge of sanity. As if it wasn't unsettling enough to have his tongue plunder her sex, he occasionally pressed it against her clit. She wanted to be silent, damn it! Needed to close silence around her. But moaning kept her from shattering, as did trying to lift her legs off his shoulders.

"No!" He lightly pinched her buttocks.

Arching her back bought her no freedom, no relief. But as long as her legs remained in place, he didn't pinch her again. And when tongue and hot breath on her about-to-explode tissues fed her thigh muscles, the resultant *punishment* slammed against her brain.

She'd just wrapped fragile self-control over her legs when he opened his mouth and sucked her labia into his moist cave. His lips closed down, captured her.

"Ah, ah," she cried into the gag. More heat than she'd known was possible rolled through her sex and caught her entire body on fire. She shuddered now, shuddered and shook and trembled as if a storm had overtaken her, and still he sucked.

Her brain spun out a comparison between what he was doing to her sex now and had done to her breast earlier. It all came together, stirred into a frenzied whole, sliced her into small pieces.

"Ah! Ah!"

The other men were speaking, their words thudding around her. But her captor continued his relentless hold, and that became her all. Everything.

Belly clenching, she struggled to push herself at him. Helplessness surrounded her, yet she reveled in it. He'd taken her apart and was putting her back together.

Or maybe she was on the brink of shattering.

Coming.

Yes, coming!

On and on and on. Legs screaming. Her mind pulsing. Trapped pussy tightening endlessly.

Laughter, male laughter. Her captor lapping at her, and her pussy endlessly filling him with liquid proof of his knowledge.

She hated him and feared herself.

15

"Remember what I said?" Nakos was somewhere far away, his voice faint and fading. "That when I was done with you, I'd expect you to show your gratitude by telling us what we want to know."

The words slowly gathered around her, and although they didn't all make sense, she comprehended that something was expected of her. He'd lowered her onto the ground again but hadn't allowed her to close her legs. A hand rested against tissues so sensitive that her brain couldn't distinguish between pain and pleasure. She couldn't feel the rest of her body.

"Where are they?"

Tau's voice grating on her nerves, she rolled to the side a little to take what pressure she could off her arms. Doing so earned her a wave of dizziness. When her vision returned, she turned her attention to Nakos. He was close enough that he could touch her if he wanted, but his hands were flat against his thighs, and he didn't return her gaze. She belatedly recalled that he'd been telling her something when she regained consciousness.

"Tell us," Tau repeated less patiently than the first time. "I've already waited much longer than the spirits promised I would have to."

"Tau." Nakos sounded irritated. "This is between her and me."

"No, it isn't! You wouldn't have taken her if I hadn't ordered you to."

"That's it. *I* caught her, not you."

"Nakos, enough," Sakima interjected. "Have you forgotten that we have only one use for her? As long as she tells us what we need to know, it doesn't matter how that knowledge is gained."

Nakos wiped his mouth clean of her juices. "Do you understand what this is about?" he asked her, sounding weary and wary at the same time. "Freedom is behind you. Your choice is simple. Either you lead us to the falcons' home or Tau will find a way to force that information from you—a way you won't enjoy and might not survive. Because of who he is to me, even if I could, I won't try to stop him."

She couldn't go on looking at Nakos, not with the memory of the climax he'd just pulled out of her still overwhelming her. But neither could she bring herself to acknowledge the shaman. Nakos was right. Freedom belonged to yesterday.

Or did it?

When she nodded, Nakos removed her gag. She opened and closed her mouth repeatedly until it was no longer numb.

"Falcons?" She made the word a curse. "They are nothing, small and insignificant birds. Eagles rule the sky, eagles and buzzards."

"Buzzards? Do not insult me with the word."

Judging by his outburst, Tau was reaching the limit of his self-control. If she could push him a little more, bring out the violence she sensed lurked in him, Nakos would be forced to protect her, wouldn't he? Afraid she might not survive the alternative, she made herself study the shaman. He put her in mind of a coyote, a predator capable of both killing its own food and stealing from other predators if the opportunity arose.

"Buzzards are as vital to this land as any falcon, maybe even more because without them, the dead would make the air and ground unbearable," she told him. "That's what your spirit dreams are about, not trying to train some small bird with no value but taking buzzards back with you so the stench of the dead no longer pollutes. That will be your legacy."

His breath hissing, Tau kicked her in the side. Because she'd seen the blow coming, she managed to deflect it by turning away. Just the same, pain bloomed around her ribs.

"Tau, no!" Jumping to his feet, Nakos positioned himself between his shaman and her. "That's not the way to—"

"It is! We were wrong to treat her like a slave when she's an animal, a simple, groveling creature. The only thing she understands is pain."

"Tau!" Sakima warned. "Your impatience is blinding you."

His expression still harsh, the shaman turned toward Sakima. "Of course I'm impatient. The longer we stay here—"

"I know. We want to return home, before winter if possible."

"But not empty handed. Never that, never."

She might be wrong, but the shaman sounded desperate. If he couldn't turn his vision into reality, maybe his position within the tribe was in jeopardy. Although she didn't want to feel sorry for him, in a small way she did. If he wasn't respected, and believed, what was he?

"Nakos," Sakima said. "Take her to your place."

Instead of pulling her into his tent, however, Nakos led her over to Lamuka's cooking fire. The slave wasn't there, but a small pig carcass hung from a stick suspended over a bed of coals. The smell of hot fat and meat reminded him of how long he'd gone without eating. And as was Lamuka's way, a clay pot filled with water was nearby. Fortunately, the water was clear, proof that the slave hadn't used it in his food preparations. After repeatedly dipping his cupped hands in the pot and quenching his thirst, he indicated he wanted Jola to kneel near it. He started to fill his hands in preparation for helping her drink when he changed his mind.

"Don't try anything you'll regret," he said as he untied her.

She said nothing, only winced as she brought her hands in front and tucked them against her body, rocking. He'd already regretted his outburst against his shaman, but seeing her in pain made him reconsider.

"How long were you tied like that?" he asked.

"Too long."

After rocking a little more, she shook her arms, then dipped her hands in the water and drank deeply. She eyed the sizzling carcass.

Lamuka never left meat untended, which meant he'd probably gone after more wood and would return shortly. In the meantime, however, there were two hungry people with growling stomachs. Lifting the stick off one of the vertical branches that held it above the fire, Nakos turned the carcass so the side that had been closest to the coals was now on top. A couple of slices with Lamuka's knife and he'd cut off two good-sized chunks of hot pork. He handed the smaller one to her.

After blowing on it, she ate quickly, licking her fingers when she was done. He was cutting off more meat when he noticed that she was studying the sky. Whatever she'd told Tau about how worthless falcons were, it was a lie.

"This changes nothing," he told her as he gave her another slice. "Just because I refused to turn you over to my shaman earlier doesn't mean it won't happen."

"I know."

"Then tell him what he wants you to. Take him to the falcons' nests. Do that and he'll have no further use for you. And the Ekewoko will leave your people alone."

"Will they?"

"You don't believe—"

"He won't be satisfied until he has gathered all the eggs and hatchlings he can."

"So? If, as you said, falcons have no value here, you shouldn't care what happens to them."

She turned on him, eyes blazing almost as fiercely as they had when she was climaxing. "I will *not* betray—No matter what happens to me, I will *not* do that."

Even if it costs you your life? he wanted to demand, but her eyes supplied the answer. The falcons' safety was more important than her own. What he didn't understand was why.

They ate in silence. Even when Lamuka returned, Jola said nothing, and Nakos had little to contribute to the slave's questions about the meat's quality. He was trying to decide whether he wanted more when movement to his left distracted him. His lord was leaving the shaman's tent. Although Sakima didn't look his way, the older man's presence was enough to get him to his feet. Sakima hadn't detailed what he wanted Nakos to do with Jola once he'd taken her back to his tent because it hadn't been necessary.

She hadn't been broken down, yet. But it would happen, soon.

Jola, too, must have seen Sakima, but she didn't acknowledge the lord. Instead, she again glanced skyward. What he'd concluded had been rage faded from her features, and in its place bloomed a deep longing.

"Come," he said. "Do as my lord ordered."

Lowering her head, she fixed him with yet another expression. This one whispered of resignation along with a hint of rebellion that instantly brought him to her side. "Don't," he warned.

"You can't stop me from being who I am. No one can."

* * *

All too soon, Jola was asking herself whether she'd lied when she'd warned Nakos not to try to change her. Once again her hands were tied, one wrist over the other, in front of her this time. He'd ordered her to kneel before him, and when she'd refused, he'd picked her up and deposited her on her back on his mat. With his scent drifting up from the bed to envelope her, she'd lain there waiting, anticipating even.

That had been before he'd clamped a warrior's hand over her crotch, his grip so firm it bordered on the painful. She tried to slap his arm away only to have him grab her bonds and force her arms over her head and against the mat as he'd done too many times.

"Move them and I'll tie them in place."

That she couldn't handle.

As soon as he released her hands, his hold on her pussy tightened. A finger slid past her cunt and between her ass cheeks, trapping her anus under his heated strength. He lifted her until her buttocks barely brushed the bed and held her there, the moments beating on and on, his finger pressing against her rear entrance. His heat was everywhere on her, storming past her labia and slipping deep into her. Then he settled his other hand between her breasts, separating them, claiming them. She felt disfigured by him, her breasts molded into shapes and places they didn't belong.

But if she tried to stop him, he'd anchor her arms, and she'd be even more helpless than she was.

She'd wait, anticipate, feel, breathe, fight for control.

Maybe mostly anticipate.

"There's more than one kind of force, Jola, more than one way to compel someone to speak."

"Torture?"

He didn't immediately answer, and when he did, his voice sounded strained. "Not the kind of torture you're thinking of."

She nearly laughed at that because his handling of her was

taking her past being able to think. Her existence began and ended with his hands. Not only did he rule her body, she didn't want it to be any other way. In some respects this was like being wrapped in a soft, warm blanket. Even with her nerves snapping and humming in anticipation, she was content to live in the moment—his moment.

Had she ever felt this way with Raci? Could she even pull her dead mate's image into her mind?

"A woman's body is far different from a man's," he went on. "In some ways I envy a woman's ability to experience pleasure after pleasure without having to recover in between, but as much as I might want endless pleasure, it is better this way."

"Do you know what I'm talking about?" Cupping a breast, he drew it upward. "A climax is a powerful thing, a wonderful moment. But when it never ends . . ."

Never end? Was that possible?

All too soon, he'd pulled her into a deep swirling pool without beginning or end. He began by lightly slapping her sex. The flat-handed taps echoed deep inside her, reaching not just her pussy but her belly. They came faster and faster, each slap a little stronger, and the echoes seeped clear to her spine. Once there, they spread up her back, flowed over her shoulders, gripped her neck and sent hot fingers to her mind.

Her breasts caught fire. Flames licked at her thighs and buttocks and still he forced teasing blow after teasing blow on her system. She barely noted when he stopped slapping and buried a finger in her hole.

In and out he drove, in and out. Faster and faster he fucked her, heating and heating and heating her already overloaded channel. Lowering her arms, she scratched his shoulder.

"Ah, so that's where you are," he exclaimed. "Reaching the edge. Trying whatever you can think of to keep from falling into space."

What space? What edge?

Claiming one breast and then the other. Pulling up on them and pushing down. Taking hold of a nipple and painting crude, uneven circles with her so-pliable flesh. Finger fucking her at the same time, going deep, so deep. Reaching her depths only to pull out only to rush in again. Fire everywhere. Crying and screaming and sometimes howling like a wild thing.

Climaxing. Body shaking. Teeth clenching and jaws aching. Body exploding, flying off, flying apart, pieces lost.

Air! Everything became about getting enough air into her lungs. But as soon as the light-headedness faded a bit, her body started screaming again.

He hadn't stopped. Hadn't let up on his attack.

One thing had changed, a little, and not that it mattered. His finger no longer filled and owned. Instead, he caught her throbbing clit between thumb and forefinger and rolled the nub about.

"No!" Closing her fingers around his shoulder, she struggled to leverage herself off the bed.

"Yes!"

Her back slammed against his bed, shaking her entire body. Her eyes couldn't focus, and her mind struggled to hold on to something, anything, in answer to the question of what had just happened.

Then she knew. He'd pushed her off him, simple as that. Struck her with undeniable proof of his superior strength, his goal.

By the spirits, he hadn't released her clit!

Knowing nothing except that for this moment he wasn't rolling it about, she tried to breathe her way to the other side of this overwhelming explosion. But she kept climaxing, pussy tightening and tightening again.

Then he gripped her hips and flipped her onto her stomach. Her arms were trapped under her, useless. She couldn't see him, could only feel as his fingers crawled over her buttocks.

He spread her wide, exposed her in a way she'd never been exposed.

"No, please!"

"Yes, Jola, yes."

Working with a speed that rocked her, he bent her knees so her ass was forced up off the bed and into the air. She tried to straighten her legs only to jam her feet against some part of his body, maybe his knees.

Anchored, face to the side and worthless hands against her cunt. The proof of her not-yet-done climax seeped between her fingers and too much of her weight was now on her shoulders and flattened breasts.

But those things didn't matter because he was spreading her ass cheeks again, seeing everything.

Not just seeing, touching.

No! No! Not his finger there. Not pressing against tight, puckered flesh and invading a little.

"No!" the beast she'd become shrieked. "No!"

"I won't hurt you, but by the time I'm done, you're going to belong to me."

At the thought of what he was both penetrating and studying, shame shook her. This was the private, most personal part of her body, or rather it had been before he'd claimed ownership of her. Maybe, if she fought hard enough, and he let her, she could regain some of what modesty belonged to her. But every muscle still hissed with the aftereffects of the climax he'd forced out of her.

Not only that, she longed to hold on to the sensation, to wrap herself in it, to climb onto it again and die in the middle.

Defeated and desperate at the same time, she stopped trying to sit up. Her focus closed down until there was nothing except his hands on her. His mastery.

"Not fighting anymore, Jola? Because you know it's useless,

or because you want this?" Pulling out of her asshole, he stroked the space between her two openings.

"I—hate you."

"Emotions are extreme, Jola. Disbelief, self-hatred, horror: they can all be the same."

What was he talking about? Any other time, she would have insisted on an explanation and if she could hold on to the question, maybe she'd draw the truth out of him. But this was now.

"There are other emotions, not all of them bad."

Wondering whether he might be speaking more to himself than her, she lifted her head and turned it so when she again rested her cheek on the bed, there was less discomfort. The instant the strain let up, her focus shifted back to her ass. He was still caressing her, not invading, the potential and promise flowing between them.

"Our bodies are precious," he all but whispered. "Their well-being vital to our survival. We'll do whatever it takes to safeguard them, and when they're filled with pain, nothing else matters."

Once again she had the sense his words were designed more for him than her. He might be thinking of his grandparents' deaths. If he was, she wished she knew how to hand him the compassion and understanding he needed. But maybe the only way she could was by telling him about Raci's death, and she wasn't strong enough for that.

Right now she had strength for only one thing: surviving his plans for her.

"A slave has no right to her body. It belongs to her master. He can do whatever he wants to it, reward or punish it. What do you want, Jola? To be punished or given pleasure?"

She wouldn't respond, wouldn't!

"Pleasure comes in many forms. Food, water, a place to sleep. Being touched by someone who knows everything he needs to about the other person. Answer me this. Do you believe I know what I'm doing?" Diving deeper between her legs, he stroked her labia once, twice.

"Yes! Yes!"

"Ah. And is this pleasurable?" A second finger joined the first, the two gliding over flesh still so sensitive and hot from her last climax she was desperate to escape him.

"Damn you!"

"No, no, my little captive." Cupping his palm around her labia, he drew the loose flesh toward him. "No swearing. Only the truth. Do you like this?"

"Like" was a breeze on a hot day. His hand claiming her was the same as a raging winter storm.

"No!" She tried to lift her head. Failing, she stretched out her fingers. Finding his hand, she tried to scratch him, but her hands were already going numb. Either that or she didn't want to hurt him after all. Needed him to continue.

"I don't believe you."

Don't believe what? What were we talking about?

He was changing position, his body shifting, that all-knowing hand no longer between her legs. Terrified, maybe, she touched her labia with a single finger and then her entire hand. Everything quivered. Unnerved, she nevertheless touched a tentative finger to her clit. Alive, waiting! She swore she heard it sigh, and if she'd been alone, she'd already be curled on her side, everything focused on reaching the incredible edge once more and leaping out and over.

"What's this?" He engulfed her fingers in his. "I'd think you'd be satisfied after what just happened. But you're not, are you? You'd love to climax again."

"You—don't know anything about me."

"Yes, I do. And as soon as you stop lying to yourself, you'll admit it."

16

He was right, damn him! Just the same, determined not to give her need anything to feed off, she curled her fingers so they pressed against her belly instead of her sex. She might not be able to stop him from playing her, but she wouldn't help him, she wouldn't!

Playing her? Yes, that's exactly what he was doing. Feeding her fantasies and killing her vow to ignore his manipulations.

With his hands boldly roaming over her, her prominently displayed ass no longer embarrassed her. Neither did she feel compelled to try to resist anything he did to her. Instead, she felt a kind of disconnect from her body. Yes, she was acutely aware of every inch of her system, but it was no longer her responsibility. Her nerves and veins and muscles, mostly her pussy, belonged to a woman concerned with nothing except sex.

It was all his doing, his hands on her thighs, breasts, and pussy.

Then he concentrated on the one place she had the least amount of control over, and for long, aching moments she shivered and moaned as he stroked her loose, heated hole. Her head seemed to expand, lose form, swirl off into space. Instead of being frightened, she accepted; more than accept, she embraced. Whatever happened was good, all good.

Then, using her buttocks to brace himself, he got to his feet and walked around her. Confused, she tried to sit up.

"No!" He pressed down on the back of her neck. "Stay where you are. I want to study you like this."

Resenting his arrogance, she nevertheless complied. From her position, she only occasionally spotted his feet and saw nothing of the rest of him. She, who'd always loved what she was, couldn't pull up a single memory of being able to change form and take flight. Her family and clan members were little more than misty images in what remained of her mind. A man had taken their place, a man with ropes and knowing hands and a take-charge voice.

That wasn't all, she acknowledged as he began his second circuit. Most of all, he was a stranger with a cock she'd willingly spend the rest of her life dancing on.

Only half caring that she keep her ultimate weakness from him, she closed her eyes. Her back ached as did her arms. Her buttocks and the backs of her thighs were becoming chilled. Other than that, she had no connection with her body.

"Beautiful," he whispered. "A female subdued and accepting her new lot in life. This is what my shaman and lord wanted you to become."

"Keep them out of this."

"How?" He trailed a knuckle from her neck to her tailbone, compelling her to arch her back and mewl. "You and I wouldn't be here, doing this, if not for them."

Hadn't he already told her that? If he had, what, if anything, had she said in response? It might not have mattered then, and it certainly didn't now.

"Even though we had to flee our homeland, the Ekewoko have survived because we know how to exploit those we come in contact with," he continued, his knuckle retracing the just-finished journey. "I tell you this not because Tau and Sakima ordered me to, but because I believe I owe you that one thing. Do you understand what I mean by exploit?"

He expected her to answer? Maybe, if he stopped touching her the way he was, stopped standing over her and let her sit up. Maybe, if his cock had never completed her.

"It's this." He pressed down on the base of her spine, his knuckle grinding into her.

"Stop! Ah, stop!"

"I can't. Don't you realize that? As long as I live, I can't."

She wanted to ask why but then it didn't matter because he'd again pulled her ass cheeks apart and was sliding his knuckle over hot, damp territory. By rocking her shoulders from side to side, she managed to remain on top of the sensations gathering and threatening to explode inside her. Her small victory might not last, but if she gave up this battle she'd be lost.

Lost. Ah, stepping off into space, flying without wings, soaring and floating.

"You're relaxing," she vaguely heard him say. "That's good. Go inside yourself, Jola. Find the woman in you and celebrate her."

His words were meant to distract and consume. Much as a night bird's throaty song enchanted her, this man's voice cradled her.

She didn't care, didn't want back what she'd once been. Needed his hands touching her ass as it had never been touched.

A firm yet gentle stroke centered on her cunt. Holding her breath, she waited.

"This is what I was talking about." His voice still had that faraway quality. "The woman in you. No matter what else you are and do, at your core you are female."

Just as you are male.

"Did you hear me, Jola? You can't escape your sexuality."

"What—do you want me to say?"

"That you agree."

She couldn't do anything else and remain true to herself, but admitting that to him was dangerous, maybe fatal.

"Is it so hard?" he continued, the pressure on her cunt increasing, heating. "What are you afraid of?"

You. And myself

"You might not want to hear this, but your silence is speaking for you. That and your body. You're overflowing here." His finger easily penetrated. "I'm swimming inside you. It's not the same as having sex, but exciting for me nevertheless and maybe safer for both of us this way."

Both of them? With so much power and control in his hands, she found it all but impossible to believe he had any hesitancy about what he was doing. Quite the opposite. Surely he was reveling in his mastery over her. Mewling again, she lowered her haunches. Just the same, he remained inside her. Disconcerted, she shook her ass. "Stop it. Damn you, how can you—"

"Give it up, Jola. It'll take a lot more than that for me to relinquish ownership of you."

"You don't own me!"

"Look at yourself." The hand not penetrating her pussy cupped her left ass cheek and squeezed, sending a series of shocks through her. "Be honest with yourself about what's happening. Then tell me you're still in control."

She still couldn't, and he knew it. Tears born of frustration, weakness, and something she couldn't define burned her eyes. If she said anything, he'd hear her hunger.

"You're uncomplicated. That's what makes you such a plea-sure to work with: your simple nature."

His comment nearly forced a laugh past her clenched teeth. If she could, she'd change form this very moment. Then, swooping and soaring above him, she'd challenge him to repeat his lie. If he tried, and even if he didn't, she'd dive and fasten her talons in his flesh. Watch him bleed and listen to him scream. But she was trapped in this woman-body and he under-stood it as well as she did, maybe more.

"How does it make you feel when I say that?" He punctu-ated his question by lightly slapping her ass while probing deeply with the finger she hadn't been able to dislodge. "Do you like being uncomplicated? Maybe that frightens you."

She was afraid, all right, but not because of what he'd just said. Rather, her sweating body was again crawling danger-ously close to the cliff it fell over every time she climaxed. Maybe if she tried hard enough, she could draw cool air deep into her lungs and fuel her muscles and veins with cold instead of the heat she couldn't control. That would be her salvation.

Turning her head a little more, she inhaled. Her neck ached from the strain and his scent coated her nostrils. He repeatedly drummed his palm against her buttock, his finger dangerously deep inside her, teasing and claiming.

Again she tried to lower herself to the ground. He immedi-ately stopped pummeling her ass and slid his arm under her belly. Muscles straining, he pulled her up once more. Even though he'd taught her the folly of resisting, she tried to shake free. Her pathetic rebellion resulted in him drawing her back toward him. She stopped with her ass and thighs pressing against his legs and the pussy invasion unending.

"I'm going to ride you," he warned. "And when I can no longer stay astride you, I'll herd you until you're exhausted. If you can't take it, tell me what we want to know, now. Otherwise, I'll drive you into the ground and force everything from you."

He'd already made that threat, hadn't he? Already gone over this and said certain words. Before she could decide how to respond, he dropped to his knees. Her pussy was empty, free. Lonely. A moment passed. Shaking, she started to lift her head only to let it drop as his cock speared her. He ground deep and even deeper, burning past her drenched tissues, filling her to overflowing, pushing.

Of their own volition, her fingers unfolded and reached between her legs for him. Finding the union between cock and pelvis, she lightly scratched the sleek flesh. He growled. Sensing a subtle shift in their relationship, she scratched him again. His growl became a low howl that resonated throughout her. Her mouth sagged and she began to drool. Her cheeks all but caught fire, and her inner tissues closed down around him.

A new fire, this one centered on her spine, pulled her attention there. Using both hands, he raked her from the base of her neck to her buttocks, undoubtedly leaving fine white lines in her tanned flesh. The thought of those thin marks and how they came to be pulled a growl from her own throat. Then he abraded her again, long and slowly, so deliciously slowly, and she screamed, the sound lasting as long as his nails' journey.

Even though he must be acutely aware of his bone-deep control over her, he said nothing. *Slave*, she silently spoke for him. *I've turned you into my slave.*

Responding in the only way she could, she pushed around their joined bodies until she found his balls. Instead of scratching him, however, she painted his scrotum with gentle fingertips. Every time he pulled back, she lost contact with him, but then he'd drive forward and into her, and she'd meet him, teasing and tickling, breathing harshly and loudly.

Her spine burned from his continued assault on it, the heat

running deep into her until she couldn't distinguish between that and his pummeling cock. She rocked under him. Shoulders and neck and thighs throbbing, she rode the baser sensation. They were fucking, powerful male claiming helpless female and both of them screeching like winged predators.

Was it possible? He was becoming like her?

Before she could pull the question into her, he locked his fingers around her middle and pushed into her with all the strength in his warrior thighs. Half believing he'd reached her throat, she met him with every bit of strength she possessed.

She flew off into space again, lost command of her body. Heat collected and began rolling throughout her, taking her high and fast.

"Damn you, damn you," he chanted. His body shuddered, froze, shuddered.

Hers did the same, following him on his journey and showing him the way to her own. Maybe she was wrong, but he seemed to reach his mountaintop the same moment she hit her own.

Then she was off. Gone. Soaring.

Muscles starting to shrink. Vision becoming keener. Legs disappearing and arms lengthening and sprouting feathers.

No! Terrified, she fought herself. *No.*

But it was too late.

Climax. Nothing else mattering. Nothing else possible.

There wasn't any part of Jola's body that didn't ache and hum. Without the overriding sensations, she had no doubt she would still be asleep. Or unconscious.

Not moving, she took inventory of herself. Her spine burned from where Nakos had scratched her, but if she could touch herself there, she suspected she'd find no broken flesh. She couldn't, of course, because her hands were bound in front. Because she was lying on her side, her arms were relatively comfortable, and she felt no compulsion to try to free herself. Although it was night and she was naked, thanks to his heat she wasn't cold.

She'd never felt like this before, not disconnected from her body after all but overwhelmed by it. It hadn't so much turned against her as it had become more than she could manage.

A memory tugged at her consciousness. When it remained misty, she started to shrug it off only to freeze and then concentrate. Somewhere in the midst of fucking and being fucked, she'd started to become a Falcon. She'd managed to end the transformation before she gave away everything, but the time might come when she couldn't. Instinct would win out and when it did, *he* would know.

Was that so terrible? Even if Nakos learned the truth about her, he couldn't control her nature. Instead, he'd be forced to admit he hadn't dominated her after all and that by shifting from human to falcon, she could easily escape.

Not just escape, she allowed with a small smile. Her talons could do far more damage than his nails had. Even though as a human he was many times larger than her, her speed and killing nature would be far superior.

She could easily kill him.

Shocked, she quickly but silently sat up. After scooting away so she no longer touched him, she rubbed her eyes and then her breasts, thinking.

In Falcon form, human thoughts no longer existed. Instead, she embraced a predator's nature. With wings instead of arms and a beak in the place of lips, she would become a deadly foe. She'd see Nakos as one thing and one thing only: a threat to her existence.

Despite the shudder washing over her, she stood and tiptoed to the far end of the cramped enclosure. Raptor's Craig was the only place the change took place; at least she'd always believed that. But her body had never been under assault the way it had been when Nakos was pushing her to her sexual limits. In times of extreme threat, or excitement—

"I don't want to hurt you," she whispered. "Maybe it shouldn't matter. After what you've stolen from and done to me, I should want you dead?"

But she didn't.

Earlier, taking deep breaths had helped her to at least delay her climax. But although she repeatedly inhaled, she remained tense. If she lay back down beside him, which she wanted to, he'd wake and continue his assault on her. And when he did—

"I can't stay here. I can't."

Except for the sound of snoring from a nearby tent, the Ekewoko camp was silent. Dying coals from Lamuka's cooking fire blended into a sky filled with stars and moon to illuminate her surroundings. Although she'd taken care to study the camp earlier, night and her desperate need for freedom conspired to confuse her. A breeze coming from her right reminded her of the lake's location, but what was the best way to head to maximize her chance of escaping?

Not moving, listening intently while straining to see, she reluctantly acknowledged something she never believed she'd have to. For the first time in her life, she was among the enemy naked and without use of her arms. Not only that, she was about to leave someone who'd become important to her.

No! She wouldn't let herself think that!

Turning slowly, she located the shaman's tent. Lord Sakima's was farther away and lost in the night. Whoever was snoring let out a series of blasts that set her feet to dancing. How could anyone sleep through that racket?

Deciding that leaving now was more important than choosing the most advantageous route, she turned her back on the shaman's tent. She'd taken maybe five steps when something behind her rustled.

Spinning around, she covered her throat with her hands.

"It's me," came a faint, deep whisper. "Lamuka."

The slave!

"Don't run, not yet."

Leg muscles screaming, she started in the direction the voice had come from. A mound near the dying fire stirred. Then Lamuka sat up.

"Don't run," he repeated, still whispering. "You have nothing to fear from me."

Much as she wanted to believe him, she didn't dare. Neither could she think of anything to say.

"I knew you'd try to escape," Lamuka continued. "Of course you would. Without your freedom, what do you have?"

What was it Nakos had told her, that Lamuka had been a slave for many years and didn't seem to be interested in any other existence. "What do you want?" she managed, her voice squeaking.

"To wish you well. And to help."

"I . . ."

The elderly slave slowly stood. "If I wanted to do you harm, I would have already called out."

"Then what—"

"I told you, I wish you well."

"Why?"

"Because—" He took a step toward her, then stopped. "Maybe because I don't want you to turn out the way I have."

Walking toward him might well jeopardize her freedom, but something in his tone made it worth the risk. "Why haven't you tried to leave?"

"I did several times at the beginning, but I came from a small, poor tribe. We never had enough food in our bellies, and other tribes, sensing our weakness, often attacked us. Here I'm seldom hungry and I usually sleep warm. Are you cold?"

Strange. She'd stopped thinking about her nudity, perhaps

because Nakos had taken her so deep inside herself. However, now that Lamuka had asked, she nodded.

"And you need to be able to use your arms."

Holding up her bound wrists, she nodded again.

"That is how I can help you."

She might be mistaken but thought he'd smiled.

"Wait here," he continued. "I have extra clothes in my tent, and my cooking knife will easily cut off those ropes."

Grateful, she blinked back tears. "Thank you."

"No, I thank you."

She was still pondering what he'd said when he emerged from his small tent holding a well-worn shirt she guessed would reach to her knees. She'd moved closer to the coals and had turned her back to the fire so she could both warm herself a little and still watch for him. In some respects, he reminded her of her clan's elders. Although age had slowed them, they still moved gracefully. Wanting to weep, she extended her hands toward Lamuka and watched as he sliced through the strands and threw the rope into the coals. Then she slipped into the shirt.

"I don't know what to say," she admitted, torn between the need to leave and an even stronger desire to embrace this man. Man, yes, that's what he was. "You'll be all right? No one will suspect—"

He indicated the already smoking rope. "You escaped. That's all they'll care about."

"I just don't want you to jeopardize—"

"Maybe it's time I took a chance. Go where you need to. Resume your life. But never forget, Nakos is not a cruel man. He is simply who he is, an Ekewoko."

17

Nakos stood before the assembled men. One at a time, he met their gazes and then fixed his attention on the one who'd raised him. Tau sat glowering next to an expressionless Sakima.

"I fell asleep," Nakos said. "I have no other excuse."

"You didn't secure her to you?" Lord Sakima asked.

"No, I didn't."

"Why not?"

"Carelessness," he said because the truth was between him and Jola, if he ever saw her again. "I was tired. I let my exhaustion take over when I shouldn't have."

"Tired, why?"

"A long day of travel followed by getting past her defenses."

"Getting past them?" Tau repeated scornfully. "If you had succeeded, she would still be here."

Several others muttered agreement, and in their expressions, he read doubts as to his right to call himself a warrior.

"You are right, all of you," he said. "I allowed myself to be blinded by—"

"Does it matter?" his friend Ohanko interrupted. "So she has escaped. When she returns to her people, what will she tell them? That the Ekewoko are skilled and well-armed warriors. I say we have nothing to fear from her kind."

"Perhaps not." Tau spoke slowly. "Perhaps she will indeed warn her kind not to risk their lives trying to attack. But have you forgotten why she's valuable?"

No one immediately answered, which Nakos took as proof that none of them wanted to risk being seen as in opposition to Tau.

"I heeded your words," Nakos said. "That's why I went in search of a Wilding and why, after I'd captured her, I brought her here. You talked to her, Tau. You know better than anyone how determined she is not to help us."

The discussion swirled around him with Tau repeating his conviction that the future of the Ekewoko depended on turning his dream of training falcons to attack the Outsiders into reality. Ohanko and Nakos's other close friend, Farajj, while not calling Tau's dream foolish, quietly agreed that Ekewoko warriors didn't need help from the spirits to reclaim their birth land. Other warriors, mostly the older ones, agreed with Tau, while the younger men were more likely to question the accuracy of the shaman's dream. Much as he appreciated not being universally condemned for letting Jola escape, Nakos hated being the cause of so much disagreement.

Even more he hated having failed and being made a fool of.

Wishing he was the carefree boy he'd been before his grandparents' death, he stood. As he did, all conversation stopped. But even with everyone's eyes on him, he was slow to begin. He'd trusted her. What it all came down to when he'd let sleep steal over him instead of securing her to him was that he'd believed she wanted to spend the night nestled against him.

He'd been wrong. She'd simply been biding her time, and

while she had, she'd enjoyed everything he'd done to her. Instead of fighting him, she'd opened her body to him and welcomed him in. Used him.

And now she was probably washing his cum from her sex and scrubbing her skin until she could no longer remember what his touch felt like.

"I failed," he said. "But it will not happen again."

"What are you saying?" his lord asked. "You're going to try to capture another—"

"Not another, her."

"But you don't know where she is, do you?"

Lifting his head so he could see beyond the camp, he stared at the endless barren horizon. "Several times when she and I were together, I caught her looking at the massive peak north of the great lake. When she did, her expression filled with longing. It was important to her, maybe more important than anything else."

"That mountain?" Ohanko questioned. "It is nothing; solid rock where not even a single bush can grow. If she made you believe it is special, she was lying."

That was possible. After what had happened last night, he'd believe anything of her. But her eyes had come alive with love and loss when she'd stared at the peak. He'd seen a hunger as strong and inescapable as what he'd endured when he would have given anything to save his grandparents.

"We've already been at Screaming Wind far longer than we believed we would be," he said. "We've gone on countless searches and, although we've spotted Wildings any number of times, until I nearly drowned Jola, none of us has ever gotten close enough to capture one. More important, we've never found where either the Wildings or falcons live."

Nakos expected the shaman to blame their failure on the warriors' inability to garner the spirits' goodwill. Instead, Tau only cocked his head, obviously waiting for him to continue.

"That's because we've been searching as Ekewoko, not Wildings."

"What are you saying?" Tau demanded.

"We've looked at Screaming Wind through Ekewoko eyes. As such, we saw that mass of rock as worthless, but what if the Wildings have made it their home?"

Quiet muttering followed his comment. Hoping the others were truly listening to him, he pointed toward his tent. "I intend to arm myself. When my preparations are complete, I will head for the mountain. I hope some of you will join me but do so only if you agree with what I just said."

"Why should we?"

Much as he hated hearing that question from his lord, he understood the reason behind it. Sakima wasn't going to give up his leadership role without proof that his successor, at least for today, had no doubts about what he was doing.

"I failed when I let her escape," Nakos admitted. "But I learned a great deal while we were together. Our bodies became one, and when they did, I saw the world through her eyes and slipped into her mind. We were wrong to call her people Wildings. They're much more than that."

He looked around at the men who made up his world. Even Lamuka, who usually kept to himself whenever the Ekewoko gathered, was there, although standing back from the group. "They know this land as we never can. They know where they are safest."

"No human would want to live up there," someone said.

"Wait!" Tau insisted. "Maybe—if you're right, whoever is up there can see you approach. They'll have more than enough time to plan and execute an attack."

"I know. That's why only I will make the climb."

"What will be gained by you sacrificing your life?"

Filling his lungs took a long time. Then: "If she's there, she won't want to see me dead."

Tau looked about to say something but didn't. For several moments, silence surrounded him, giving him no choice but to ask himself if he was right.

It didn't matter. He was an Ekewoko. A warrior who'd made a promise to his people.

The air was cooler up on Raptor's Craig, cleaner, clearer. Standing with her arms outstretched, Jola tilted back her head so her hair slid down her spine.

Freedom! No one controlling her movements or body, no ropes restraining her limbs.

"Do it. Let yourself go."

Opening her eyes, Jola stared behind her at her chief. Cheyah, lean and muscular despite his advanced age, stood watching her. Like most Falcons, he was naked. Although she'd long ago become accustomed to Falcon cocks, she couldn't help but compare Cheyah's to Nakos's. By Falcon standards, Cheyah's penis was large. Even at rest, it was longer and thicker than most, which said a great deal about why he'd been made chief. The most virile men made the most commanding leaders.

If that was so, Nakos would be considered Cheyah's logical replacement the moment he revealed himself.

No! She wasn't going to think about the man who'd stolen her freedom and more.

"I will celebrate my heritage," she belatedly responded. "There were times when I wondered if I'd ever be able to change again. Knowing I can become a Falcon whenever I want brings me incredible pleasure, and I'm savoring the moment."

'You feel alive, then?"

"Of course. Why do you ask?"

Cheyah shook his head, gray hair flying about. "After Raci was killed, I wasn't sure you'd ever embrace life again."

"Did you think that of me?"

"You thought I wouldn't?"

"I'm sorry. I was so wrapped up in my grief that I couldn't think about anything else."

"I know. Watching you, I wondered if you wanted to follow Raci into the Otherworld."

She'd seldom had a private conversation with Cheyah. As chief, he was responsible for the well-being of all Falcons and spent most of his time with the other senior men. As soon as she'd reached Raptor's Craig, she'd gone to him and told him everything about what she'd learned and observed during her time with the Ekewoko—or rather, she'd told him almost everything. Other than admitting that her captor had tried to turn her body against her as part of his attempts to get her to betray her people, she'd insisted that her captor's specific techniques didn't matter because he hadn't succeeded. To her relief, Cheyah and the other elders hadn't pushed for further explanation.

"Jola? I still worry about you. Are you all right?"

"I am." She'd lowered her arms during the conversation but now lifted them again. Her entire body, even her lungs, felt clean and renewed this morning. "I can't bring Raci back. I accept that."

"And do you accept that you're free to choose a new mate? More than free, you're expected to make a choice."

A Falcon to spend the rest of her life with, to mate with. "Soon," she admitted. "Right now I just need to be me."

"Because your captor stole that from you." Cheyah extended his hand as if he was going to touch her, then let it drop to his side. "Fly with the sun this morning, Jola. Feel life pour through your veins. Hunt and kill and become strong again."

She could do that! In truth, she'd ached for that strength ever since Nakos had captured her.

Nakos.

Even more determined not to let him invade her thoughts, she stepped to the edge of the craig. She'd taken off the garment

Lamuka had given her before changing into a Falcon and flying to the top of Raptor's Craig. Then, because she'd needed to communicate with her kind, she'd shifted back into human form. Now the breeze sweeping over her body put her in mind of a lover's caress.

Silent, she leaned out and jumped. The instant she did, her body started to compress in upon itself. At the same time, it became lighter. Instantly, her ability to see became keener. Feeling herself fall, she lifted her head and opened her mouth. Instead of a scream, a sharp cry erupted. Reveling in the change, she pressed her lips together, only they were no longer soft flesh but hard, capable of tearing the meat from a kill's carcass.

She no longer had arms but wings longer than the length of her body. The wind rushed over her feathers in a harsh caress. Breasts, waist, belly, and hips were gone, and in their place, a compact form created for speed. Floating now, she fanned her tail feathers and acknowledged how superior her tail was to legs.

The breeze cradled her. Trusting completely, she held her wings out just as, a few moments ago, she'd extended her arms. Back when she was still learning what it meant to be two things, she'd wondered what happened to her human weight and size when she cast off that shell, but she no longer cared. Now she accepted, gloriously accepted.

When she wanted it to happen, her Falcon body would fade away so the human one could take its place, but right now she couldn't imagine being anything except what she was. A predator.

Free.

The ground was so far below that if she'd been looking at it with a woman's eyes, it would be nothing except a distant blur. Fortunately, her raptor vision afforded her absolute clarity. There, an ant hill undoubtedly alive with the tiny black creatures. Over there, a spider making its way over a dry leaf. Further out, a gray snake slithering around a rock. If she wanted, the snake would make a meal.

Instead, she'd wait for larger prey. Fly south or maybe west looking for other birds or perhaps a rabbit.

Usually while in Falcon form, she didn't think. Instead, burying herself in instinct, she'd fly and float and dive. But, maybe because the air was cold this morning, maybe because she hadn't cleared her mind of her captor after all, his image returned. He might be looking for her, might even think to come here.

At least she wasn't concerned with his thoughts or emotions. She'd had enough of that weight during her long walk home. All that night she'd wondered what he'd think and do once he discovered that she was gone. Maybe fury would rule him. He'd be consumed with the need to make her pay, perhaps by killing her.

And maybe he'd vow to capture her again.

It wasn't going to happen! Not while Falcon blood heated her veins.

The sun, which had been behind Raptor's Craig, lifted over the top and touched her back and head. Energized by the warmth, she headed higher. The universe stretched out before her. Memories of Nakos and Raci faded. She was alone, a predator in her prime with one overriding purpose in life: to reproduce. Her chief had encouraged her to find a new mate, another Falcon, someone to unite with and then feed her while she incubated their offspring.

Tomorrow. That's when she'd go in search of Raci's replacement and when she'd put an end to all memories of Nakos.

Today she'd hunt.

Although Nakos preferred that he alone should bear the responsibility and risk of either recapturing Jola or finding another Wilding, he took a couple of warriors with him. Sakima had wanted at least half of the men to accompany him, but Nakos had stood his ground, explaining that the more Eke-woko the Wildings saw, the more likely they were to perceive their presence as a threat and either attack or flee.

Silently, his friends walked beside him. Both Ohanko and Farajj were well armed. In addition, they carried packs filled with dried meat and water. Neither had said anything beyond agreeing when he asked them if they'd accompany him. As they were taking off, Ohanko had asked if he really thought the Wildings might attack. Influenced by Jola's courage, Nakos had said it was a possibility. Agreeing, Farajj had pointed out that even creatures who were more animal than human would defend themselves. And if they managed to recapture Jola, or any Wilding, the others might try to free her.

Unless Jola begged them not to.

Splitting his attention between his footing and the crystal-clear sky, Nakos pondered whether she'd care whether he lived or died. If they were still together, he might have no trouble convincing himself that his life meant as much to her as her own did, but she'd shattered that illusion with her escape.

"What I most hate about this place," Ohanko said, "is the lack of hiding places. I've never felt more exposed."

"The Wildings must feel the same way," Farajj replied. "Granted, they know more about this forsaken land than we do, but they also know how few hiding places there are. Nakos, what do you think? Are we going to find her?"

"I told everyone—"

"I know what you said about that craig, but what if she was trying to throw you off by looking at it?"

It was possible. Anything was, where she was concerned.

"If we don't find her," Ohanko said, "any female will do, as long as they're built the way she is. What was she like to fuck?"

Nakos had expected the question from his outspoken friend. He just wished he could come up with a reply that wouldn't leave him feeling exposed, or as if he was betraying a confidence.

"She's fully human, if that's what you're asking," he replied.

"I know. Don't forget, we saw her, all of her. I'm talking about her responses. Tau and Lord Sakima were right? Her sexuality is her greatest weakness?"

"What weakness?" Farajj snorted. "I'd say her body is her greatest strength. At least it got in the way of what Nakos was supposed to accomplish."

"Enough!" Nakos exclaimed. "What happened, happened. I'm moving forward, not back."

"No one said you weren't." Farajj's tone softened, and he tapped Nakos's shoulder. "What if we locate and are able to capture her? Are you willing to turn her over to someone else, or will you insist on keeping her?"

Stopping, Nakos stared at the man he'd hunted and fought beside since they'd completed their manhood ceremony. A brother couldn't know him better. "She's mine, no one else's."

"Because you're determined to finish what you began, or because of what she's become to you?"

Suddenly the vast plain surrounding them became too small. He needed to be alone—just him and her.

"You aren't answering." Ohanko tilted his head to the side, his gaze intense. "Farajj's question is a simple one."

"Is it?"

"You tell us. Nakos, don't keep what you're feeling closed up inside you."

"If I do, what then?"

"What do you mean?"

"Will you tell our shaman?"

The two men exchanged a look. Then Farajj cleared his throat. "I never thought I would keep something from Tau. Without his wisdom, the Ekewoko might not still exist. But I value our friendship as I never have anything else. Whenever I think of what you had to face when your grandparents were killed, I wonder if I would have run away instead of staying with their bodies. I've always judged my courage against the standard you set."

You don't know the truth. No one does.

"I agree," Ohanko said. "To be that young—"

"It was a long time ago,"

"Yes, it was. Still—you're right. We aren't here to bring the past back to life. We're here to try to get our hands on a wild woman."

Jola was a wild woman, all right, yet she was more than that, something he didn't fully fathom and might never. Bombarded by thoughts he couldn't handle, he started walking again, followed closely by his companions. Although the craig was still a half day's walk away, he couldn't shake the sense that they weren't alone out here.

Looking up, he scanned the sky for something, anything that might explain the sensation. A few clouds rested along the horizon, but other than that, everything was a relentless blue. There was no place even a single Wilding could hide, and why was he studying the sky instead of the ground?

Maybe because of Tau's belief that controlling falcons would insure the Ekewoko's future.

Maybe something else.

Wings and tail folded back, the Falcon dove. Her legs were tucked against the small body, the third eyelid cleaning her eyes, making it possible for her to keep the gray bird beneath her in sight. Tiny bone tubercles guided the tremendous air pressure through her nostrils and eased her breathing. She flew faster than an arrow, faster than her prey could comprehend.

At the last instant, she extended a clenched foot and struck the bird a killing blow. It started to fall, but she easily caught up, snagged it, and brought it close to the ground before letting

it drop. Landing beside the kill, she immediately started pluck-
ing feathers. That done, she began feeding.

She'd nearly finished when a riffle of alarm sped through her
system. Not waiting to see what had caused it, she took flight
but remained closer to the earth than she usually flew. Her superior eyesight spotted movement at odds with what usually
took place here. Her predator brain told her nothing specific,
but that wisdom insisted she keep distance between herself and
the unaccustomed movement. Curious, she floated closer.

Three creatures were moving along the ground. They bore
no resemblance to deer or antelope. Another sensation stirred
her and took her beyond the primitive. More than just a killer
now, she caught hold of the bits and pieces floating in her brain.
When they came together, she accepted that the three weren't
among the Falcons she shared her world with.

Confused and even more cautious, she flew higher before
continuing her examination. She now acknowledged that when
she ceased to be a bird of prey, she became one of the humans
that called themselves "Falcons." That was acceptable, part of
the nature of things.

Who, then, were these strangers?

Blinking repeatedly, she began circling above the newcomers. Her keen sense of smell brought a hint of familiarity to
her, and the longer she studied the creatures, the more she accepted that she'd seen them before. Instead of questioning her
inability to have detected that earlier, she took her new knowledge as her starting point.

So they weren't strangers, one less so than the others. He
walked with a familiar rhythm, and when he spoke to the others, the notes and tones settled easily inside her. Her small body
heated, and the need for more movement touched her wings.
She was growing restless. Hungry.

A shadow from the past closed around her. In the middle of
the shadow lay a dead Falcon with something long and thin

driven through its body. The dead predator had been her mate, her everything.

The creatures below had been responsible.

Her mind pulsing from the strain of trying to process everything, she pushed herself into the sky. But even as she broke free, a bond remained. One of the newcomers was responsible for it.

18

Although he had no intention of telling the others, Nakos's shoulders and back ached from the weight of the pack he'd brought with him. His legs were tired, and he had a headache, probably from the sun. If he'd been more alert, he'd have come up with a way to do something about the various discomforts by now, but walking took up a great deal of energy. Either that, he reluctantly admitted, or concentrating on his worn-out muscles was easier than asking himself what he was doing here and what he hoped to accomplish once he reached his destination.

If Jola indeed lived on or near the mountain, she certainly wasn't there alone, and undoubtedly her people had devised an effective way of keeping an eye out for would-be invaders.

So he, Farajj, and Ohanko couldn't storm the craig without being seen. What, then, did he hope to accomplish?

Ask her to talk to him?

And then what, grab and subdue her?

He should have sat across from Tau while the shaman spoke to their ancestors' bones about what to do. Putting aside his pride and whatever else had sent him out here, he should have prayed to Tau and maybe his lord for guidance. But he hadn't.

Feeling nothing like the warrior he'd long believed himself to be, he lifted his head and tried to focus on his surroundings, but as had happened too many times before, his eyes strayed upward. The few clouds had rearranged themselves and showed no sign of disappearing—or providing water.

Stopping, he reached behind him for his water bladder. Sighing audibly, his companions did the same. They drank sparingly.

"Enough," Farajj announced and dropped to the ground. "Whether we reach that cursed place today or tomorrow isn't going to make any difference."

Agreeing, Nakos settled himself on his knees and then his buttocks. He removed his pack but resisted the impulse to massage his shoulders. Ohanko had already taken off his pack and was using it to prop the back of his head against as he lay sprawled on the dirt. For three warriors, they looked more like footsore wanderers.

Nakos flexed his fingers. Then he studied his hands, thinking not about their expertise with weapons, but what it had felt like to run them over Jola's body. She'd been soft, so soft. Granted, at first she hadn't wanted him to touch her, but he'd persisted and bit by bit she'd let him come closer.

And not just physically close. Even though he probably couldn't get her to admit it, the barriers between them had broken down. He'd controlled her body, and yet it had been much more. He hadn't told her the whole story of his grandparents' death, but he'd told her things no captor ever needed to tell a captive.

Lids drooping, he tried to recall what she might have said, but much of the time she hadn't used words. Instead, she'd opened her body to him, revealed her woman-weakness, stripped herself down. He might have invaded her personal space, but she hadn't tried to hide her reaction to that invasion from him. At least he didn't believe she had. She'd climaxed and climaxed, not simply because he'd forced them from her but because she'd wanted them—from him.

Unless he'd deluded himself.

Sleep threatened to steal over him, but before it could succeed, something touched his nerve endings. Even before he looked up, he knew what he'd find.

Falcon.

The three men bedded down with the base of the craig so close Nakos had noted where it broke free of the ground and began its upward thrust. He still wasn't sure what he was going to do in the morning but then staying awake during his turn to stand guard took most of his concentration. He was also plagued by an erection that had come upon him as the sun was setting and refused to retreat despite his half-hearted attempts to masturbate.

Before eating, they'd gathered enough dried brush to keep a small fire going throughout the night, but the low flames provided only a limited amount of illumination. Darkness was so close.

He'd have to discuss it with Farajj and Ohanko, but it made the most sense to remain where they were for a while tomorrow and see if any of the Wildings approached. Although Jola's behavior had convinced him that the Wildings weren't animal-like, they might have an animal's curiosity. If that was the case, one or more of them might slip close for a look at the strangers.

Either that or the Wildings were out there at this very moment planning their attack.

Picking up his knife, Nakos reassured himself that the rest of his weapons were within easy reach. One thing about the question that had just reared its head: he was now wide awake.

Even if they hadn't stripped him of fear, countless journeys over the years into unfamiliar land had conditioned him. Fear, he'd concluded over time, was an essential element when it came to staying alive. Without ragged nerves and heightened senses, he might relax, and relaxation could kill him. Granted, he'd never admit his insecurities to the others, but he'd guessed that he wasn't the only one to walk with his belly clenched.

And yet he wasn't afraid of dying.

Dying, his grandparents had taught him, came to everyone.

It was the manner of that death that kept him tuned to his surroundings.

Straightening, he listened as Farajj's slow breathing slid into a low snore. If it became any louder, he'd have to shake his friend. However, by turning away from Farajj, he found it easier to isolate the night's sounds. Countless insects were singing their ageless songs. For a change, right now there was only the faintest breeze, which allowed him to catch the whispery footfalls of the creatures that came out after dark. He heard the whir of an owl's wings; something, a rabbit maybe, nibbling; a snake's slither. The familiar sounds eased his nerves a bit, and he studied the contrast between firelight and night. The line between the two was indistinct, a blend really. Shadows waved and wavered, looking more and more unreal the longer he gazed.

Suddenly there was something else. Alert and alarmed, he gripped his knife tight. The unexpected sound was repeated, then it disappeared. Still, he didn't relax. It seemed to come from the earth itself, perhaps something walking or sneaking closer.

Farajj gave out with a snorting snore. Then the warrior flopped onto his side and fell silent. Too many uneasy moments later, the earth sound came again. By turning his head this way and that, Nakos determined that it was coming from his right, but if he got to his feet, he'd give himself away.

Not breathing, and with his heart trying to pound its way to freedom, he narrowed his awareness until nothing existed except for the faint sound. Whomever or whatever it was wasn't coming closer. Rather, it seemed to be circling the campfire, careful to remain in the shadows. Moment by slow moment, he made the circuit with what he'd come to think of as the invader. Only one thing made sense: a Wilding was out there.

It could be more than one, he reminded himself, but the sound appeared to be a solitary one. And the longer it went on, the slower his heart rate became. His palms were still sweaty, and now it hurt to breathe, but at least fear had stopped crawling up his throat. In its place, a warrior's need to pit himself against the enemy surfaced.

What are you? Who are you? Are you armed, because if you aren't, I'll kill you.

A cold smile lifted his lips. His shoulders felt stronger, his back straighter—proof, he told himself, that the boy who'd buried his grandparents no longer existed.

Certain now that he knew exactly where the stranger was, he measured the distance between them. Because of the firelight, the stranger could undoubtedly see him, which meant he'd have to rely on every bit of speed he possessed when he made his move. But he would! He would.

Smiling again, he sprang to his feet. Four quick strides and he reached his destination. But although he'd been positive surprise would give him the advantage, he found nothing, touched no one. Confused, he darted left and then right, slashing with the knife as he did. When that, too, accomplished nothing, he stopped, confused. Only then did he realize he was now in utter darkness. Unease ran through him.

"Where are you?" he demanded, albeit with a hint of hesitation. He turned in a slow, unproductive circle.

From where she stood back in human form, a short distance away, Jola sensed more than watched Nakos. Because she'd guessed what he planned to do, she'd easily moved farther into the night before he reached her, but before long his senses would alert him to her location. In the meantime, however, she'd let his presence—his essence even—touch her.

It shouldn't be like this. In truth, she should either be asleep at the top of the craig or replenishing her sense of self by surrounding herself with other Falcons. Instead of either of those things, however, she was here. Remembering so much.

Nakos's tension reached out to touch her. Although she didn't want to, she couldn't help but feel sorry for him. Unlike her, who carried a predator's soul against her heart, he feared for his life. He might go to his death not letting his companions know he was close to panic, but he couldn't keep that from someone who'd been born knowing how to take advantage of a prey's weakness.

She could, if her need for revenge was strong enough, terrify him. Instead, she spoke.

"It's me, Nakos. Jola."

He took a gasping breath. "You? What are you—"

"You shouldn't have come here." She hurried to avoid being asked why she'd sought him out. "This place is sacred, for my people alone."

"My shaman will never believe that."

At first she didn't know what he was thinking about. Then she remembered what Tau had said about his determination to find and capture falcons. Thinking how little the shaman knew, she nearly laughed.

"And you do whatever your shaman tells you to?" she asked. "Even if the task frightens you."

"I'm not afraid."

She nearly told him she knew better but what would that accomplish? In spite of—or maybe because of—what had taken place between them, she could never see Nakos as simply the enemy. How could she, when her body kept reminding her of those things? She didn't want those reminders; at least, she struggled to tell herself she wanted nothing to do with heat between her legs and swollen breasts.

But that heat was so sweet, all softness and wanting. He'd taken her places she'd never known she could go, expertly guided her from one climax to another. Granted, those explosions had left her in awe of him and frightened of her body.

Afraid? Wasn't that what she'd just accused him of being?

"Are you alone?" he asked. "Maybe you won't tell me, but I have to ask."

"I'm alone."

"Why? I'm not."

"I know. Your friends—"

"They're more than that. They're warriors who've committed themselves to turning our shaman's visions into reality."

"It won't happen."

"You don't know that."

They'd already had this argument, hadn't they? But she didn't want to touch on the subject. Instead, against all reason, she ached to put an end to the distance between them, to feel his arms around her, to pull him into her body.

"Did you hear me, Jola? You need to know what you and your people are facing. The Ekewoko are proven—"

"So you've told me!" The instant she'd spoken, she knew she was fighting herself and not his words. "But the Fa—those you call Wildings are far different from what you believe we are. I came here tonight to ask one thing of you. Leave. Before it's too late."

"Too late? You think your people's weapons are superior to ours?"

"There are weapons far different from knives and arrows. No matter how skilled you are, you can't succeed against us."

He didn't immediately respond, which gave her too much time to ponder whether she'd said more than she should have. Unfortunately, because she hadn't left enough distance between them, she couldn't concentrate on finding the answer. At least she could no longer see him. Watching him illuminated by the firelight had been hard and had brought back too many memories of the time they'd spent together. Just thinking of coming in to his arms and under his control after he'd pulled her out of the lake caused her juices to flow.

"Is that the only reason you came here tonight?" he asked.

"Did you think there'd be any other?"

"No." He spoke slowly. "And now you've said what you believe you needed to, are you going to leave?"

He might be warning her that he'd try and stop her, only she didn't think so. Just the same he was right. She had completed her mission.

Feeling lost, she again fought the impulse to touch him. "Listen to me, Nakos. If you want to live, if you don't want to risk your companions' lives, return to your camp. Tell the Eke-woko that they don't belong at what you call 'Screaming Wind'."

"So I can tell my shaman and the man who raised me that I failed?"

They spoke the same language and yet they didn't. It had been the same for their bodies.

Her eyes burning, she wrapped her arms around her middle. "What means the most to you? Staying alive or bowing to your leaders' commands?"

"That's not what it is! I want the same things my shaman and lord do."

Was that true, or had the two men ruled him for so long that he no longer asked if there might be another way? "Then I feel sorry for you."

"Don't!"

Instead of saying anything more, he took several deep breaths. Remembering when she'd been so close to him that she could feel him exhale brought fresh tears. She'd been unable to get through to him tonight. There was no longer any reason for her to remain here. If his decision brought on his death, she'd live with it—somehow.

"Good-bye, Nakos."

Before she could take a step, a flicker of light distracted her. Another bright spot in the middle of all that darkness joined the first one. It had just occurred to her that Nakos's companions were approaching when something struck her with such force that she was knocked to the ground. Acting instinctively, she tried to bury her nails in the flesh pushing down on her. Powerful fingers circled her left wrist, but although her attacker tried to do the same to her right, she managed to keep it out of his reach. Even as she put every bit of strength she possessed into the uneven fight, she knew who was responsible: Nakos.

The twin lights bounced closer, but the danger they represented barely registered. Nakos was above her, pressing her left arm against the ground while trying to straddle her waist.

"No! By the spirits, no!" Sinking her nails into his naked chest, she struggled to buck him off her. Grunting, he tore her hand off him. That done, he captured her right wrist and forced her arm down along her side. Her wild thrashing briefly prevented him from resting his weight on her middle, but all too soon, he had her.

Again.

"It's her, isn't it?" one of the men holding the burning branches asked. "The Wilding you caught earlier. What is she doing here?"

"She tried to warn me not to look for her people." Nakos sounded as out of breath as she was.

Nakos's companions stood on either side of her with their fires so close she could make out his determined expression. Another emotion simmered beneath it, one she couldn't fathom.

He leaned over her, nearly blanketing her body with his. As his breath caressed her cheeks, she stopped struggling. She'd been here before, his helpless and willing prisoner, her body responding to his and her pussy softening.

"What now, Jola?" he asked.

She didn't answer because the truth was, nothing mattered except this moment. She vaguely recalled the determined woman who'd come here tonight, but that woman had been pushed aside by a creature who wanted only one thing.

"No answer? Then I'll tell you what's going to happen." He ground himself against her until she gasped and squirmed under him. "Right now we're going back to where my companions and I are camped. In the morning, you'll show us the way to the top of that peak of yours."

His edict made her laugh.

"Don't do this, Jola. Your response, to say nothing of your opposition, won't change the outcome." Still tightly gripping her wrists, he leaned even closer. "Have you forgotten what I can make your body do?"

How can I? "My body, maybe, but not my head or heart."

"Which means?"

"That I will never betray my people."

She should be accustomed to his silences, but this one gave her too much time to think. They were close to where she'd spent her entire life. She was surrounded by memories both good and bad about what it meant to be Falcon. Until he'd entered her world, she'd never questioned that existence, but now—

"I'll tell you what I'm thinking," he said, breaking into her thoughts. "If the only thing you cared about was your freedom, you wouldn't have come here tonight. But you did because I succeeded at certain things."

Before she could react, he'd crossed her wrists one over the other. Easily holding both with a single hand, he reached behind him. Because the dress she'd retrieved from her home had ridden up around her hips during their struggle, it was a simple matter for him to slide a practiced hand between her legs. The moment he touched her cunt, she tried to lift herself off the ground.

"You're wet there, Jola. No matter what you say or do, you can't keep that from me."

Much as she wanted to deny his words, she couldn't. Maybe her only salvation lay in telling him nothing, not moving. But although she forced her legs to relax, her pussy twitched. When he slid a finger past her wet labia, she suspected he'd felt the movement. Concentrating on not reacting to his exploration got her past the next few moments but then she lost focus.

He knew so much about her, how and where to touch her, what covered her in heat. And yet his command of her body went deeper than that, triggered her heart somehow and made her long for what she and Raci had briefly experienced. Most of all she wanted to give back. To belong.

"What are you thinking, Jola?" he asked, not sounding as harsh as he had earlier. "Maybe you're full of hate for me. If that's what it is, I understand. But I'm not convinced it's that simple."

His features were drenched in red from the flaming branches, and she guessed her features were illuminated as well. His grip no longer threatened to cut off the circulation in her hands, and the finger at her entrance simply rested there. Earlier today she'd reveled in the joy of flight. Now another sensation claimed her.

"Still not answering?"

"I have nothing to say."

"Because your body is saying everything? Never mind." He sighed. "I know you better than that."

Before she could mull over what he'd said, he pulled her to her feet. One of his hands forced her right arm behind her and against her spine while the other gripped her hair and pulled her head back so she had no choice but to again stare at him. His companions hadn't said anything, but even if they had, she probably wouldn't have paid attention to them. She still felt loose and easy, far from the muscled predator she'd been not long ago. In human form as it became dark, she'd grown chilled, but having Nakos this close warmed her.

If only she could forget what he represented.

19

Sitting cross-legged on the ground near the now snapping campfire, Jola turned her shoulder toward the heat. Nakos had tied her hands so they were crossed before her. Another rope led from her wrists to his right hand. The other two men had stretched out on their sleeping blankets but showed no sign of being interested in going back to sleep.

"The last thing I expected," Nakos said, "was to see you tonight. Why?"

"I told you, I had to try."

"Try what?"

"To get you to leave."

He considered that for a moment, then idly scratched his flat belly. Thanks to the loose garment that reached from his waist to knees, she couldn't tell whether he had an erection.

"Does anyone know you're here?" he asked.

"Do you think I'd tell you?"

"Probably not. Another question. Did you really believe we'd give up and walk away simply because you asked us to?"

"I had to try."

"Why?"

She needed to concentrate on her every word, not let his presence distract her, which was no easy matter. They hadn't been apart from each other for long, yet the time had dragged. Now that she was looking at him again, she knew looking wouldn't be enough. It shouldn't be like this! She shouldn't want him.

"Tell me again, what did you believe you needed to try to accomplish?" he pressed. "You risked a great deal, and for what?"

"You don't understand. You're the one who has risked his life by coming here."

His companions tensed. "Just *his* life?" one of them asked. "Or all three of ours?"

"All."

"What is she talking about?" The question came from the other man. "What has she told you about this place?"

Nakos frowned. His fingers crawled along the rope he held. "Not much. Not, it seems, nearly enough. What takes place here, Jola?"

She was weary of this conversation, exhausted from trying to defend herself against his impact on her. In the morning, maybe, she'd have found the words to turn these men around and start them back toward where they belonged.

"I was born here," she whispered. "I've never wanted to be anywhere else. When you talk about traveling here, there, and everywhere, I don't understand. Why aren't you content to remain in one place?"

"We have a home: Ekew."

"But you gave it up. Why?"

Now it was his turn to place silence between them. Finally one of the other men spoke. "We haven't given up on Ekew. All of us want to return and fight the Outsiders for it. But Tau—his dreams and visions—"

"Not just dreams and visions," the other man interrupted. "We *must* have the right weapons if we're going to succeed."

"Have you tried fighting with the weapons you have?"

"Of course."

"And what happened?"

"We lost."

"That's why you gave up, because of a few failures?"

No one spoke for a long time, making her guess that each was asking himself questions maybe he hadn't before.

"You're a woman," Nakos finally said. "As such, you can't be expected to understand what it takes to insure a tribe's safety."

"I know what it takes to remain alive: vigilance."

"Ha! Perhaps if you'd been more aware of your surroundings, you wouldn't again be a prisoner."

Unable to argue with him, she shrugged and patted the ground around her looking for the most comfortable place to stretch out. Nakos could prevent her from doing so, but if he didn't, she'd at least get some sleep. After her long day, rest was more important than anything else, even having sex.

Maybe he guessed what she was doing because he shook his head and tugged on the rope. "I'm not a cruel man. You don't have to sleep on rocks and dirt with no covering."

There was only one alternative: next to him, sharing his sleeping pad. Shivering, she tried not to look at it.

"What are you afraid of?" he asked.

"Nothing. But neither do I want—"

"I know you don't want me, but it doesn't matter. Come here. It won't be the first time we've spent the night together."

She'd been wrong. He hadn't insisted on fucking her after all. In fact, once he'd secured the rope between them to his wrist, he'd stretched out on his back while she'd lain on her side facing him, because that was the only way she could stay on his pad and under his blanket. At first he'd been so tense that she'd been tempted to try to massage some of that tension out of him. Fortunately, he'd fallen asleep, snoring lightly. Listening to him breathe, she wondered at his ability to ignore her.

She, on the other hand, couldn't separate herself from him. Oh yes, she managed not to touch him, but his heat not only touched her skin, it seeped into her. Every time she let down her defenses, she relived his hands boldly exploring her. Most unsettling were memories of the night he'd taken climax after climax from her.

She wanted him to start her on that journey again, wanted his hands on her naked flesh and his cock housed deep inside her. Just thinking of how it had felt when he'd finally stopped teasing her and taken her stole her breath. If she thought she could do so without waking him, she'd roll onto her back and bend her knees so she could touch herself. She'd try to bring herself along slowly so the pleasure would last. As she lightly stroked herself, she'd imagine Nakos was guiding her along that delicious journey and, as he had in the past, he'd know exactly what she needed.

Something in the fire snapped, making her start. In the aftermath, she berated herself for losing sight of why she'd come here. In the morning she'd try again to convince Nakos and the others that their being here wouldn't bring them the success Tau was looking for. The problem was, she didn't know how to get her message across to them without betraying the Falcons.

Only the elders could decide whether to let outsiders see what it truly meant to be a Falcon. If the right was hers, she'd stand before the Ekewoko and demonstrate that it was possible to be both human and predator—and that in predator form, a Falcon became a powerful killer.

It wouldn't matter that the Ekewoko were many times larger than a Falcon—because only a Falcon possessed the deadly speed, talons, and beak needed to tear flesh apart. A Falcon could blind an Ekewoko or tear out his throat before the enemy knew what had happened. Once that had been accomplished—

A new sound splintered her thoughts. This one hadn't come from the fire but was closer. Focusing on Nakos, she again imagined touching him in a way men and women everywhere understood. Instead of waiting for him to arouse her sexually, she'd make the first move, maybe by running her damp tongue over his chest. As she did, she'd press his arms against the ground so he couldn't touch her. It would be his turn to squirm and gasp, to—

"No, by the spirits, no!"

Nakos's outburst brought her upright. Careful not to put strain on the rope that had turned them into one, she glanced at his companions, but they remained motionless. Concluding that they considered what was going on none of their business, she turned her attention back to Nakos.

He muttered something she couldn't understand, and his legs jerked. Much as she wanted to step between him and what had to be a nightmare, she waited.

"No," he repeated. "Ah no, please."

His legs still moving, he began punching the air. He might be trying to ward off an imaginary attacker, but she didn't think it was that. A grim look contorted his features so much she barely recognized him.

"I can't, please, don't ask me . . ."

Don't ask you to do what? she longed to say. Instead, she pressed her arms against her chest. He'd started rocking from side to side. If he turned over, the rope would be trapped under him and she'd be forced against him. Fortunately, he only continued the strange rocking motion, and she was put in mind of a mother comforting a frightened child. Perhaps he was trying to comfort himself.

"I know, I know. By the spirits, I can see but . . ."

Propelled by the pain and horror in his voice, she closed her fingers over the hand closest to her and held it against her breasts. She couldn't be certain but thought the gesture calmed him a little. He was still speaking, the muttered words no longer making sense. Having fallen apart after Raci's death, she understood grief, but what he was experiencing went beyond that.

Determined to do what she could without endangering the Falcons, she hadn't told the Falcons of her plan to get close to the strangers camped near the base of Raptor's Craig, which meant no one of her kind knew what had happened to her. As a consequence, just like the first time Nakos had captured her, she had only her own resources to rely on. When he'd jumped her earlier today, she'd reassured herself with the knowledge that she could change from human to predator now that she was on sacred land. As soon as the timing was right, she'd shift form and be free. Tonight, however, freedom was the last thing she was concerned about.

"You aren't alone," she muttered as she continued to hold Nakos's hand between her breasts. "I'm with you, and if you need to talk about your nightmare, I'll listen."

His legs continued to churn, albeit less violently than earlier.

"Is it one you've had before? If it's new, maybe it'll fade away and become nothing, never return."

"I love—love you. Please, no."

Who was Nakos saying that to? Surely not her.

"It's only a dream," she continued. "Nothing to be afraid of."

"Don't ask me to—no, I can't. Anything but that."

"No one is asking you to do anything, Nakos." Although she was whispering, her throat burned, and if anything, the ache in her heart became more intense. "It's a late summer night, peaceful, perfect for sleeping." *And sex.*

Bit by bit his legs quieted. The muscles in the hand she held were still taut, and every time he took a breath, he held it until she thought his lungs might burst. She shrank before the possibility that this warrior was dependent on her to keep his nightmare at bay, but if she didn't try, maybe it would destroy him.

A faint whimper pressed past his lips. There was something—a femininity maybe—to the sound that made her wonder if whoever was in his nightmare might be responsible for it. Then he moaned, the note masculine and yet not one she'd ever heard from his throat. She became convinced that he wasn't alone in whatever horror he was caught in, and that she wasn't part of it.

Another soft whimper pulled her thoughts off herself.

"Don't cry. Please, don't cry," Nakos begged. His fingers were so tightly clenched she was afraid his nails would pierce his palms. "Atch, I see. By the spirits, I see."

"What are you seeing, Nakos?"

"Their burns. No, please, no."

"Whose burns?"

"The smell—their screams. Stop screaming! Please, no more."

Galvanized by the agony in his voice, she pressed her body against his. Her arms went around his head. His heart pounded.

"I'm here, Nakos," she soothed with her mouth against his ear. "There's no screaming. Everything's quiet, and it's night. You need to sleep, only sleep."

A shudder rolled through him, prompting her to spread her legs so they were on either side of his. With her dress askew, her pussy kissed his thigh. Before she could think of more to say, he took a long and deep breath. Although she couldn't make out his features, she sensed he was no longer asleep. Tuning into the sound of his breathing, she imagined air going in and out of his lungs as reality returned to him. His heat against hers quieted her. Hopefully the same thing was happening to him.

"What are you doing?" he muttered.

Risking a great deal. "You were having a bad dream. I was trying to—I didn't know how to make it end."

"What did I say?"

Surprised by the question, she considered sitting up, but before she could, he wrapped his arms around her. An arm pressed against the small of her back while the other warmed her shoulder blades. One thing she knew: he was concerned he might have said too much. Was he determined not to let just her into his private world, or was his nightmare indicative of something he kept from everyone?

"What did I say?"

"Not much that made sense," she assured him. "You muttered a lot, and from the way you moved, it was as if you were trying to get away from something. Do you remember? Maybe you were running from an enemy."

"Enemy?"

Even before she'd mentioned running as a possibility, she knew that wasn't right because she'd concluded that he'd been carrying on a conversation with one or more people while staring at something that horrified him.

"Someone was screaming." Although she lifted her head so she could make out his expression, she was content to remain against him. Keeping her pelvis still wasn't easy. "I don't think it was you because the voice you used wasn't familiar. And you said something about burning."

With a sound somewhere between a grunt and a sigh, he sat up, pushing her off him as he did. She didn't try to scoot away but remained close so his heat continued to reach her.

"Is that what I said?"

About to tell him no, she nodded.

The fire had again turned to little more than coals, but now the moon was up. Between it and the stars, she noted how intently he was watching her. Men, even Falcons, were private creatures when it came to their emotions. They were loathe to reveal any more of what they were thinking or feeling than they absolutely had to, but maybe if she waited him out, she'd find a way to break past his defenses.

"I seldom remember my dreams," she said, hoping the admission would get him started. "And what I do makes little sense. Fortunately, I hardly ever have a nightmare."

"It wasn't—"

"Yes, it was!" she snapped, then looked around to make sure his companions were still asleep. "Don't lie to me, or yourself."

Instead of replying, he picked up the rope that held them together and stroked it. Watching his hands at work calmed her. Just the same, she couldn't distance herself from memories of when he'd touched her and how she'd responded. They'd been physically close most of the time they'd been together, and yet the connection had never felt as strong as it did right now.

"When I look back on my dreams," she continued, "I realize that most are triggered by something that happened earlier. Everything gets jumbled together so it becomes bits and pieces that don't make much sense. From the things you said, I got the feeling it wasn't bits and pieces at all. Instead, and I could be wrong, your nightmare was part of a single experience. You were stuck in one place, unable to get free."

"No, I couldn't."

He hadn't been looking at her when he spoke, but now he lifted his head, and what she saw tore at her heart. He had this incredibly vulnerable expression, almost as if he were standing at the edge of a cliff trying to decide whether to step off into space. If he'd been a Falcon, the decision would have been a simple one.

"That wasn't the first time that happened, was it?" she prompted. "You've had that—dream before."

"Too many times."

Wondering if she'd have to pull things out of him one word at a time, she rested her hands on his knee. At the touch, her body jumped and came alive. Fighting the warmth tightening around her throat and between her breasts, she squeezed his knee. "Something about your voice—you sounded younger than you do now, like a boy."

"I was."

I was. As even more heat slid over her, she ground her teeth to keep from stroking him. Much as she wanted to help him take the next step, she wasn't sure how. If she pushed him too hard or said the wrong thing, he'd retreat into silence. Either that or too much would become about sex. "I'm sorry to hear that," she came up with. "As children we don't have much control over our lives."

"No, we don't."

Timing her breathing to his, she again squeezed his knee. "We envy the adults in our lives because we think they have the control we lack. Then we grow up and discover that isn't true. There'll always be things none of us can anticipate or plan, that happen whether we want them to or not."

"Like this." He indicated her bound wrists.

Nodding, she dropped her gaze and studied her fingers resting on his knee. The bone was barely beneath the surface, large and hard, superbly conditioned and yet part of a vulnerable man.

In her eyes, Raci had been handsome, but next to Nakos, she now saw him as what he'd been: young and untested. Until the Ekewoko had arrived, Raci's life, like all Falcons', had been an easy one dictated by whether he was hungry or full. She, too, had timed her changes from human to predator to fit her stomach's dictates. Granted, she sometimes became a Falcon simply because flying was more interesting than walking.

In contrast, Nakos could never be anything except what he was: an earth-bound man.

"What are you thinking?" he asked.

"I'm not sure. So many things have changed since I learned you and the other Ekewoko exist."

"And you wish we'd go away."

"I didn't say—"

"You don't have to. You can't possibly want people who have disrupted your way of life around."

"Maybe we became complacent," she offered. "Maybe we need change in order to grow."

"But shouldn't it be change you have a say in?"

Not only hadn't she expected the conversation to take this turn, she couldn't think how to return it to his nightmare. "I've learned many things," she admitted.

"Such as?"

That it's possible for Ekewoko and Falcon bodies to come together. "That—that your shaman wields a great deal of power."

"It isn't that simple."

Thinking of things to say was becoming more and more difficult because what did words matter when there was this terrible/wonderful heat between them, and her body kept crying out memories of when they'd fucked?

"What—do you mean?" she stammered.

"Tau's visions give us guidance, but they aren't law."

"You don't always do what he says you should?"

"Once, when I was a child, the Outsiders came to Ekew. That first time they didn't stay long but . . ." He took a long, deep breath, and his features tightened. "Tau's father, who was shaman then, declared that those people were peaceful and we should welcome them with food and gifts. He was wrong."

Nakos had been a child then. Did that experience have anything to do with his nightmare? Lifting her hands from his knee, she ran her knuckles over his cheek. Her arms buzzed, and her cunt felt loose and hot. No matter how she tried, she couldn't think of a thing to say.

Using the lead rope, he drew her hands off his cheek and pulled her toward him. Leaving her off-balance, he untied the knots and started massaging her wrists. Her entire body was loosening, flowing. She waited for him to end the silence, but when he didn't, she looked up again. The stars and moon had been there her entire life. They'd outlived Raci and would out-live her and Nakos.

But tonight they existed to reveal him to her, and her to him.

The muscles along her shoulder blades rippled to remind her of the transformation from human to predator, forcing her to concentrate on staying in human form. That done, she gently pulled free so she could touch his cheek again. Then she ran her fingers down the side of his neck. A vein there jumped, and she pressed her thumb against it.

"Are you trying to choke me?" he asked.

"No. I'd never—"

"No, I don't think you would. You're beautiful, Jola. I never thought I'd say that of a Wilding, but you are."

"We don't call ourselves Wildings."

"Then what?"

If she told him, would he guess the truth about Falcons? The greater question was whether she wanted him to know more than the little he did. Dragging her gaze off the heavens and back onto his shadowed features, she decided the timing hadn't come. But it might.

"It doesn't matter," she told him as her fingers began a jour-ney over his shoulders. She'd been right. This was a mature man's body.

He allowed her to explore his arm, but when she placed both hands flat against his chest, he closed his hands around her wrists, the grip more commanding than the ropes had been. She thought he might pull her off him, but he didn't, only matched her pace as she circled the hard nub of his nipples. His breath caught; so did hers. Her head swirled, and the knot in her belly tightened in contrast to the flowing sensation in her womb.

Using his thighs to support herself, she knelt beside him. As her hair slid over his chest, she first rubbed her cheek against his nipple and then raked her teeth over it. That done, she moved to his other nipple and took it between her teeth in memory of what he'd done to her.

"By the spirits!" he gasped.

Not wanting to harm him in any way, she contented herself with holding on to him while bathing the nub with her tongue. She leaned toward him, still pressing her hands against his thighs and feeling the powerful muscles there, mind spinning and her pussy dripping.

Perhaps he knew because he slid his hand between her legs and delved into her hole. She waited for him to say something or use his knowledge to his benefit, but he only swirled his finger inside her.

"Ha!" she breathed, not letting go.

"You're more than beautiful." He sounded as out of breath as she did. "You're going to be my ruin."

She could say the same about him, not that the admission was necessary with her nipples rock hard. When her jaw started to ache, she released him but drew out the leaving by first drenching both nubs. She started to straighten only to stop because she needed his finger filling her. After a moment, she rested her head against his chest, her hands splayed over his thighs. He was so much larger than she, strength in contrast to her weakness. Granted, if she changed form, everything between them would change.

Would she let him see what she was capable of? Did she dare take the risk?

"I thought I might never see you again," he muttered.

"Maybe that's why I was so angry when you escaped, that and believing you wanted nothing to do with me."

"Not because you couldn't get certain information from me?"

He sighed, the gesture resonating throughout her. "That doesn't matter."

Wondering if he no longer shared his shaman's goal, she tried to ignore the burning sensation down her back, but moment by moment the strain increased. Sighing, she sat back up. As he did, his finger slid out of her.

"What?" he asked, taking her around the waist and tugging her close. "You aren't thinking of leaving, are you?"

Earlier he would have simply made sure she couldn't, but this was now and a great deal had changed between them.

"I won't, not tonight."

"But later, maybe?"

"I don't know what the morning will bring. Neither do you."

His grunt made her wonder if he was keeping something from her, but whatever it might be would have to wait until the energy between them had been tamped down. The side of her knee pressed against his thigh, preventing her from getting any closer. At the same time, his hands remained on her waist. After assuring herself that she'd fully regained her balance, she let go of his thigh and stroked his chest.

Moisture from her mouth still dampened him there, but it had cooled, giving her reason to roll her palms over him. Friction built to add to the heat she was transferring from her to him. Although he tensed a bit, he made no move to stop her until she tried to capture a nub between her fingers. Then he lightly slapped her rump.

"Some things a man can handle; this isn't one of them."

"You don't like—"

"That's not what I said."

She tried to capture his nub between her thumb and fore-finger, which earned her another teasing slap. Smiling in the dark, she again leaned into his strength, this time aiming her mouth at his shoulder. Her teeth raked his collarbone.

"Ah woman! I should have left you tied."

"It's too late for that."

20

He could have pointed out that that his superior strength would dictate the outcome of any *battle* between them. What hopefully he understood was that she didn't want to fight him, or be treated as she'd been in the past. Tonight was about the new. Them. Not tomorrow.

Losing herself in the vibration rolling from pussy to breasts, she alternated between kissing and playfully biting his collarbone. As she did, he patted her buttocks. A faint drumming sound accompanied his gesture to again bring a smile to her. She was in the moment, alive in the now, every inch of her afire.

Her teeth came down on him with more and more strength. She understood the drumming on her ass and the sensations reaching from there to her sex, nothing more. Night or day, winter or summer, safe or dangerous didn't matter because there was him, only him.

Her pussy so alive she was forced to press her thighs together, she bit down.

"Ah!" He jerked back, freeing himself.

Before she could apologize, he collapsed onto the ground,

bringing her down with him. She was on top of him, chest to chest with her lower body off to the side. Reaching under his loincloth, she cupped his erection.

"You've changed," he said, tight lipped, his hands around her upper arms. "What happened to the woman who didn't want to touch me?"

She pressed her palm against the hard mound. "You'd tied me, don't you remember? There was little I could do."

"Then you would have done this if it was possible?"

"I don't know."

"Why not?"

With her cheek resting on his chest, she drank in his familiar and yet overwhelming scent. Tasting it throughout her, she acknowledged that she'd taken some of it with her when she'd fled. Maybe his unique essence would never completely leave her.

"The first time between us," she started, "I was nearly a virgin. I didn't know what to expect, or whether I could trust you."

"Nearly a virgin. How many men have there been?"

"One. Only one."

Not giving him time to probe, she began massaging his thick length. Her hand barely fit around him, giving rise to the need to explore every inch. As engaged as she was in her task, her mind kept sliding back to what she'd just told him. She hadn't wanted the conversation to take this turn, but did she expect it to be any different? After all, she was Falcon, a woman who a short time ago had believed she'd found her mate. Was that why she was being so bold tonight, because fucking her former captor was better than reliving her loss?

"Jola?" His fingers dug into her arms as he lifted her off him. "What are you thinking?"

"Nothing. Nothing."

"Don't lie."

She was lying? What about his refusal to explain his nightmare? "I don't want to think," she admitted with her fingers still on him and her gaze locked on his deep-set eyes.

"Neither do I."

That said, he let her down so her breasts were once more flattened against his chest and her cheek absorbed not just his heat but his heartbeat. Instead of settling her attention on what her hand cradled, she ran her lips over his chest. Her eyes started to burn, compelling her to close them. Still, a tear broke free.

"Are you crying?" he whispered.

Unable to answer him, she kissed the flesh over his heart and lightly stroked his cock.

"Wait a moment," he hissed.

"What?"

"My garment. Take it off."

Silently thanking him for giving her something to do, she straightened and tugged the rope-held waistband down over his lean hips. Moonlight centered on the dark rod waiting for her. With his help, she dispensed with the loincloth and tossed it aside. Tears still blurred her vision, and her heartbeat carried a command she'd never heard. Giving into the message, she sank down and took his cock head into her mouth.

"By the spirits!" he gasped, fisting her hair.

Maybe he intended his grip as a warning for her to stop, but until he did, she'd cling to him. Unsure of what she was doing, she drew more of his length into her. His breadth filled her mouth, and she became light-headed. The sensation, both overwhelming and wonderful, captured her full attention. She was vaguely aware of an ache in her back but next to her pleasure of the taste and smell of him, the discomfort was nothing.

Still holding her hair, he cupped a hand over a dangling breast. Feeling possessed by him there, she vowed to hand him the same experience. Because she needed her hands against the ground to hold her balance, her mouth became her only tool, and she opened it to pull yet more of him into her damp warmth. His cock head touched the back of her throat, sending a shock through her. Once she'd adjusted to the new sensation, she lifted her head and slowly let him slide out. The grip on her breast increased.

Thankful for the silence, she took a moment to swallow. Then, turning her head to the side, she licked. Her tongue glided over ridges and silken skin. Again and again she trailed over his length. When she applied so much pressure that she pushed his cock to the side, she followed it, nipping playfully.

His hold on her hair tightened yet more. Her breast now ached, a delicious sensation that floated through it before sliding into her chest wall. From there the pleasure/pain spun down her body. Even as the mix of joy and discomfort settled into her pussy, she fought to keep it manageable by again clamping her legs together. Her hips moved in a primal rhythm.

"Do it," he commanded, pushing down on the back of her head. "Suck my seed from me."

"No." She shook her head. "I want that in my sex, nowhere else."

"What if I commanded—"

"Your time for that is behind us."

"I could—"

"Don't." Determined to end the argument, she ran her tongue over his tip. His cock shuddered. Capturing it between her lips, she lifted her head, stretching him. Another drawing sensation, this one centered around the breast he held, distracted her. Potent heat spun through her.

They began a dance of sorts, a contest perhaps. Every time she tried something new, he did the same to her breast. Once when she tapped his cock with her chin, he released her breast only to claim the other. She arched her back.

He released her hair, then finger combed it until it lay across her shoulders. The gentle gesture had her fighting more tears. After running his finger down her spine while she mewled and fought the tickling sensation without releasing him, he gripped her left ass cheek and drew it away from the other.

Undone by the sensation, she lifted her head and stared. The moon and stars, however, offered her no escape, if in truth she wanted one. The power was in his hands, in the fingers claiming her breast and buttock. If she hoped to regain command of her body, there was only one way.

Fighting her body, she opened her mouth. His cock now rested against her tongue, pushing it flat. For a moment she thought she might gag, then her throat relaxed and the taste of him slid down it.

He guided her buttock back into place only to draw it out and away again, making her mewl once more. As determined as she was to meet him challenge for challenge, he was now one step ahead of her because every time she started to suck or lathe his cock, he either flattened her breast against her chest or slid a finger between her ass cheeks.

No more! She couldn't handle—

Furious, she touched her teeth to blood-swollen veins. He responded by pressing something, maybe his thumb, against her rear opening. She nearly howled.

"Who's going to win?" he demanded. "And if this is a battle, why?"

Releasing him, she shook her head. "I don't want to fight."

"Then what?"

Before she could begin to formulate a response, he took her waist with both hands and lifted her up and over him. She helped by positioning her legs on either side of his hips, then stopped with her ass in the air and his cock poking her belly. A moment later, she rocked forward and then down so his cock slid along her sopping sex lips. The sleek glide brought her within a breath of climaxing. She gasped.

"What?" he demanded. "Are you—"

"Not yet."

"But soon?"

"Yes."

She didn't want to be in control, needed his strength over and around but mostly inside her. Following instinct, she reached between her legs and guided him into her. Yet desperate as she was to be filled, she willed herself to take him slow. Slow and strong. Her mouth hung open, and she breathed as if she was dying. Taking hold of her hips, he guided her downward journey. Thighs straining and hot, she opened her sex to him, took him one inch at a time. It couldn't be, of course, but her womb felt as if he were nestled in there. Then her belly greeted him followed by her breasts. Next would come her throat and she'd be lost. Gone.

"Yes!" he grunted. "By all that's sacred, yes!"

Finally her buttocks rested on him with his length caught and sheltered inside her. Even as hunger screamed at her and her pussy burned, she simply held him. Learned his contours and made them hers.

Hands planted on his chest, she tried to do the same with his features, but even with the moon's help, there was too much shadow to make out his mouth, nose, and eyes. Shoving aside her unease, she rose slightly. Her clenched cunt muscles brought him with her.

"By the sacreds—"

"Hush," she warned. "The others—"

"Will envy us."

She rewarded him by settling back down, but with need clawing at her from every direction, she couldn't remain still, prompting her to once more lift herself a little. This time she relaxed her muscles, causing his cock to slide along her channel. Even with her mouth tightly closed, a low moan drifted into the night air. She followed the sound upward, maybe clear to the top of Raptor's Craig, then her thoughts, and more, returned to the man under her.

Still trying to comprehend the change in their relationship, she set about bringing pleasure to both of them. Muscles working endlessly, she lifted herself, then slowly collapsed, rose and retreated. Sometimes she brought his cock with her. Other times she fantasized she was giving it freedom only to settle down, his maleness stretching her inner walls and tearing more moans from her.

Even with cool air all around, she started sweating. Unable to pace herself, she pushed her thigh muscles to their limit. Faster and faster she fucked this man, her hair flying about, sweat sticking to her, her cunt on fire.

A climax rolled over her, a quiet thing that suddenly exploded, forcing her to close her teeth over her lower lip to keep from crying out. The explosion was still tearing at her when he pulled her down on top of him, his cock lodged tight inside her.

"Nakos?"

"Quiet."

Quiet was a place she could go to ride out her climax. It still pulsed deep in her core as he rolled onto his side, taking her with him. Then he was on top, his cock sliding out but back in again a heartbeat later. She stared at him, let the moon distract her.

Under him.

His.

Now it was his turn to plow into her. His greater strength rocked her, and she bent her knees and planted her feet on the ground, clinging to him all the while. Instead of pausing while she repositioned herself, he continued to thrust. His cock completed her, retreated, completed her again.

She couldn't stop moaning, couldn't close her mouth. More sweat joined what was already there, and she closed her arms around him, holding on to him as if he were life itself. Her pussy caught fire.

Another explosion. Sparks flying skyward and shooting through every vein, muscle, and bone. The combustion rolled through her, slipped off into space only to slam into her again. His hot seed flooded her. She smelled his sweat, his cum, heard his sobbing breath.

Then it ended. Slowly.

Groaning, Nakos lifted himself off Jola and settled himself on his side with an arm flung over her breasts. Before long he'd have to go in search of the blanket they'd shared, but for now he was content to have the sleeping pad under them and her beside him.

Judging by her breathing, he surmised she was nearly asleep. If she slipped over to the other side, responsibility for her warmth would rest with him, something he hadn't imagined concerning him when he'd first accepted his assignment. He wanted to let her go into that place where nothing mattered or registered, but if he did, he suspected he'd never tell her what he now wanted—no, needed—to.

Not giving himself time to ponder why, with her, he'd decided to share something he thought he'd always keep to himself, he reluctantly moved his arm from her breast to her shoulder. Marginally less consumed by her than he'd been a moment ago, he watched as her eyes opened.

"I've always lied," he blurted, dragging his attention to the night. Feeling protected by it, he continued. "To everyone."

"About what?"

"My grandparents' deaths." The words had been said. There was no taking them back.

"They weren't killed by invaders? Their hut wasn't burned?"

"It had been torched. Nothing was left." In contrast to how

he felt, his voice was emotionless but maybe that was the only way he'd get through this.

Rolling toward him, she lay small, warm fingers on his upper arm. "But you weren't the first to see what had happened? Was that what you'd lied about? You wanted everyone to believe—"

"That wasn't it."

"Then what—"

"Let me talk." Eyes unfocused, he slipped into the past. "My grandparents had built their hut near the river because the earth there was rich. They grew a great many things on that land and fished year round. Although many considered the location the best Ekew had to offer, it meant they lived some distance from the rest of our people, who'd chosen a higher elevation."

"They were vulnerable."

"Yes. The invaders had come by water in small, well-made boats they carried around rapids. When they saw my grandparents' garden and the deep, quiet pool where generations of fish fed, they must have decided they wanted the place for themselves."

"You weren't there when the invaders arrived? But weren't you a young boy?"

"I was in my tenth summer." His throat threatened to close up, and he couldn't shake off the memory of a too-slender youth with feet and hands better suited on someone much older.

"Ten. Between youth and man."

She already understood more than he thought she would. Maybe she sensed where the telling was taking them. "I wasn't there because I'd wanted to attend spring's celebration. My grandparents insisted they needed my help in preparing the land for planting, but I argued that another two days wouldn't make any difference. By the time I returned . . ."

"It was too late."

It was, but not for the reason he'd told her earlier. "I spotted the smoke before I reached the hut. I kept telling myself that they were burning weeds, but I knew better. Then, when there was no hiding from the truth, I was afraid to go any farther."

Still resting her hand on his arm, she leaned back a little, and he guessed she was trying to study his expression. Hopefully the night would keep its secrets because these might be the hardest words he'd ever spoken. He still didn't understand why tonight, with her, everything was spilling from him.

"Scouts had alerted us that strangers had come to Ekew, but the shaman—Tau's father—said we had nothing to fear from them. Seeing the smoke, I knew he'd been wrong. Horribly wrong."

"Couldn't you have gone back to the village and asked the warriors to come with you?"

With both of them on their sides facing each other, their knees touched. Although they'd recently fucked, her presence so distracted him that he rolled onto his back and stared at the sky. After a moment, she sat up, took his hand, and held it between hers.

"I don't know what you want from me," she said. "Would you rather I say nothing? Wait for you? Or maybe you need me pushing you a little."

How could he have once thought her less intelligent than him? "I need to get this out, but it's hard."

"You've started. That was the hardest part."

Not sure she was right, he nevertheless nodded. Then, staring at the stars, he pushed on. "I wanted to turn around and run back the way I'd come, but before I could take the first step, I heard my grandmother scream."

"Ah—she was still alive?"

"Yes." His tone became flat and emotionless. "They both were. Burned. Badly burned."

Her ragged breath was nearly a twin of the one he'd just taken.

"Somehow they'd gotten outside, but they'd collapsed. They were holding onto each other, my grandmother screaming and my grandfather—he kept making a sound I've never heard from a human throat."

Jola's hold on his hand tightened. Pulling this proof of her strength into him, he continued. Although he plowed through the telling as quickly as possible, he left nothing out. When he saw what had been done to them, he'd tried to get his grandparents to stand so he could help them into the river with its cooling water, but neither had been able to move. They'd begged him not to leave them, but he made a number of trips to the river, filling the family's water bladders each time and dragging them behind him. He'd poured the water over the worst of their burns, beseeching them not to cry out as he did. But they had.

"Then Grandfather ordered me to stop. He grabbed me with what was left of his—and . . ." The old memory of the stench of burned flesh stopped him.

"I'm here, Nakos," Jola muttered as she settled his hand on her soft thigh. "Don't forget, I'm here."

And because you are, I'm saying things I never believed I would. "He—he begged me to end his wife's agony, and then his."

"Nakos? Are you saying—"

"Yes." His eyes became hot coals while ice clogged his veins.

"It was you who killed them, not the enemy."

Much as he needed to thank her for saying what he still wasn't sure he had the strength for, he couldn't because his throat had closed down again.

"Nakos, don't blame yourself."

"They were my life," he managed. "Before—before they

died, I'd been upset at them for expecting me to work instead of sharing in the festival. On my way home I'd realized how selfish I'd been. I was feeling guilty because they had to do my share of the labor, and I had decided to apologize. I never got the chance."

She'd kissed the back of his hand and returned it to her thigh before the gesture registered. "They know."

Thank you for saying that. "I pray they do."

"Believe me, they do. My parents, particularly my mother, tells me that when I become a mother, I'll understand how deep a parent's love is. It must be the same for grandparents. Besides . . ."

"What?"

When she didn't respond, he rolled back toward her. Looking at the night had been easier, yet he needed her gaze on him.

"What were you going to say?" he prompted.

"That—that you did what they couldn't for themselves. You put a swift end to what would have taken a long time."

Yes. "Who was I to decide when they should die, to take the decision in my own hands?"

"Don't do this to yourself!" She started to scramble onto her knees; then, perhaps seeing something he wasn't aware of in his expression or voice, she sank down beside him, resting her head on his chest. "I'm sorry. I didn't mean to try to stop you from talking. You've kept this inside for so long. It's time for the truth to come out. The words, your doubts—those things don't matter as much as leaving nothing behind does. There isn't more, is there?"

He hadn't told her what he'd done to stop his grandparents' hearts from beating, but that would have to wait for another time, if it ever happened. "No," he managed.

"How do you feel?"

His feelings? He almost told her that he'd had years in

which to reconcile himself to what he'd done, but holding the truth to his heart was far different from what had just happened. "I don't know."

"More at peace, maybe?"

She was right, in a way. Even with pain still tearing at his throat and his heart in agony, he experienced a sense of freedom he'd never expected.

"I hope you are," she continued. "Nakos, thank you for trusting me with this. Do you want to say more? Details maybe. I don't know what to ask, or whether to say nothing."

"Say nothing." Night air pressed against his shoulders and legs to remind him of the world beyond the two of them. When he ran his hand over her back, she shivered, and although he wanted to tell himself that his touch was responsible, he couldn't. "It's getting colder."

Rolling away from him, she grabbed the blanket and pulled it over both of them. Having her move against him like that sent erotic messages to his cock, but although it stirred, he didn't try to encourage it. Truth was, he felt more exhausted than he had just after they'd had sex. His mind was drained; his emotions had slipped off into a place he couldn't reach.

Drifting, he again rubbed her back. This time he found no goose bumps, just a long, slow shudder that spoke of an emotion that had nothing to do with the cold. Leaving her to deal with it, he studied one star after another until his lids closed. His breathing lengthened out. A moment later, he heard himself snort. Instead of turning onto his side so, hopefully, he wouldn't snore, he concentrated on one slow breath after another.

Sleep drifted over him. This time no nightmare waited.

21

She didn't love Nakos, nothing like that.

Still, as she watched him get ready for the day, Jola acknowledged an emotion she'd never expected to feel where the Ekewoko were concerned. She still didn't understand why he'd shared his deepest secret with her, but even more important, she hoped he didn't regret it. They'd said nothing when they'd woken up. Instead, they'd rolled away from each other and sat with their backs still to each other. But before that, she'd felt his erection against her belly and acknowledged the soft warmth between her legs. Those responses, she told herself, were primal and primitive. They had nothing to do with what she felt for Nakos or whatever his thoughts about her might be.

As soon as he'd relieved himself, Nakos had joined his friends in rekindling the fire and pulling out strips of dried meat to eat. Assuming they'd share their food with her, she got dressed and walked off by herself so she could urinate. Then she returned and knelt before the fire warming herself.

Farajj had been tying his sleeping mat into a bundle, but

now he stopped and studied her. "What happened to her ropes?" he asked Nakos.

"I took them off her."

"So I see." Farajj exchanged a look with Ohanko. "I told you. The Wilding has been tamed."

"Maybe," Ohanko muttered. He handed her a piece of meat. "Is my friend right?" he asked her. "You've become Nakos's pet?"

Although she wasn't sure what "pet" meant, she sensed it was less than complimentary. "I belong to no one," she replied.

"Maybe. Maybe not. Why aren't you running away?"

"Stop it," Nakos interjected.

"Stop what?" Ohanko asked.

"Whether she stays or leaves is between her and me."

Ohanko and Farajj exchanged another look. "Our orders—" Ohanko started.

"You heard our lord," Farajj broke in. "And Tau. They're determined to learn where the falcons nest and where, maybe, her people live."

"We're here." Nakos pointed at Raptor's Craig. "We can find the trail."

Despite the seriousness of the moment, Jola couldn't stifle a small smile. How little Nakos and the others knew. The Falcons had nothing to fear from three men many hundreds of feet below them. They never would.

"What will it be, Jola?" Nakos asked her. "Do you guide us, or do we find the way on our own?"

She stared up at the man who'd impacted her life in so many ways. A part of her longed to show him what it meant to be Falcon, to be as honest with him as he'd been with her last night. But his revelation about his grandparents had touched just the two of them, while anything she said or did impacted her people's future.

"You came armed," she told him. "I will never expose my people to your weapons."

At first she couldn't read his reaction. Then he shrugged and turned toward his companions. "You heard her," he said.

Farajj grumbled that Tau and Sakima would be less than pleased, but Ohanko only nodded. "Her loyalty for other Wildings is no less than ours is for the Ekewoko," Ohanko said. "Can we expect it to be any different?"

"If he"—Farajj indicated Nakos—"had turned her into a sex slave as our leaders wanted him to, she'd be on her knees before him and eager to do whatever he commands."

Jola scrambled to her feet. "I'm not a beaten animal."

"That's not what I said," Farajj insisted. He planted himself in front of her. "I never called you an animal. But you're female. A slave to your sex."

Sometimes. And only around Nakos.

"If that's what you think of all females," she told him, "then you know nothing."

Farajj looked as if he'd like nothing better than to backhand her, but before he could make a move—if indeed that had been his intention—Nakos grabbed her arm and pulled her behind him. Furious, she stepped around him only to be forced to stop as Nakos extended his arm in front of her. "Enough," he said. "Do what you believe you must, Farajj. Are you going to join Ohanko and me or—"

"I'm with you," Farajj said. "I've always been. I just need to know what's going on inside you."

Wondering what Farajj would think if he knew the man he considered a close friend had spent years keeping something from him, she nevertheless envied the relationship between the three. Long seasons in each other's company and acknowledging that their lives depended on each other had forged close ties. In contrast, all she and Nakos had was mutual physical need. She loved Falcon Land while he considered it worthless.

As the men set about arming themselves, another thought struck her. Since waking to find Nakos's bonds on her and lake water coating her body the other day, her mind had only briefly and occasionally turned to her family. Granted, as an adult, she no longer lived with her parents and didn't see them every day. But since Raci's death, she'd felt the need for their company. In Falcon form, she'd flown to the outcropping where they lived almost every day, and if she didn't make the short trip, one or both of her parents would fly to the nest she'd set up with Raci.

Undoubtedly they'd been looking for her. When whichever Falcon had been keeping an eye on her told the others what he or she had seen, they would have gathered as many Falcons as possible around them and maybe tried to plan her rescue. Whatever their decision, she'd be surprised if keen predator eyes weren't on her and the men right now.

As for why the Falcons hadn't attacked Nakos before now, the answer lay in what it meant to be a Falcon. Although they all shared a common bond, Falcons were by nature solitary creatures. They came together to mate, breed, and raise their young, but Falcons hunted alone. Flew alone. Not only that, never before had their existence been threatened. Even if the Falcons understood the danger, they might not know how to respond.

She tried to study the sky without drawing attention to what she was doing, but between the bright morning sun and her weaker human eyes, she couldn't make out a single dark speck in the heavens. However, thinking about how much more she could see when in raptor form filled her with sharp longing. She'd never occupied her human body this long before meeting Nakos and needed the swoop and sway of freedom, the reckless dive through hundreds of feet of air. Needed freedom.

Forcing her thoughts off what made her want to cry out, she focused on Nakos and his friends. Yes, his form was still familiar to her, but he stood across the campfire from her, dressed in the trappings that proclaimed him as Ekewoko. He was here because he and the others believed they could claim Falcon Land and rob the Falcons of their future. He was wrong, of course; none of them had that right!

She wanted him gone.

"What are you staring at?" Nakos asked, startling her.

She met his gaze. "I'm trying to understand what makes you so arrogant."

"Arrogant?"

"You and your companions, you're all strangers to this land. Just because you've been forced to leave Ekew, that gives you no right to claim mine."

"Yours?" Walking around the campfire, he stopped a few feet away. She should have prepared herself for his impact, but maybe that would never be possible. "Why is this"—he pointed up at Raptor's Craig—"any more yours than mine? If the birds Tau is after are up there, what do you care?"

Steeling herself against his body's draw, she stood her ground. "Your shaman is wrong. He has no right to—do you agree with him? Falcons are necessary if you're ever going to go home?"

"We have to try something."

"Nakos?"

Recognizing Ohanko's voice, she reluctantly acknowledged the other warrior who'd joined them.

"What?" Nakos asked.

"We're ready."

"I know." Turning back toward her, Nakos brushed his fingers over her forearm. At the touch, she jumped. It took all her strength not to touch him in return. "You're not coming with us, are you?"

She shook her head.

"What if I forced you?"

"You won't."

* * *

She was still where Nakos had left her that morning when he and his companions returned. In her own way, she'd already told him good-bye and could have slipped off to a secluded place where she could become Falcon, but she'd wanted to know if they'd come to the only conclusion they could. Not only that, if they told her what they'd found, or rather what they hadn't found, she might be able to tell her kind that they were truly safe. As for how Nakos would deal with his discovery—no. That wasn't her concern.

"You knew, didn't you?" Nakos said as he drew close.

"Yes."

"But you didn't say anything. Why not?"

"Would you have believed me?"

His eyes were weary, his expression sober. At the same time, a spark flamed inside him, prompting her to wonder if it was a flame she'd ignited. Maybe, even if they never saw each other again, they'd always feed off that unique heat. Her body hummed the way the earth sometimes did when a thunderstorm was approaching, and she didn't dare get any closer to him. Neither did she risk a downward glance.

"No," he said. It took her a moment to recall what she'd asked him. "I wouldn't have believed you. I had to see it for myself."

"Tau is wrong." Farajj's voice was heavy with disbelief. "The Ekewoko can never reach where falcons nest."

A glance in Farajj's direction left her feeling sorry for the young man. He'd always believed his shaman. His entire life revolved around Tau's visions, dreams, and *wisdom*. It was Tau who'd helped Lord Sakima decide where the Ekewoko would go and what they needed to do after invaders forced them from their home, but now Farajj and certainly Ohanko and soon everyone else would question Tau's guidance.

What would that leave them with?

"We looked everywhere." After dropping to his knees, Ohanko sat cross-legged on the ground. He stared at the bits of ash that were all that remained of the morning's fire. "There's no trail up, not the smallest path. Nothing but sheer rock."

Which was why Falcons had chosen Raptor's Craig to raise their young.

"What are you going to do?" She wasn't sure whom she was asking her question. "Will you return to—"

"To camp, yes. We have no choice," Nakos said wearily. He was looking at her, yet she doubted that he actually saw her. Maybe his eyes had been just as unfocused last night when he'd told her about his grandparents. A wave of sympathy threatened to swamp her. "Our warriors are waiting for us."

"And once you've told them everything?"

Nakos glanced at his companions, then shook his head. "I want to say that Tau will find a new direction to guide us, but I don't know."

"All Tau's visions and dreams," Ohanko interjected. "How could they have been so wrong?"

Strangely, she wanted to offer an explanation, but what would it be?

"A dark spirit maybe," Farajj offered. "If one has stolen Tau's soul—"

"Then maybe the Ekewoko are doomed," Nakos said.

Doomed? With no future? Knowing Raci's life was over had devastated her, but the rest of her world had remained the same. But what if everything she'd always believed turned out to be a lie and she couldn't even return to the land of her birth?

Hurting, not just for Nakos but all Ekewoko, she searched her mind for something to say, but no words filled her throat. Even offering her body to Nakos wouldn't shelter him from reality.

"I should not have said that," Nakos said. "I won't accept that we're doomed. I can't. As long as strength remains in him, a warrior doesn't surrender."

"I agree," Ohanko said after a too-long silence. "But what are we fighting? Not the Outsiders; they aren't here."

Studying the men's somber expressions, she guessed that the argument, if that's what it was, wouldn't go on much longer because no words could erase the reality of what they'd discovered about Raptor's Craig. One thing she'd learned while watching them: they were barely aware of her presence. She should, could leave. Now, before the walking away became even harder than it was.

"Tell Tau what you found," she suggested. "The rest is up to him and Sakima, not you."

Nakos stared at her from under thick lashes. The silence between them stretched out and became heavy. Then a mist slid into place, blocking him off from her. Much as she ached to tear it apart, she was grateful for it. Turning toward the wilderness, she took her first step. Her legs trembled, forcing her to fill her lungs before going on. Her feet thudded dully on the packed ground, and her arms hummed in anticipation of becoming wings.

"Listen," Ohanko said, the unexpected word spinning her back around. "Something's coming."

22

From what she could tell, the entire Ekewoko warrior camp had followed them to Raptor's Craig. Even the slave Lamuka was there. Other than exchanging puzzled looks, Nakos and his friends hadn't said anything as the group approached. Tau and Lord Sakima walked slightly ahead of the others, each man wearing bright capes she assumed signified the importance of today's events. Every warrior was armed.

Studying their somber expressions, she wondered if she should have run the moment she'd heard them, but if she had, what would she have been able to tell the Falcons? Much as she wanted to take strength and courage from Nakos's presence, she refused to get closer to him. For his part, he acted as if she didn't exist.

"My lord," Nakos said when the newcomers were close enough that he could speak without raising his voice. "We didn't expect you."

"When you left, I didn't know we'd be doing this," Lord Sakima explained as the others gathered around. "But a decision has been made." He looked pointedly at Tau, who was glaring at her.

Instead of immediately speaking as Sakima obviously expected him to, Tau came to within a few feet of her. He folded his arms over his chest and stood as tall as he could, but she refused to shrink back from him. "I was right," he announced. "She *has* cast a spell over him." He pointed at Nakos.

If there were any spells, Nakos was the one who'd spun one over her, not the other way around. With an effort, she managed not to look at the man who'd changed what she'd always believed about humans.

Tau cleared his throat. "What further proof do we need? A true warrior would have already obeyed his lord. He would be up there." He jabbed a long, bony finger at the top of Raptor's Craig. "Instead this *warrior* who has surrendered his manhood to a Wilding is with *her*."

"It isn't—" Ohanko started. Then his voice trailed off.

"What?" Tau insisted. "Has she poisoned your mind as well, taken you into her body and made you equally weak?"

"Is that why you're here?" Nakos demanded. "To accuse her of—"

"Accuse?" Tau interrupted. "*You* are proof. You shouldn't be here. You should be—"

"How?"

At Nakos's question, Tau's mouth sagged, and he blinked repeatedly. "How? What do you mean?"

"What are you saying?" Sakima demanded before Nakos could respond.

"That I have no choice but to ask my shaman something." Nakos's tone was measured. "He expects us to have already reached the top of that peak, maybe have gathered up every falcon egg we found, but how is that possible when there's no trail?"

"No—trail?"

The others, who'd remained at a respectful distance from their lord and shaman, now pressed close. Male gazes darted from one figure to another, with most staring at either Jola or Nakos. Feeding off the tension, she recalled a winter afternoon last year when the sky had filled with black angry clouds and thunder rolled. Any moment now the first lightning bolt might strike.

And when that happened—

"I have to ask this," Nakos said to Tau, his voice loud in contrast to the silence. "I have no choice. Your visions convinced you that we would regain Ekew once we'd turned falcons into our personal war weapons. Instead of allowing the Outsiders to keep us from Ekew, we would return with our new allies flying beside us. Those allies would chase the Outsiders from the land of our ancestors, killing anyone who resisted. But how is that possible if there's no way to reach the nests?"

Jola couldn't say what was happening to Tau. The shaman seemed to be shrinking and expanding at the same time, his features darkening while his gaze darted here and there. She'd heard of shamen who went into trances and wondered if that was what she was seeing.

"This is not possible!" Tau's voice echoed off the nearby rock. "You haven't—instead of fulfilling your mission, you let her, a witch, capture your body and soul."

"There was no spell," Nakos retorted. "She's a woman, only a woman."

"Ha!" Spinning away from Nakos, Tau planted himself in front of her. The shaman wasn't much taller than her, but the years and his position within the tribe had given him a powerful presence. Even she felt his confidence, his arrogance.

"Only a woman?" Tau continued. "Then why didn't she

drown that first day? How did she recover so quickly after you'd paralyzed her?" His eyes widened, then narrowed. What little she could see of his pupils chilled her.

"I don't know," Nakos answered. "All I can speak to is the truth. No human can climb that damnable craig."

"What have you done, witch?" Tau took another step toward her, forcing her to curl her toes against the ground to keep from backing away. "I know what my visions revealed. How can you, a simple creature, steal what was there?"

Tau's refusal to believe Nakos so angered her that her fingers burned. Perhaps another word from Tau and she'd bury her nails—or even better, her claws—in his throat. "Maybe I'm not as simple as you want to believe," she taunted. "A witch, you say. Perhaps."

Fury contorted the shaman's features. "Grab her! Bind her."

A glance assured her that no one had moved, but these warriors were accustomed to obeying their shaman. "Do it yourself." The moment she'd spoken, she wondered if she'd made a mistake by challenging Tau.

"You are nothing, nothing! A witch perhaps, but one whose so-called powers will shatter before mine."

"Tau," Lord Sakima said warningly. "Today isn't about her. You told us—"

"That we have one destiny, and it is up there." Tau pointed to where Jola had once believed she'd be raising her and Raci's offspring. "Nothing has changed. As soon as I've removed the threat she represents, our destiny will be fulfilled."

Because she'd been focusing on what the shaman was saying, she'd been slow to realize he'd unfastened his cape and was drawing it off his shoulders. The moment he exposed his chest, her heart began pounding. Around his neck he wore a simple necklace made from a narrow leather cord. The cord held a single feather.

"What?" Tau demanded when her gaze riveted on the long, narrow, bluish black feather distinguished by thin black bars.

"You!" she managed. "You killed him?"

"Him?" Nakos echoed. "Jola, what are you talking about?"

Until this moment, every time she heard Nakos's voice, her body had responded. Now, however, she had room for only one emotion. One thought. "Where did you get that feather?" She spat out each word.

"This?" Tau held it up as if taunting her with it. "From a falcon carcass after I'd shot it."

Not long ago something had reminded her of a fierce winter storm about to explode. Now, staring at what she had no doubt had been Raci's tail feather, the storm raged around her. "Why?"

"Why did I take—"

"No! Why did you send an arrow through him?"

"Him? The bird was on the ground, feeding. I knew I'd never be able to kill the predator while it was in the air." Tau's expression had been tentative, even guilty maybe. Now, holding up the feather as if it represented an honor, his features hardened. "This is proof of my power, of how much the spirits favor me. Only a great shaman could send an arrow into such a creature's heart. Other falcons will see what I have done and bow before me."

She couldn't listen to him, couldn't! Not with her body now shaking as if in a blizzard's grip. Maybe she should be relieved knowing Nakos hadn't killed Raci, but in some ways this was worse. Realizing that Tau had ripped the feather from Raci's still-warm body sickened her.

"You're surprised?" Tau went on. "Ah, I understand you believed I have no more power than you do, but now you know how wrong you were."

She opened her mouth.

"See what I've done, Wilding!" Tau held the feather even higher. "Look at this proof of my greatness. My spirit-given skill stopped the earth's swiftest creature. You have one choice, slave. Either you show us the way to where falcons nest, or my arrows will find more predator hearts."

His words no longer made sense. Oh yes, she understood that he was trying to goad her into saying or doing something reckless, but it didn't matter. Only this horrid reminder of how Raci's life ended did—that and understanding that nothing would stop Tau.

A blip of awareness alerted her that Nakos was coming closer, his arms extended, perhaps in preparation for imprisoning her. Not long ago she would have relished the surrender of body and mind to him, but he'd become a stranger.

As much of one as the others who called themselves Ekewoko.

Her gaze remained riveted on Raci's feather. Just the same, she couldn't stop her lungs from drawing in air that Tau had soiled. Nakos's ropes and strength had never trapped her as she was now.

Only one thing would assure freedom.

And revenge.

Mostly revenge!

A high, thin cry escaped her throat. Recognizing it as a Falcon's alarm, she sank into the sound. As she did, her muscles, bones, and veins began to contract and change. She drew in upon herself, arms and legs morphing into something else as she did. Wings replaced useless human limbs, and her vision became keen. Most of all, she stopped thinking as a human does.

Shouts and cries from male throats briefly penetrated her consciousness. Then a sudden wind surrounded and lifted her. Wings widespread to embrace the strong current, she headed skyward. Climbing rapidly, she split her attention between the few clouds above her and the men staring up at her. At first she believed she only wanted to be free, but as she began circling high over the Ekewoko, a human thought tore through her.

A man who believed he was his people's spiritual leader had murdered her mate and stolen a feather from his maybe still-living body.

Screaming, she tucked her wings tight against her body. She couldn't bring Raci back to life, but she could make his killer pay. Punish him.

Another scream, and she dove. At the last possible moment, she pulled up and spun so her talons slashed Tau's chest. Blood bloomed from several gashes. Bellowing, the shaman dropped to the ground and curled into a tight ball. Hovering, she tore at his back. Again her talons sank into flesh. She hung on, dug deeper, screamed. So did Tau.

"No! Jola, no!"

Not Tau but another man's voice.

"Jola, don't! No!"

Nakos!

Now suspended over the shaman's quivering body, she focused first on shredded and bleeding skin and then on her surroundings. Except for Nakos, the men had all backed away from Tau, who sobbed and shuddered. Although the warriors gripped their weapons, they seemed frozen, their eyes disbelieving.

Nakos alone stood next to his shaman, his arms outspread in an attempt to protect Tau. He stared unblinking at her.

"Don't. By all that's sacred, don't!"

As a boy, Nakos had risked his sanity by obeying his grandparents' desperate pleas. What would he do now, offer his body to save his shaman?

A lonely cry slipped past her beak. Facing the heavens again, she flew away.

23

—————

"What are we going to do?" Lord Sakima asked.

Incapable of uttering a word, Nakos shook his head. Then, because he needed something to do, he lifted the bandage off Tau's back and reassured himself that the bone-deep gouges had stopped bleeding. The shaman lay trembling on his side with his legs tucked against his middle. He still stared at nothing and, except for crying out as the others had tended to his wounds, he hadn't uttered a sound. In too many ways, Tau's behavior reminded Nakos of how he'd reacted after he'd granted his grandparents their awful request. Tau had shut down.

"What happened couldn't have and yet it did," Sakima said not for the first time. "She's more than a witch, more than . . ."

Because he couldn't explain what had happened any better than his lord had, Nakos made no attempt to finish what the older man had begun. Even with his eyes resolutely open, he clearly saw everything that had happened starting with Jola turning into a falcon.

A falcon! A killing predator.

Why, he needed to know, hadn't she changed form earlier? She hadn't had to endure his treatment of her after all. Instead, she could have killed him.

"We can't stay here," Sakima muttered.

Although the others were crowded around them, Nakos wasn't sure everyone had heard, but maybe it wasn't necessary because surely they'd all come to the same conclusion. Whenever he looked at the peak's sheer walls, he shuddered and, although maybe he'd saved Tau's life, he'd been unable to convince himself that Jola—or the falcon she'd become—wouldn't return to finish what she'd begun.

She hated Tau. It was as simple as that.

But she didn't hate him. Otherwise, he'd be dead. That, too, was simple. And unbelievably complex.

"Can he be moved?" someone asked. "Even if he can't walk, we can carry him."

Where would they go, Nakos wondered. Yes, it wouldn't take long to return to their camp, but what about after that? Only one option presented itself. The Ekewoko warriors would make their way to the sea, where they'd rejoin the rest of their clan, all of them refugees, homeless.

Everything Tau had told them about their future had slipped away like ice with the sun beating down on it. Instead of being able to cling to the dream of returning to Ekew, the Ekewoko belonged nowhere.

"He isn't going to die," Sakima belatedly replied. "And even if he did, none of us wants to remain here. If we leave now, we'll be back in camp by dark. Our people—it's time we return to them."

"And then?"

Locking gazes with Ohanko, Nakos silently acknowledged his friend's courage in asking the hard question.

"I don't know." Lord Sakima sounded like a weary old man. When Sakima crouched before Tau, Ohanko nodded at

Nakos, indicating he wanted him to join him. The two walked away from the others.

"Of course we'll go to where we left the women and children," Ohanko said when they were out of earshot of the others. "Then we'll tell them that that place must become our new home."

"No one wants to hear—"

"I know. By the spirits, I know! But what choice do we have?"

"None," Nakos reluctantly admitted. His lord had looked and sounded ancient, but Sakima wasn't the only one weighed down by their new reality. Nakos hadn't felt this beaten since his grandparents' death.

"Something frightens me," Ohanko continued. "What if *she* gathers the other Wildings around her? If they attack . . ."

"Attack?" Nakos muttered.

"You saw her fury." Ohanko shuddered. "If it wasn't for you, she would have killed our shaman."

Ohanko didn't have to say anything more for Nakos to know what his friend was thinking. "I still can't believe what I saw," he admitted. "For her to be two things, human and predator—"

"She can't be the only one, can she?"

Although he didn't have the answer, Nakos suspected Ohanko was right. After all, Jola had told him about the first *man* to have sex with her.

"Will she and others of her kind let us go?" Ohanko asked. "Or will they tear us apart? Even now they might be gathering—"

"Yes, they might."

The rest of the Ekewoko had undoubtedly come to the same conclusion Ohanko had because by the time Nakos returned to his people, someone had placed Tau on Farajj's back. The other

Ekewoko warriors had positioned themselves around Farajj and, with Lord Sakima at the lead, were all leaving.

Spotting Nakos, Lord Sakima stopped. "This place isn't safe," he said.

"I know," Nakos agreed.

"The mysteries here—ha, Wilding spirits are far more powerful than anything our shaman has. I pray Tau will survive, and that his magic will show us what we must do."

Lord Sakima's expression said he needed Nakos to agree with him about a shaman's magic, but how could he when nothing like what he'd recently seen had ever happened? Jola, a woman who'd impacted him in ways he'd never expected, was capable not just of changing into a falcon, but nearly killing an Ekewoko.

"What are you going to do?" Ohanko asked Nakos as Lord Sakima started walking again.

"What I have to, to insure that there won't be another falcon attack."

His features grim, Ohanko hugged Nakos. "You think that's possible?"

"I have to try."

Ohanko shook his head, then nodded. "You're right. Only you stand a chance of reaching her."

"If she's in human form. But if she's a falcon . . ."

"I will pray for you. So will everyone else."

Although she'd been at the top of Raptor's Craig and in human form for hours, Jola's muscles were still energized. After gathering the Falcons around her, she'd told everyone what had happened, starting with the Ekewoko's discovery that no human could climb Raptor's Craig. Chief Cheyah had pressed for details about the damage she'd inflicted on the shaman, but she'd kept her explanation brief. No one had argued that she shouldn't have attacked Tau; everyone understood why rage and grief had turned her from human to predator.

"Maybe peace will now fill your heart," her chief had said. "From now on, you'll look forward, not back. Raci's death has been avenged."

Grateful for her chief's understanding, she'd nevertheless expressed concern that the Ekewoko might not feel the same way. Agreeing it was possible, Cheyah had ordered his oldest son, Dai, to locate the Ekewoko and report back on what he found, which he'd done a short while ago.

He'd learned nothing that concerned her, Jola reassured herself as she sat by herself watching the sun begin its downward journey. According to Dai, the Ekewoko had shown no sign of planning an attack. Instead, they were hurrying back the way they'd come from, taking their wounded shaman with them.

"I meant it. I believe we have nothing to fear from the strangers. In fact, they reminded me of mice or rabbits scurrying for cover."

Pulled out of her thoughts by Dai's unexpected voice, she looked up at her fellow Falcon. Dai, who was next in line to become chief, sat down across from her. "I didn't say this before because only you need to know."

"Know what?"

"That one Ekewoko remained behind."

Her full attention on Dai now, she waited for him to continue. Dai, who was several seasons older than her, had lost his mate to a wasting disease, but before her death they'd raised one brood, and those children had given Dai a reason to go on. After Raci's murder, she and Dai had talked about how vital the love of those around them was in the face of grief. Some, her mother among them, had wondered if she and Dai might mate, but with Raci's death so new and raw, she hadn't been able to concentrate.

"You saw me watching over you after he captured you, didn't you?" Dai asked before she could respond.

"That was you?"

Dai, who in human form had little hair and big feet and buttocks like his father, nodded. "If I'd believed your life was in danger, I would have done what you did to Raci's killer."

"Knowing I wasn't completely alone helped."

Dai was silent for several seconds. "I wasn't there all the time, but enough that I saw what took place between you and your captor."

Remembering her and Nakos's frenzied sex, she lowered her gaze. "Ah, you said not every Ekewoko left."

"Yes." Dai drew out the word. "*He* remained behind. What, if anything, are you going to do?"

A million possibilities swirled through her. Most of all, she wished Dai hadn't told her what he had. Then, her emotions shifting, she wished Nakos had left with the others because the last thing she wanted was to see him again, to hear his voice or look into his eyes, to remember his skillful handling of her body and her wild responses.

"What are you going to do?" Dai repeated.

On the brink of shrugging, she took note of her hands. Her short, smooth nails showed no sign of having penetrated human flesh and striking bone, but she clearly remembered her frenzy as she'd avenged Raci's death. These slender female hands also served as claws. They had two roles, two purposes.

Standing, she walked over to the edge of the craig. When she lifted her arms, a sharp wind tossed her hair into her eyes, but it didn't matter because in a moment, she'd change.

It had to be her.

One arm lifted to shield his eyes, Nakos studied the small shape circling high overhead. Even as his heart raced and his throat threatened to close down, he admitted he'd never seen anything more beautiful.

Beautiful and deadly.

His fingers twitched. If she maintained the same measured pace, he could aim an arrow at her before she reached him, but not only could the lazy float turn into a breath-stealing dive in a heartbeat, he couldn't shoot. Not her.

His arm still lifted, he widened his stance. She was little more than a speck, a piece of nothing in a pristine sky. Maybe the wind toying with him didn't reach that high. Otherwise, wouldn't she be tossed about?

Questions about the nature of things at Screaming Wind flowed out of him because, against all odds, he'd hoped this would happen, that the two of them could talk once more—but what if she refused to shake off her predator body?

What if she hadn't satisfied her need for revenge?

This ability to change from one thing to another was a gift from forces the Ekewoko knew nothing about. How ignorant he and the rest of his people had been to think they had a right to come here.

But Tau's dreams and spells—

She was now so close that he could make out her beak and the claws pulled up against her body. Those same claws had nearly killed his shaman and might do the same to him.

His lips pressed together, he watched as she settled to the ground a few feet away. In contrast to a falcon's deadly dive, her slow landing had been magical, but maybe he only thought that because the woman living inside the predator body had captured his soul.

After shaking herself so her feathers shimmered, she folded her wings. She was small and deceptively fragile looking. If he was quick enough, he might be able to strike her before she could react. Protect himself.

Then she shimmered again, and nothing else mattered.

There Jola was, inch by naked inch. Watching her emerge from the sudden mist that had been a predator numbed his legs while lifting his cock. He should have guessed she'd be nude, should have prepared himself for lean arms and legs and full breasts. Instead, gaping, he stared at what was both familiar and new.

Her dark hair floated over her cheeks and against her throat. Staring at her neck, he cursed himself for having placed a rope around it. Then he turned his attention to her hands and memories of those slender wrists hidden beneath loops of rope filled him with self-hatred.

But if he hadn't restrained her, would her fingers have become claws?

"What are you doing here?" he asked, belatedly finding his voice.

"I wanted to ask you the same thing."

She seemed to have disconnected herself from her body. It was as if her physical form didn't matter. He, on the other hand, had all he could do to keep from cradling his too-heavy cock.

Damn her! She was responsible!

"What am I doing here?" he finally responded. "Maybe because I believe I deserve an explanation."

"You what?"

Realizing she wasn't as in control as he'd initially believed allowed him to relax a bit. She wasn't going to kill him, because if that had been her goal, she would have already torn him apart.

"An explanation," he said. "Why didn't you show me what you're capable of at the beginning? You didn't have to submit—only, it wasn't submission, was it? You wanted sex as much as I did. Maybe more."

Her eyes seemed to be narrowing. If she started changing again—

"That's it," he threw at her. "For reasons I don't understand, you wanted me. My body anyway. Maybe you were going to prove how superior your kind—"

"We're Falcons."

Falcons. Of course. "All right. Your intent was to beat me down. Make me believe I was in control when all along it was the other way. What was it, you were going to throw my supposed superiority in my face? Then you'd return to your—to the Falcons and tell them what fools Ekewoko are?"

"I wouldn't do that."

"Why should I believe you?"

"You're right. You shouldn't." She ran her hands down her sides, then folded them over her belly as if she didn't know what to do with them. "Do you know why I did what I did?"

"Change into a Falcon, you mean?"

Looking weary, she shook her head. "I had no control over that. It happened, it simply happened. As for why I remained a woman until today, near Raptor's Craig is the only place Falcons can leave one body and enter another."

"Why should I believe you?" Even as he spoke, he regretted his outburst. But his emotions were wild things, maybe as wild as she was. "I should thank the spirits that you didn't rip me to shreds."

"Maybe you should."

"If I'd known what you were capable of, none of this would have happened. From the beginning, I would have known how wrong Tau was to believe he could control—"

"Would you have told him?"

The conversation was making his head pound when he had all he could do to control the knots in his belly and between his legs. "I don't know."

"Is he going to live?"

"Do you care?"

"He killed my mate," she whispered. "When I saw the feather on his chest, I knew."

"You nearly killed him."

"There was no decision behind what I did," she continued in that same barely audible voice. "The part of me that lives to kill took over." She pressed a hand to her forehead, then wrapped her arms around her middle.

"You didn't deliberately—"

"I knew only rage."

Because he'd witnessed Tau's mauling, he understood how deep her fury had been, yet that stood at odds with the dark confusion now in her eyes.

"Unless infection takes hold of him, Tau will live," he told her. "But he'll be changed."

"The scars—"

"Not just that. His visions turned out to be nothing. Everything he said about how the spirits wanted us to use falcons to force the Outsiders to leave Ekew—maybe there never were any visions. Maybe he only said what he believed we wanted to hear."

"I don't know."

"Things will change for my people," he muttered. "So many things."

"Where will you live?"

24

The wind at the top of Raptor's Craig had been so strong she'd had to fight it, but down here she barely noted it. But then she had other things to concern herself with.

Most important was hearing Nakos's answer.

Waiting for him to break the silence, she acknowledged the courage it had taken for him to stay behind. After all, if she'd seen her shaman all but destroyed by a raging predator, she probably would have fled, herself.

"Don't you know?" she asked when she concluded that Nakos wasn't going to answer her question about where he and the rest of the Ekewoko would go.

He glanced down at his hands. "We can't return to Ekew."

"Because the Outsiders—"

"Even if we set up our tents on some remote part of Ekew, they'll destroy them."

Burn them, he meant. Burn them with innocent men, women, and maybe children inside. "Then you'll go somewhere else? Find new land—maybe settle where you and the other warriors left the rest of your people?"

"Near the sea?" He shook his head. "There isn't enough open land. Trees and steep hillsides grow up to the shore. Besides, what do you care?"

"I do," she said, but so low she wasn't sure he'd heard.

She'd flown down here to try and explain the powerful emotions that had led to her attack on Tau, but now that didn't seem to matter. In truth, she couldn't think of anything to say. Maybe the only thing she could do was turn back into a Falcon and leave.

"I envy you," he said. "What's it like to have no cares beyond filling your belly?"

Her belly needed not food but his hand on it. Just thinking about his fingers on them made her breasts ache. And if he slid his hands between her legs in that knowing way of his—

"You're right. You should envy me and the rest of the Falcons. I'll never know . . ."

"You'll never know what?"

She'd nearly blurted that as a Falcon she'd be spared the kind of pain he'd endured and the decision he'd made when his grandparents' house had been set on fire, but neither of them needed to hear those words.

"Nothing. Nakos, I became a woman today so you might understand why I attacked Tau."

"Because you're a killer. It's in your nature, your blood."

No!

"Is that why you ended your grandparents' lives?" she shot at him. "Because, as a warrior, that ability was in your blood?"

His face went pale, and his fingers knotted. At the same time, his head snapped back as if she'd struck him.

"I'm sorry." Barely aware of what she was doing, she stepped toward him. "I didn't mean—by the spirits, I'm sorry."

His arm snaked out. Grabbing her wrist, he yanked her against him. "Don't."

"I said I was sorry." Her breasts, flattened against his body, heated. "I shouldn't have, Nakos, I'd never—"

Before she could finish, he'd pushed her away but continued to hold on to her wrist. An odd quieting along with a familiar excitement slid into her. Was it possible she'd missed his rough handling?

"I wanted to talk to you again," he said. "That's why I stayed behind. Now I wish I hadn't—no, that isn't right. I'd regret it for the rest of my life if I didn't try to see you one more time."

One more time. "I felt the same way. Nakos, I won't ask you to forgive me for attacking your shaman because you're right, it's part of my nature."

"An extremely complex nature."

"Not to me, it isn't," she said as something hot flowed from him to envelope her. Earlier today she'd been filled with a savage fury that blocked out every other sensation. Now much the same thing was happening—only instead of fury, need claimed her.

His hold on her wrist let up a little. "I've always thought of myself as a warrior. Knowing I was a valuable Ekewoko helped me forgive myself for what I did all those years ago. But I'll never come close to what you are: a creature designed to kill."

"I'm more than that." She wanted to continue, yet she didn't. Words built upon words could never say everything or change his mind. Weary of trying, she lowered her gaze and stared at her hand in his.

"Can you break free of what the spirits dictate?" he asked.

"As a woman, no."

"But if you became a Falcon—"

"I don't want to. Not now."

He tugged on her arm, and she stepped toward him again. Her heart rate kicked up. When they were so close that his features blurred, she placed her free hand on his shoulder. "Let me go."

He did after a moment, his arms dropping to his sides but his gaze not leaving her. The wind riffled across her back. Resting the hand he'd been holding on his other shoulder, she leaned into him. Her breasts again caressed his flesh, and her already hard nipples throbbed.

"Do you know what you're doing?" he asked, his body tense and unmoving.

"I'm asking you to see me as a woman."

"A woman."

The simple words vibrated through her as he cupped her buttocks and pulled her against him. Sliding her arms up so they circled his neck, she rubbed his collarbone with the side of her face. He'd become precious to her, part of the air she breathed, the reason her pussy flowed.

Now it was his turn to slide his hands over her, working slowly from her ass cheeks to the small of her back, then up her spine as she whimpered and nibbled on his collarbone. Arching her spine, she tried to read his expression, but they were too close, and she couldn't begin to think how to put distance between them.

"Naked," he breathed. "You came to me naked."

"Yes."

"Why?"

"Because this is who I am." Blushing, she ducked her head. As she did, her chin struck his chest, causing her to bite her tongue. Eyes burning, she breathed deeply until the pain receded.

But even if she couldn't get her body to work as it should, she knew it belonged against his. Granted, the contact might not last, but she'd take everything she could into her.

Because of him, she was looking at her world and life in

ways she never would have otherwise. She owed him her gratitude.

And her body.

A burning sensation along the back of her calves prompted
her settle onto her heels. As she did, she ran her tongue over his
chest, leaving damp warmth behind.

"You're seducing me," he muttered.

"Am I?"

"You know you are."

"Because I'm a woman?"

"Is that what this is about?" Cupping her upper arms, he
pushed her back a little. "You want me to never forget that part
of your nature?"

"Yes."

"Don't worry. I won't. I can't." He reinforced his words by
thrusting himself at her so his cock ground into her belly.

Reaching between them, she fumbled with the tie to his
loincloth. Freeing it, she leaned away long enough to tug the
garment down around his knees. Then, surrendering, she once
more closed in on him. He held her hard against him for a long
time while her head swam and hot pinpricks of sensation
chased over her. His cock again prodded her belly.

"Wait," he muttered just as she rose onto her toes. "Let
me . . ."

Hating every moment of the separation, she nonetheless
stepped back so he could kick out of his loincloth. He stumbled
a little, causing her to chuckle. So she wasn't the only awkward
one.

Before she knew what he had in mind, he'd wrapped an arm
around her back and turned her slightly to the side so her left
shoulder kissed his chest. Masculine fingers circled a breast repeatedly while she reached for his cock, touching only to draw
back. When he left off her breast and began a slow, hot journey
down her ribs and from there to her waist, strength flowed out

of her, leaving her gasping. Her gasps turned to pants the moment his fingers slipped into her pubic hair.

"You want this, Falcon woman?"

"You know . . ."

"Yes, I do."

Sunlight melted the snow that sometimes covered the ground all winter at Falcon Land. She was like snow, slipping away and becoming nothing. At the same time, she fed off the warmth that was Nakos. Determined to share what she was experiencing with him, she ran her hand under his cock and closed her fingers over it. Her fingertips were numb; her wrist ached. She couldn't think what else to do.

He turned her some more so his larger arm fit into the space he'd created between them. Even before he ran his hand between her legs, she'd widened her stance, welcoming him in. Yes, he'd touched her here before, tested her readiness, taken her moisture, and slipped his fingers into her, but it was all new. All overwhelming!

She jumped, shivered, knees threatening to buckle. In her attempt to keep her feet under her, she released his cock and gripped his shoulders with both hands. Still he kept after her, dipping into the secret welcoming place.

"Ah!" she groaned. "Ah."

"You're so wet. Drenched and hot."

A woman. I am a woman.

As much as she loved revealing what made her heart beat, the predator blood running through her demanded to be in control so she again went in search of his cock. She cupped and cradled it, their arms rubbing together as they claimed each other's sex.

"You're killing me, Jola."

"No. I'd never—"

"Not that way. But I want you so damn bad."

Holding him with one hand, clinging to his shoulder with

the other, she stood on her toes. She was swimming, churning, being thrown about and wanting to take him on the same journey. Something clawed its way up her throat to press against her clenched teeth. She barely heard her thin cry.

"By all that's holy!" Nakos exclaimed. "If you're going to—"

Not change. No, not that!

Tears flowed. Thinking to wipe them away, she pressed her face into his chest. She blinked, blinked again.

What was that? His hand no longer between her legs but sliding along the back of her thigh, lifting and bending her knee at the same time. She now stood on one leg. He drew her toward him, close, closer yet. A sudden spark of clarity and she understood what he had in mind. His cock slid along her mons, glided over hot flesh. By thrusting her pelvis at him, she offered her pussy to him. His tip kissed her opening.

Then he was in her, going deep and strong, stretching and filling her. Her cheeks became flushed. She couldn't breathe.

Ah yes, Nakos driving himself ever deeper inside her body. Pulling back again only to plow her once more. She hung on to him, trusting him to keep her erect, one leg dangling uselessly, the other hard and strained.

In he ran, deep and full, sliding out a little only to ram anew while she hissed and cried. His cock caressed everywhere, laid claim to each inch of her, blew both her mind and body apart.

"Yes, yes! By the spirits, Nakos, yes!"

Sweat still clung to Nakos, but with the sun soon setting, before long he'd get chilled. Looking down at Jola's naked body from under heavy eyelids, he wondered if she was equally vulnerable. She might need his arms around her to keep her warm. Of course, she could always change form.

"I'm not going to stay." He had to work at getting the words past his throat. "My companions—they'll worry if I don't catch up to them."

"Is there any chance they'd return ready for battle?"

Now that both of her feet were planted on the ground and she and Nakos no longer clung to each other as if they were starving, she seemed smaller, frail even, when he knew she was anything but. His fingers ached with the need to stroke her hair so he tucked his hands under his armpits. Maybe he should have first put his loincloth back on.

"They'd be armed," he told her. "But how can they prepare for an enemy they've never encountered?"

"Falcons aren't the enemy, Nakos. We never were."

He wanted to believe her, needed to. But trust could be dangerous. Besides, what did it matter?

Looking up at him, she ran her hands over her hips and then her thighs. "Sex happened so fast. I didn't know we'd—"

"Didn't you? Where is your dress?"

"I didn't think to bring it with me."

How a Falcon could carry any garments was beyond his comprehension. Maybe, if he had a lifetime in which to learn what it meant to be one, he'd understand, but he didn't have that.

"Thank you for this last memory," he made himself say. "I'll never forget what happened between us."

Moisture glistened in her large, expressive eyes. "I don't want you to leave. You and your people have nowhere to go, nothing to return to."

"After everything I did to you, you don't hate me?"

"Because of you, I'm alive again. The past is that, the past."

"You've forgiven Tau?"

"I don't—maybe. Forces I don't understand rule him. Who am I to judge them?"

Her words, coupled with the tears she didn't try to hide, put an end to his vow not to touch her again. Still, as he ran his fingers into her hair, he cursed his weakness. Leaving her was going to be even harder.

"Do you also forgive me for what I did to my grandparents?" he asked.

She covered his hand with hers. "Of course. What matters is that you do."

They'd said so many things since she'd joined him a little while ago, and yet it didn't seem nearly enough. But maybe it didn't matter because he belonged with his people and she with hers.

A wind gust blew her hair over her face. When he brushed it back, her tears dampened his fingers. Touching them to his lips, he tasted her. He'd never forget her.

"Do it," she whispered. "Leave, if you must."

"Jola—"

"Now. Before I try to stop you."

For an instant, he felt nothing, did nothing. Then a deep chill spread through him. His limbs were numb, his chest so tight he could barely breathe. Acting without thought, he stepped back, his fingers combing her hair one final time as he did. Then he leaned down, snatched his loincloth, and stepped into it. He looked at her without truly seeing her as he gathered up his weapons. His world no longer had any depth. He couldn't speak.

But as he started to turn his back on her, movement above caught his attention. Motionless, he watched as two small birds circled above him and Jola, floating closer with every circuit. The pair landed soundlessly. Piercing gazes cut into him. Then, as one, they shook off their Falcon bodies, and two un-abashedly naked men stood before him. Their features were similar although one appeared to be much older than the other.

"Chief Cheyah," Jola said. "Dai."

The older man nodded at Jola. "We watched," he said. "We saw."

"Everything?" she asked.

"Yes."

Instead of being embarrassed, Jola waited for her chief and his son to continue. She'd sensed that Nakos was shutting down emotionally and, taking her cue from him, she'd struggled to do the same. As a result, everything now seemed unreal to her, as if she was removed from what was happening.

"Nakos," Cheyah said to the man she'd recently fucked. "It's a strong name, a good one for a warrior."

"Thank you."

"I understand why Jola returned to you," Cheyah continued. "When your bodies became one, they created their own storm."

Nakos nodded, once.

"You're wondering why my son and I are here. It's not just to let you know that the two of you didn't have privacy after all, but because we want you to realize we respect you."

"Respect?" Jola said when Nakos remained silent.

"We're predators," Cheyah said. "But that doesn't mean we can't admire humans. After all, we're that, too."

Cheyah wasn't saying anything all of them didn't already know so what was he getting at? She was afraid Nakos would grow impatient. Either that, or he'd want nothing to do with others of her kind. But when she gathered the courage to look at him, his expression was attentive, his gaze steady.

"Jola," Cheyah continued. "Thanks to you, the Falcons have begun to understand what the Ekewoko are. We like what we see."

"All Falcons feel that way?" she asked.

"Dai and I aren't the only ones who watched the two of you. Even before you had sex, we studied the way you looked at each other. We heard the things you said."

Nakos whirled on her. "Did you know?"

"It didn't enter my mind," she admitted. "Please believe me. Otherwise I would have never said—"

"She speaks the truth," Dai reassured Nakos. "I'm certain

the last thing she thought about was Falcon ears. You're the only thing she cares about."

The look of betrayal faded from Nakos's eyes. Much as she tried to recall what they'd said to each other, she remembered only their sex, their mating.

"Nakos," Chief Cheyah said, "What made the most impact on me about that conversation is how rootless the Ekewoko are. You truly can call no place home?"

His eyes sober, Nakos shook his head.

"It could be here."

Everything seemed to stop for Jola then. Maybe it was the way Cheyah had measured his every word, maybe because Nakos stood still as stone. In contrast, her heart pounded wildly.

"Here?" Nakos said at length.

"Falcon Land isn't a kind place," Cheyah went on. "That, in part, is why our ancestors chose it. We needed space and privacy to be who we are. But the lake has always provided, as have the animals who make this their home. Yes, the wind almost always blows, but at the base of Raptor's Craig on the other side from where we're standing, it is quiet."

"I noticed that when we were trying to find a way to the top, but then I forgot," Nakos said. Although he was speaking to her chief, he now returned to her gaze. "Grasses grow taller and there are trees."

"Because the soil is richer."

Once again everything slowed down for Jola. This was Nakos's decision. His and his people's.

"Did—all Falcons agree to this?" Nakos asked. "You speak with everyone's voice?"

"Nakos, Jola lost her mate to an Ekewoko. When she discovered who was responsible, she exacted a Falcon's vengeance, but when she came looking for you today, she did so with a woman's heart. Her human body sought and found yours.

When we saw that, we all understood. Ekewoko and Falcon aren't enemies."

A moment ago she hadn't believed she was capable of moving, but as she stepped toward Nakos, strength guided her. Her head high, she extended her hands toward him. "My chief knows me better than I know myself," she admitted. "I don't want you and me to be enemies, ever."

Nakos's jaw sagged. Then he pressed his lips together. "If I tell my people what your chief said and they agree to make Scr—Falcon Land their home, you'll welcome us?"

"Yes," she breathed. "Yes."

His hands covered hers, warming and challenging her at the same time. "Will you travel with me?" he asked. "Speak for the Falcons?"

"Yes."

"As my—my mate?"

She could ask him if that's what he truly wanted, but his eyes and body had already spoken so she answered by taking another step and offering herself to him. "Yes," she managed, "as your mate."

Turn the page
for a sizzling preview of
PURELY SEXUAL,
by Delta Dupree!

Coming soon from Aphrodisia!

1

"Marriage?" Donnie shouted. What the devil would he do with a damn wife? In his current state of sexual affairs, a wife would be nothing but a frigging hindrance.

"Fontana, listen, goddamn it." Paul Tedesco settled his elbow on the desk, propped his cheek against his fist. "Spouses can't be forced to testify against significant others. You need to think about the issues. Think about the future. Survival. A number of people saw you with Susannah, and Challie saw you upstairs together."

Fists clenched at his sides, Donnie said, "I don't give a damn what the maid saw. I didn't beat the hell out of Suze." No way could anybody claim he'd hurt Pearson. Any woman. And why had every time he'd heard the maid's name or he'd caught sight of her, his dick jerked? "Suze was fine when I left her. Angry, but fine."

He marched over to the window and stared through the sheer curtains, then snatched a length of fabric back. Across the expansive courtyard, Paul's Silver Cloud was parked along the circular driveway. The driver/bodyguard, a humongous Samoan dude named Tupa, polished smudges off the Rolls-Royce. Bright sun rays enhanced July's blue skies, but thunderheads rolled in from the southwest. Dark. Ominous. Threatening as this damn situation.

Donnie spun around as the curtains fell back into place. "This is bullshit."

"Look," Paul said, holding his hands up. "Calm down. We'll get to the bottom of it. Soon, I hope. The police want to interview everyone who attended the party last night. I've got a list to turn over soon. Meanwhile, you have to keep Challie from testifying if things escalate to a trial."

Earlier this morning, the new maid had found Susannah. What idiot would attack a woman? The only thing Donnie attacked on the female species was the hot snatch between her legs.

"I don't have anything to hide." Damn it, why wasn't Paul listening or understanding? Abuse was not Donnie's game. He'd never laid a hand on a woman. Well, not maliciously. Maybe a good swat or two when she misbehaved. Or to get her undivided attention. All in fun and foreplay.

"Okay, okay," Paul said flatly. "The problem is Challie can point the finger at you, make your life miserable. Unlivable. If she tells the cops about the argument, you're in for some real problems. Mayhem I don't need."

"Exactly, an argument. Suze was pissed because she caught me with Ellie Brewsters. But I didn't fuck Brewsters, Paul," he said before his boss spit out his next belittling words. "Too many buddies are talking about her. She just has a mouth that—" Obviously he'd said the wrong shit again.

Paul's eyes narrowed. "Is sex all you ever think about? Jesus Christ." He was married, had two kids and an imaginary white picket fence surrounding this huge mansion, living ideally in loving matrimony.

Donnie's two-bedroom condo was pretty damn sharp, but it

was no comparison to Paul's modern-day castle. Pool, spa, pricey artwork, a library that gave the Phoenix metro area's bookstores a run for their money. Donnie would give anything to live high and mighty on unlimited resources.

"Your dick's gonna get you into a lot of trouble one day . . . correction . . . it already has. Where did you go after leaving here?"

"I didn't take off right away. Um." Paul was sure to jump in pissed.

"I don't think I want to hear this." Perceptive, Paul gazed back, his dark eyes filled with annoyance. "As long as you keep your damn hands off *my* wife."

"I'd never touch Tina." He'd thought about it a few times. She flaunted dangerous swaying hips. Silky blond hair, one tiny dimple piercing her left cheek, vivid blue eyes, she was hot, boasting honkin' knockers. Sure as shit, her sexpot was . . .

Hostility gathered in Paul's dark eyes. He snapped the chair forward with a loud bang, as if he'd seen the burning lust in Donnie's gaze. "Picture this. Your balls stuffed, lacquered and rolling across my pool table before you get the chance to apologize."

Smarter than the average guy, Donnie's growing erection deflated. Clearly, Paul Tedesco had ways to control people. "I'm cool. No way would I mess with your old lady."

"Good damn thing. Saves your gonads for now." He leaned back again, rocking. "Did any guests see you to the door, wave good-bye as you left?"

He shook his head. "I took the back stairs, went out the gate. Vanessa's old man was coming up the main staircase."

"Vanessa? She's only been married to Bradley for three damn months."

"Guess he's not giving her what she wants or needs."

Sighing noisily, Paul adjusted his black horn-rimmed glasses. He lifted the half-smoked Cuban cigar from the ashtray, relit it in three big drags. The pungent aroma wafted toward air cleaners that his wife insisted they install. Outspoken Tina had iron nerves; she'd confront him, boldly defy her husband and come away unscathed.

"When I left here," Donnie continued. Why dwell on history? Think about the present, the future, his current problem becoming his biggest nightmare. "I went straight home for once, straight to bed. Alone." He never invited any hot snatch to his condo.

"Lousy alibi in my opinion. Anybody see you leave the premises or call your home phone later?"

Every bone in Donnie's body softened to rubber. Slumping, his brown-striped tie tightened around his neck like a noose. He pulled the choking polyester free, draped it over his shoulder then unfastened the top two buttons of his tan shirt as he moved across the room.

With the situation growing grimmer by the second, Donnie collapsed onto the visitor's wingchair and buried his face in both hands. "No. When I got there, I turned off the ringer as always. I needed sleep. Been out in the streets too much."

"Undoubtedly," Paul said. "The way I see it, you have two options."

Tensing, Donnie looked up. "Options? Why do I need any options? I haven't done anything wrong." He screwed up his face when Paul gave him a blank stare. "What are they, for God's sake? This nightmare has to end."

"Marry—"

"I don't want to hear that one, Paul." Donnie tunneled all ten fingers through his hair. Why the hell was he living in Scottsdale, Arizona? Of all the cities in the United States, he'd chosen one of the hottest sons of bitches. Now his ass was on the city's hotplate, ready to be fried to a fucking crisp for a crime he hadn't committed. "What if she doesn't want to marry me?"

"Not a problem. She will."

He shook his head. "Can't do it."

"Fine. Challie knows more than she's saying." Standing now, Paul adjusted his red silk tie. Combing his thinning brown hair, he moved across the room to the maple coat rack, lifted his navy jacket and thrust his arms into the sleeves. Tailor-made Italian suits were the only threads he wore, never the assembly-line creations from the business he owned. In essence, the clothes produced—part of PT Industries—was the main reason the district attorney had been sniffing after his ass. Sweatshop, as in illegal immigrants, some would say.

"Don't leave yet. What's my second choice? I'll take it, whatever it is. It has to beat marriage by a long shot."

Paul went back to the desk. He pulled the leather chair back and said, "Take Challie to the ranch. You can stay in the fore-man's cabin next to Ray's place. Then—"

"Then what?"

The cabin was located in Bum-Fuck, Montana. Good pussy was scarce in an area of dazzling fields filled with cows, horses, and manure. The great American countryside.

Paul pinned him with a level gaze. "I'll have Tina tell her you're vacationing and you need her to clean for arriving guests. I'll get a couple of my boys to join you. You've been there before, forty-odd miles away from Nowhere, USA. Clos-est neighbor is four miles downwind."

How could he forget? Other than fucking and fishing, the best part of Montana was horseback riding across 6,000 acres without a care in the world, the wind in his face, the smell of freshly cut hay filling his nostrils. "And?"

Paul yanked the desk's center drawer open. He withdrew his favorite .38-caliber S&W and set it on the gleaming wood. "Do whatever's necessary to take care of any problems."

Donnie straightened his back. *Do what's necessary? With a fucking gun?*

Was Paul really as cold and calculating as people had claimed? One particular detective had put his life under a high-powered microscope after his first wife's death. In the end, he'd pocketed millions of dollars from insurance and assets, not to mention old money Lana had brought into their marriage. When Donnie blatantly asked his boss about the incident, the answer was as chilling as an Arctic wind. *Ask me no questions, I'll tell you no lies.* Donnie's mouth had clamped shut like a trap door.

Sliding the weapon across the desktop, Paul said, "You don't have much choice. Pick one. If you have an aversion to marriage, you're looking at wearing the tears of a clown in jumpsuit orange, day in and day out, if Susannah doesn't make it."

Ah, hell. He hadn't done anything wrong, hadn't laid an abusive hand on the secretary. Now, Paul was talking jail. Hell of a choice—marriage or prison. Either way he adjusted the picture, the old ball and chain action dominated the scene with one major problem: prison meant no female activity.

"What about our lawyers? What the hell do we pay them for?" he asked.

"Real estate and commercial business mainly. I don't want them handling this particular criminal case. I can't afford to have my name or any of my businesses associated with amoral activity, not with my current state of affairs. The district attorney's been harping on my ass enough already. If you're steadfast against marriage, take the gun," Paul said. "You lack an alibi and, remember, the police have already started the investigation."

Donnie slowly got to his feet, shaking his head wildly. "You're talking . . ." Hell, he couldn't get the word out.

Paul replaced the gun and shoved the drawer closed. "I've got a meeting with the symphony directors." Straightening his tie, he marched toward the double doors. "Lock the desk when you leave and put the key away as usual."

"I'm not doing it," Donnie snapped. He might as well take the pistol and blow his own frigging brains out. "Marriage or Montana. My ass'll be sealed up in prison two decades as some sloppy jailbird's goddamn girlfriend before—"

Paul swung around. His brown eyes narrowed thinner than paper. "It's not a request, Donnie. You will go to Montana and do whatever is necessary, be it marriage slash honeymoon or curbing all future problems while the perpetrator is still walking free."